DOC AND THE DOLL

A Novel By

Stevan A Fisher

Other Books by Stevan Fisher include:
- What Happens in Roswell …
- SNAFU
- A Man Walks Into A Bar
- The Stray

ISBN: 978--1-6522-4962-7

Dedication

To all those who listened politely as I developed this
story.
To my Wife most of all for her editing and patience
&
To that runner who inspired the start of this story

Table of Contents

Chapter 1

This day began like every other day for the past few years. That wasn't a bad thing; it just meant that he had grown complacent. However, the attempted kidnapping and gun play did manage to liven up Martin's routine.

He retired some years ago but still worked as a cybersecurity consultant for an IT company in Seal Beach. The drive from Laguna Hills to his office could take up to an hour, during which time he enjoyed the peace and quiet, and sometimes the sights. At least three, sometimes four days a week, he would round the corner and see his jogger in the distance. Summer or winter, rain or shine she was out running between 5:30 and 6:00 am, her long ponytail bobbing from side to side as she ran.

He generally drove by this energetic runner without looking at her directly. He doubted he would recognize her if he brushed passed her in a store or saw her in a restaurant; yet, she was a memorable start to most days. Today should have been no different. He made the turn onto the side road and spotted his jogger about two blocks away. Then the morning took a disturbing turn.

As she approached the entrance into one of the neighborhoods, a small Ford transit van, coming from the opposite direction, made a sudden left into that same neighborhood. The turn, right in front of the runner, caused her to almost lose her balance, trying not to collide with the side of the van. Suddenly, both doors on the passenger side of the vehicle burst open, and the passenger in the front grabbed her.

Martin stomped on the accelerator, closed the distance, and hit the brakes, as he skidded into the back edge of the van.

The runner took advantage of the jarring shock to push back and partially break from her attacker. The driver, who must have been the one who slid open the side door, regained his balance, pulled a pistol, and fired at Martin, who was already out of his car.

Martin was not a newcomer when it came to high-stress situations. During those times, his view of the world seemed to shift into slow motion. From that slow motion perspective, Martin watched the assailant at the side door regain his balance, pull a gun, and fire it in his direction. Those shots went wild, and the idiot never got any additional shots off. Martin hit him with a full body block that forced the shooter's arm against the side opening, snapping the bones as the gun flew free and hit the ground.

Martin then turned his attention to the jogger and her assailant. She had managed, in the commotion, to get partially free. The thug, maybe six inches taller and easily a hundred pounds heavier, reached out to regain his grip. Instead, he found Martin directly between him and his prey. Martin grabbed him by the front of his hoodie and shoved back with all his strength. The assailant was thrust back through the door opening. Unfortunately, his head didn't clear that opening.

With a sickening crunching sound, his head snapped forward then back again. He crumpled from the opening and slid down to the ground. A small pistol dropped from his limp right hand. He must have been trying to pull it out from under the edge of the hoodie.

Silence. It was all over, and for a moment, quiet. The guy wearing the hoodie was a crumpled and disturbingly bloody mess. The driver, at the side door of the van, had passed out from the pain. He lay, part in and part out of the sliding door. Martin turned back to look at the jogger as he dialed 911. For the first time he was seeing her up close. She was still sitting on the sidewalk where she had landed when Martin moved in between her and the guy in the front.

As he answered the 911 operator's questions, he studied the jogger who was looking at the surrounding carnage. He looked up to see two police SUVs approaching from opposite directions. Someone else must have already called 911. He also noticed a fire or emergency vehicle behind one of the SUVs. It appeared the early morning event was drawing a small crowd.

He heard someone speaking behind him.

"What are you?" Unsure that she had been heard her, she repeated the question, "What are you?"

He was sure that was what she was saying. He turned back to look directly at her. She had resumed assessing the scene and was no longer looking directly at him. She turned back to him and looked like she was about to repeat what struck him as an odd question when the first of the police officers arrived on the scene.

The next few minutes were a bit tense. The arriving officers had no perspective or clue as to what had gone on. One of the officers instantly drew down on Martin. That officer, along with a second, were preparing to subdue him when she spoke up again.

"Leave him alone you idiots; he's the one who just saved me from those bastards in the van."

To Martin, this was a more realistic response than asking him what he was.

The next few hours, first at the crime scene, then at the Laguna Hills substation, were tedious but expected. In between questions and statements, he continued to ponder the "what" in her initial inquiry to him. She could have meant what are you: police, security guard, what? That would have made some sense; but, her inflection had not felt right. When he was finally released, he decided to take the day off; after all, it was Friday, and he could use the time to forget this whole incident.

He had learned a few things. The jogger's name was Dr. Karen Wing, Ph.D. and she was head of a Defense Advanced Research Projects Agency (DARPA) field office. He learned this from her aide-de-camp, a Marine Corps Captain assigned as a liaison to that office. Having a Marine Captain assigned to her seemed odd, but the Captain explained that he was with the Marine Corps Warfighting Laboratory (MCWL) and that seemed to fit. Learning the runner and her aide were government, was the only information he was able to get. He recognized stonewalling and gave up quickly. There were no thanks and no other interactions with the person he had just rescued. She had been whisked away during Martin's interview.

———————————————

Ambrose Cobb, Rosy to his few friends, sat quietly where he was parked in the substation lot. He wasn't sure what more he might be able to learn sitting here, but knew he would have to report something to Ronan Murdock, his boss.

The plan had been simple -- stage another kidnapping of a seemingly random jogger. One more abduction, in a string of recent cases, would add credence to the fear that there was a serial predator in the area. Again, no victim would be found, bringing the total to three missing joggers. Once they had Wing, his, Rosy's team would be able to extract the information needed. Her abduction as a jogger would be sad but would not be linked to her work with DARPA and MCWL. Taking this scientist was different than the previous abductions. His boss wanted access to the research this woman was doing. Her research into physical enhancements, as they related to creating a super soldier, was nearing completion, or appeared to be. So, they needed to grab her soon. This research was a salable commodity and his boss already had a buyer. Then they could send her off with the other abductees.

There should have been nothing to prevent the capture team from acquiring the female scientist.

Instead, it went wrong from the start. It was beginning to look like Wing might have perfected her research and had at least one super soldier as a bodyguard. Rosy had not been forewarned. Whoever was feeding information to Ronan had left the super soldier out of the briefing. Ronan would have let Rosy know if he had known. In which case, Rosy would have assigned a different pickup team.

As Rosy had watched the entire debacle, from a distance, this seemed the only reasonable explanation. The unknown super soldier had rammed the van, jumped out, possibly taken two rounds center mass, dispatched the van's driver and then crushed, yes, crushed the head of the lead member of the abduction team.

The next attempt would be better planned. It would need to be more direct, but now there were two potentially valuable targets. Since they were aware of the bodyguard, there would be no new surprises. He hated surprises.

Chapter 2

As he drifted off to sleep Friday night, Martin considered that his life seemed to be circling back to a previous time. He had retired from the Navy after twenty years. Now thirty-some years later, he was once again being shot at and forced to break people in self defense. He had foolishly assumed that part of his life had been relegated to the past.

When he returned home, he began peeling off his dirty and his bloodstained clothing from the jogger rescue. Paramedics and police had repeatedly asked if he was okay and at the time, he had insisted he was fine. The blood on his clothing was most certainly from the attackers in the van. At least someone had asked how he was feeling. The jogger, Dr. Annoying, had never asked him how he was or if he was hurt. She just repeatedly asked him what he was.

Now looking at the right side of his chest, in the fleshy area between the third and fourth intercostal rib, he discovered he had been shot. The damage had to be from the first round. He was sure he had sidestepped the other two. He hated this.

It had been, he did the math, forty-five years since the last time. That had been during an evac the week before he left Nam at the end of his second tour in 1974. Counting that evac, he had managed to get shot three times in eighteen months or so. Now history was repeating itself. He needed to figure out how this worked. Not the getting shot part, he was sure he knew why that had happened each time. No, he was more concerned with why being shot again seemed only a minor inconvenience, nothing more. He was now in his seventies, but through the years had always kept in shape. It annoyed some of his oldest friends that he looked like he was at most in his mid-fifties. Then again, maybe he was getting old and simply had not dodged fast enough this time. He focused back on the wound. Regardless of his age, why were his wounds so inconsequential?

He examined the puncture. It was a through and through. By now it was mostly closed, and while it hurt like hell if he poked at it, he knew it would take care of itself by morning. The same pattern as in the past. Being shot was the result of having not ducked or dodged well enough. The fact was, the pain related to having been shot was somehow masked allowing him to focus on the task at hand, not on the wound. The previous three times, the shots rarely caused him much pain or damage. Sleep was the best remedy. He would decide what to do in the morning. He took a long, hot shower and went to bed.

The next morning, he watched the news to see if there was any additional insight into the abduction attempt. Nothing new. There was a theory that it might be similar to the earlier disappearances of two other female joggers. What he did find oddly disturbing was that the attacker, whose arm he had broken, had passed away during the night due to a blood clot. That left investigators with physical evidence only, no one to question. Before he could decide why this bothered him, there was a knock at the door.

Martin opened the door and found himself facing the jogger, and her aide, keeper, head of security, companion, or whatever the Marine Captain assigned to her was for. She stood quietly for a minute, looking at the room behind Martin before she finally spoke.

"We thought we should drop by and take some time to discuss what happened yesterday. Can we come in?"

Martin stepped aside and motioned them into his living room. The room decor was 'casual bachelor' with a large flat screen mounted on the far wall. He had a worn recliner positioned for the best view. There were a few other tables and a recliner-style segmented couch that also faced the flat screen from a comfortable viewing angle. The Captain took a position at the back of the couch, and the good doctor took a moment to walk around the room looking at various items and photos.

Martin used this time to take a closer look at his guests.

Up until now, Dr. Karen Wing, Ph.D., etc., had been a pleasant diversion most mornings. As he watched her walk around his living room glancing at various knick-knacks, he considered revising that thought. In the morning as Martin drove off to work, rain or shine, she was the jogger setting a consistent pace down the sidewalk in the early hours of the morning. He couldn't see her face; she was always running the same direction he headed. There was a thick black ponytail keeping beat as she ran, always the same measured athletic pace, never faltering. When he turned the corner, he could judge if he was running a little late by how far down the road she might be. On the days he didn't see her, he figured that she had run early, or something had caused her to change her schedule. She was a representation of normalcy.

He had not given her much thought until yesterday when someone tried to abduct her and now, he had a growing collection of questions. He studied her a bit more as she finished her rounds and sat down on the couch, her guardian standing relaxed behind her. She looked to be in her mid to late thirties, light skinned, no California tan or ethnic skin tone. Her eyes had the slight hint of an epithelial fold giving her, what had been referred to in his younger years, a Eurasian look. There was no smile, more of a determined something in the set of her features.

Now was also the only time he had ever seen her in street clothes. She dressed like a middle management official from an office somewhere - no style, just function. The jogging outfits were an improvement. At least her jogging attire had color and some panache.

"Interesting home you have here, Mr. Brensen," she said looking directly at him, holding his gaze.

The tone of her voice was a cross between a middle school teacher and a tired college lecturer.

"You can call me Martin if you like," he replied, "and how would you like me to address you?"

"Ms. Wing, or Dr. Wing, whatever, you prefer. I am here to talk about yesterday. I have some questions, and then we will leave you alone. You don't mind, do you?"

"Is this a DARPA investigation? Your tone makes it sound as though you are here in some official capacity."

There was a moment of rather conspicuous silence. The Captain shifted a little at his station covering her back.

"What makes you think I work for DARPA?"

She stared at him with what he assumed to be her 'you

are annoying me, and that is not a good thing' stare. The 'what the hell, let's have some fun with this' part of Martin smiled. He decided that if she wasn't here to thank him for saving her life, at least he could bug the shit out of her.

"The Marine Officer in civvies standing behind you informed the police yesterday in my presence. So, I am a bit why there is a DARPA official here and not in DC."

Silence...

"Mr. Brensen, I had your military record pulled and have reviewed it. You had a rather exemplary twenty years of service. During the early part of your career, you spent two tours in Vietnam, and you were one of a handful of Corpsman constantly in combat situations who never got a Purple Heart. The few people I could locate yesterday spoke of you with the utmost respect and admiration. The comment was that you never lost a man and were as lucky as hell. Were you shot yesterday? Because we have recovered the three shots fired at you and one of them has traces of blood on it." The last sentence was punctuated with an 'I got you now' smile.

He didn't want to answer that question, nor had he expected it.

She stood casually, speaking as she began to approach Martin. Her tone and expression were that of a teacher trying to gain the confidence of a student, or a child, or maybe, a puppy.

"I would like it if you would come down to my office where we can talk in private."

Martin was aware that beside his relative indifference

to pain, in emergency situations his perception of the world slowed significantly. Like the pain thing, this was something he didn't dwell on or could he predict when it occurred. This time dilation phenomena which had allowed him to dodge two of the three shots yesterday, now kicked in again. As the good doctor stood and approached him, she was withdrawing and palming a device from a pocket in her slacks. At that same instant, the Marine was reaching into his coat. Briefly, Martin considered that this sucked.

As she continued to approach, she shifted her grip on what looked like an epi-pen type of injector. The Marine now had a pistol clear of his jacket and was shielding it from sight as much as he could. Martin recognized it as a dart gun; a small compressed gas operated device used to fire a tranquilizer dart. He clearly saw all of this as the time dilation was now fully engaged.

In the next and final few seconds, he turned the tables. Dr. Wing reached out as though to put her hand on his shoulder. He caught her hand and redirected the force of her move down to her side causing her to discharge the auto-injector into her own hip. The effect was almost immediate, and she began to slump, though Martin saw the surprised realization on her face.

Tranquilizer darts travel several magnitudes slower than bullets. The Captain had fired as Martin assisted the good doctor in tranquilizing herself. When the dart closed the gap, Martin caught it and threw it back, hitting the Marine in the neck. He had always been good at darts but was pleasantly surprised this had worked so well. The look on the Captain's face was priceless as he collapsed and dropped out of sight behind the couch.

For Martin, yesterday had been the start of what was not going to be a good weekend.

Chapter 3

After having re-gifted the tranq dart to the Captain, Martin confirmed that he was out and would stay so. He then searched the unconscious Marine and found the neat little waterproof case with spare darts. Those turned out to be handy later. The small case had also included an auto-injector with instructions that identified it as a counter or remedy for the tranquilizing agent. While reading the notes on the anti-tranq, he suddenly had another thought and checked outside to confirm his suspicion.

He must be getting old he thought, his guest would have brought backup. One more thing he had to take care of.

Once back in the house he stopped to check on the Ms. Wing. By now she had curled up into a semi-fetal position on the floor. Time to finish. He began by setting up the two chairs from the dining room in the living room.

Martin looked around. This would work fine. He had lifted the Marine onto the couch. The tranquilizer darts packed a fairly long-lasting punch, they were designed to keep a 250lb target down for at least forty-five minutes. He suppressed a chuckle as he tied the Marine's shoelaces together. If the Captain woke up early, that should trip him up for the moment and alert Martin.

Now, for Wing, he had stopped thinking of her as a doctor, Ph.D. or not. Right now, she looked more like a broken doll. She was still lying where she had collapsed while he was throwing the dart at the Captain. With everything taken care of, Martin could get back to ... he chuckled ... the Doll.

He paused and took a minute to review.

One chair had arms; the other did not. He gently placed the Doll in the chair with the arms. His decided to reset the stage from the earlier aborted Q&A in a manner he felt was more appropriate. He hoped to be rewarded with a suitable reaction when he referred to his female guest as 'Doll.' The results should be interesting with this self-important, smug individual. He knew he was making several assumptions, but that was half of the fun. On the other hand, she hadn't even said thanks for his having taken a bullet for her, so he would play this out his way.

He began with the zip ties. These were the standard size everyday ties, but by linking a couple of them together, he could make some reasonable restraints. Ankles to the chair legs, wrists to the chair arms, not too tight, just enough to prevent his guest from trying anything. He surveyed his handy work, then sat down in the other chair, at what he judged to be a safe distance away.

Martin took a calming breath then placed the auto-injector with the antidote against the same thigh that had received the initial tranquilizing dose. He triggered the injector; then, he waited. At just over a minute she stirred back into consciousness. Fifteen seconds after that her eyes were trying to burn a hole into Martin, as she realized that the tables had turned. She was bound to a chair and there was no help coming. She might have held out some hope but that was because she wasn't aware that Martin had tranqed the two backup support agents, or whoever, waiting outside in the obvious government sedan.

"Hi Doll, glad to see that you're awake again. You have

an odd way of dropping by to thank someone who saved your ass yesterday morning."

Martin smiled and studied the changes in her expression and body language. Just as she looked like she was going to reply or possibly shout for help, he continued.

"The two guys in the car outside are sleeping off the effects of the Captain's spare tranquilizer darts. They never saw it coming." He watched again.

"What did you call me?" She replied, after a minute more and in a tightly controlled voice.

"Doll." He was inwardly amused at that being her first point of contention.

"And what is it you plan on doing next?" She asked in the same, or maybe just a tad icier, tone than her first comment.

Martin had learned over the years that if you had the high ground, you held your position and took any possible advantage. Besides, he was enjoying this wrinkle in what had been a long boring stretch. The first ten years after he retired from the Navy had been okay, but the last twenty or so years had become a little boring and sedate.

"Well, Doll, this is how I see the situation and what I plan to do. You have the impression I know something you need to know. I base this on your actions yesterday at the police station and your un-guest-like actions this morning. I assume that after knocking me out, you would have searched my home and then taken me somewhere for further questions."

"You work for DARPA and, according to Captain Thompson's credentials, he is part of MCWL, so you can probably get away with holding me without cause for a short while." He paused for a moment watching her glare at him, then resumed before she could contribute to the conversation.

"So, my plan is as follows: I am going to head out to see a movie I had already planned to see this weekend. After the movie, I intend to have a relaxing dinner, then head back here. However, before I leave, I will place this pair of scissors on the table near my recliner. It should only take you a few minutes to crab walk your chair to that table, get those scissors, and set yourself free. Unfortunately, I will be on the road to the theater by then."

"After you have your team back on their feet, please take your time to rummage through my belongings. See if you can find what it is you are after. I will leave a notepad on the dining room table. If you still have questions, jot them down. Maybe leave me a number, and I will give you a call on Monday. I promise to be as cooperative as I possibly can. However, right now I have no clue what you are looking for and your current approach to garner my cooperation sucks."

"Finally, for the record, this is not what I expected to have happened when I decided to intervene in your kidnapping. And since you seemed concerned, yes, the first guy with the gun did manage to wing me. However, I didn't notice it until last night when I was cleaning up. It wasn't anything I couldn't take care of."

Martin then got up, placed a pair of scissors on the table, and headed for the door. A last-minute thought came to mind, so he turned back.

"Doll, before you wake up Captain Thompson, untie his shoelaces; it would have worked as an early warning for me, but he doesn't deserve to fall on his face on my account. He was only following your lead."

And he left.

Chapter 4

Martin figured the movie was a given. No matter how quickly the Doll got her crew awake and functioning, they would be hard-pressed to figure out which megaplex he had gone to, let alone which show. So, he relaxed and enjoyed the film. When he came out of the theater, his car was where he left it. That had the potential to give him away; it still bore the damage from the controlled crash yesterday. He had already made plans to drop it off at the shop and get a rental. As he approached his car, that little voice or feeling that would surface if there was impending danger remained silent. Satisfied the he was still in the clear, he dropped off his car and got a rental.

The next stop was a favorite restaurant in the Spectrum complex. Dinner, dessert, and coffee were also uninterrupted and he still felt no sense of being watched. He began speculating on what he wasn't seeing, then decided it didn't matter. Life was too short to waste time worrying. He smiled, imagining that if the Doll were watching and waiting for his return, the rental car would be an unknown.

Home ... no government sedans. He hesitated, unlocked the front door, and stepped into his living room. Nothing. Well, that was not true; everything was ... well, where it should be. No mess, no extra chairs, no cut zip ties. Kitchen, bedroom, bathrooms, spare bedroom, office, even the garage. Martin concluded that he should hire the Doll and her crew as a maid service, then made a mental note not to make that remark the next time he ran into her.

Finally, he returned to the kitchen table where he had

left a pad and pen. When he started investigating his newly cleaned house, he saw the note but figured it could wait until he had finished his inspection.

On the pad was a simple short note written in a flowing script. It read:

I was brought up with better manners. I hope you will allow me to take you to dinner at Splashes Restaurant in Laguna Beach to show my sincere appreciation of your heroic actions yesterday morning.

If you are not familiar with this restaurant, it has a spectacular view overlooking the ocean and will provide a neutral public setting. I still have some questions. Captain Thompson will be accompanying me. I was informed that I need a bodyguard for the immediate future.

Reservations are under my name at 6:30 pm Sunday, tomorrow.

It was signed in the same flowing script.

The Doll

Martin smiled and considered the note. Someone doesn't rise to a senior position in DARPA without being both intelligent and politically savvy. All the correct topics had been addressed and the signature was both a whimsical and amusing touch. The location was neutral and public. He had been to Splashes once before. It was in the Sand & Surf Resort on the Coast Highway.

Also, there was no phone number or way to decline. He smiled, "Well played, Doll."

"Back to business," Martin thought as he pulled a toy from his pocket. Usually kept in his car, this battered child's plastic radio with a bent antenna was a sophisticated electronics scanner. When he dropped his car off at the dealer, he remembered to retrieve it from the trunk. Initially he tried it in a few locations where he would like privacy.

Then he swept the rest of his home with this little toy radio and found no hidden devices. Very confident in the scanner's accuracy, he went to bed wondering where this was all headed.

His luck factor in Nam, now almost forty-five years ago, had bothered him at the time, but he came back when others did not. More than that, he was responsible for some of those good men getting back home to their families and that outweighed the other weirdness. Why was he pushing his luck again now?

He was seventy-one years old now and, without thinking, had jumped in and saved a jogger from what? In hindsight, it was evident with the guns and two-against-one tactic, this would not have ended well for the Doll. Martin made a mental note to remember the Doll had a real name ... something Wing. Yesterday and today, he had also experienced that same odd, revitalizing effect that appeared after he had escaped death. He was sure that it was just a mental sleight of hand, but it felt like an adrenaline high. That surge had gone from zero to one hundred during the kidnapping and with today's tranquilizer fiasco behind him, he still hadn't returned to a figurative zero state. He was still somewhere around a solid twenty.

He spent the next three hours trying to figure what and why. Finally, he realized he was still focusing on the 'what are you' as he drifted off to sleep. He would have a chance to get some answers at dinner, best focus on that. And, come Monday, he would be back in his office in Seal Beach.

The next morning, he was up early and jogged about two miles. After breakfast, he decided that he was now at a solid twenty-five on his made-up adrenal scale and that worried him. It wasn't a jittery adrenalin feeling; it was more of a general energy level feeling. He looked in a mirror and could swear that some of the gray stubble in his close military style haircut had disappeared. Next, he checked and the hole in his side was all but gone. Crap, it was like he was reliving part of the last year in Nam all over again and, damn, he realized he was suddenly starved. He made himself two cheeseburgers for an early lunch and took a walk around his neighborhood, ostensibly looking for anyone who seemed out of place, but mostly to vent energy.

By the time he headed to Laguna for his dinner meeting, he had the situation back under control, he told himself. If he concentrated, he could bring his respiration, pulse, and any other body functions back to a resting state. This was something he had not had to do for years but eased back into it and found that by the time he got into his car, he was at maybe a subjective 2 out of 100 on his unusual power scale. He could also sense that he was at a solid 25 on the reserve energy scale.

He parked in one of the lots near the resort. The main lot was full and it was only a short walk to the resort. Once there, he went through a maze of passages to the beach and through to the restaurant. The maître d' escorted him to Dr. Wing's table near the outer wall composed of open doors that let the ocean breeze in. As he approached their table, Captain Thompson rose and extended his hand in greeting.

"Mr. Brensen, can we try this again? As a Marine from a Marine Corps family, would you mind if I called you Doc?" The Marine held the shake for a moment longer.

They shook, took their respective seats, and the Captain, continued, "I finally had a chance to review your service records and my father, a Gunny when he retired, would have read me the riot act for my previous lack of respect."

Martin smiled, "Semper Fi and no, I wouldn't mind if you called me Doc. It has been a while, but it's still second nature to turn and respond to the title."

Both men sat and Karen Wing studied them for a minute before speaking, "Why is it that I suddenly feel outnumbered?"

Martin studied her face and decided that remark bore no added meaning or undertone.

After a moment, she continued, "I don't have the military background or upbringing but, I have noticed that in any notes related to actions you were in, it seems that the title Doc was always used instead of your given name. There were also a few comments about unusual actions, but we can discuss what those were about later. In the interim, would you be okay with me also referring to you as Doc, since my colleague has already adopted that as a way of addressing you? Somehow Martin doesn't seem to fit you as well."

Martin smiled and thought, "in for a penny, in for a pound."

"I will accept the nickname from you in return for the reciprocal right to call you Doll, in select company only, of course."

The Captain almost choked on the water he was trying to sip and Dr. Wing's face went through a gamut of expressions, from embarrassment, to anger, then frustration, and finally relaxed into one of wry amusement. To both men's amazement she nodded yes.

"At some point in time I would like to know where you drew that title from and why, but I will concede for now," was her only comment.

They made small talk, ordered, and enjoyed an excellent meal. The open doors that led out to the beach and the cool breeze off the ocean added to the relaxed atmosphere.

Eventually, over coffee, the conversation turned to recent events. Dr. Wing opened the discussion by giving Martin an overview of her position at DARPA and what she was studying and researching. She jumped past the attempted kidnapping and went directly to an unusual problem her assistant was reporting. They had the blood on the bullet and while they could tentatively identify Martin's blood type as O-negative, they couldn't get a reliable DNA pattern. They had some hair samples, from tidying up his house, but those took longer to process. Martin was concerned over the fixation on his DNA but listened as the Doll explained that all the test results were consistent with what would be a tainted sample. Finally, she smiled and asked if he would come to her office tomorrow and let them take a fresh sample.

She was about to go into further detail when all hell broke loose.

Chapter 5

The old, familiar, uneasy feeling grew, accompanied by the onset of the time dilation effect. Doc spotted the strike team as they made their way along the walkway outside the restaurant above the sand. The Doll was sitting masked from view by a waiter on the side where the strike team was approaching. Without hesitating, Martin placed his hand on her shoulder and applied pressure as he said, "Get under the table now..."

To her credit, she slid forward off the chair dropping to the ground. At this point, there were some surprised remarks from diners closer to the advancing team. Realizing they had been noticed, the team of four burst into the room from the outer walkway. Two of them fired bursts into the air with what appeared to be HK237s or something with that compact of a form factor. It didn't seem that they knew precisely where their intended targets were, as they began demanding that the customers stand up and move away from the tables. Captain Thompson was one of those who complied while nudging Martin, now also out of sight, with his right leg.

That leg had an ankle holster with a Sig 9mm, which Martin liberated. Thompson continued forward and joined with the group from the next table giving the appearance that his original table had already been cleared or that maybe he had been dining by himself. The group he had joined moved toward the center of the room, drawing attention away from their original table.

Doc took a moment to assess the assault team. They looked like professionals with dark tactical clothing, vests, and what he was now sure to be HKs. The one he pegged to be the leader was referring to a tablet, probably looking to match images on its screen with faces in the group of diners now gathering in the center of the room. Sadly, what until then had been a frightening, but nonviolent, situation took a dark turn. A security guard from the hotel burst into the room, pistol drawn, and became a target for all four strike team members.

During the exchange of automatic weapons fire, it wasn't immediately apparent that a few additional things had also happened.

The leader of the strike team had the small tablet on a lanyard and released it as he reached to steady his assault rifle. In the resulting chatter from the automatic weapons, no one noticed the tablet shattering from a 9mm round. Then the leader of the group collapsed like a discarded toy as two more 9mm rounds entered his right temple. What the assault team did notice was that a table near the bar was turned on end and two people were fleeing over the rail and down to the beach.

The wailing sound of sirens erupted as Doc and the Doll hit the sand running. He was partially carrying and partially dragging her. He focused on heading them in the opposite direction from where he was confident a pickup vehicle would be waiting for someone to deliver two captives. As they continued, he led her into a warren of paths and corridors from the beach back to the resort and the parking lots.

They made their way unnoticed through the parked cars in a secondary lot. Doc was glad he wasn't in the main lot and was driving a rental car. He was relatively sure anyone who was part of this current attempt would be looking for a late model white Ford Fusion, not a tan Jeep Cherokee. Furthermore, since he was not in the main lot, it was likely any vehicle leaving this lot was probably not going to be on their radar.

By the time they were getting into the Jeep, police cruisers had begun pulling into the lot at the Surf & Sand Resort. He motioned for the Doll to slump down out of sight in the passenger seat as he calmly drove out of the lot and down Coast Highway, away from the growing uproar.

"There was nothing I could do to help the security guard," he said quietly into the dark as they drove. "The removal of the leader of the group and the tablet with, I assume, ours and Thompson's photos, should help somewhat. The attackers looked like professionals. With their ringleader neutralized, the other three might cut their losses and lawyer up."

A quiet reply issued from the passenger seat, "In the few days I have known you, three men have died, two directly at your hand, one more under questionable circumstances. You seemed surprised when I asked you initially what you were. I still don't have an answer."

"Two days ago, two men tried to kidnap you, not me. We need to work on our communications rather than trying to finger point. I believe I am part of this mess as a collateral target because I stepped in to help you. After today, the fact that I don't play the victim well ensures that both of us are now in the same sinking boat. Do me a favor and think quietly to yourself while I try to figure an exit plan and who I can trust."

After a few minutes, she moved up into the seat and sat

quietly.

"Why do you call me Doll?"

After a moment he replied, "I saw you jogging one day a few months ago. You caught my attention. You were in one of the many jogging outfits that you appear to have, complete with matching headband and your ponytail bobbing as you ran. It was like seeing a human version of a Barbie jogging down the sidewalk. In the politically incorrect part of my brain that old guys still have, I thought, 'what a Doll.' As the months passed and I would see you on most weekday mornings, the name stuck in my head. Depending on where you were, in the several blocks that I know you covered as part of your run, I would judge my morning commute. I would amuse myself with 'the Doll is near the end of her run,' that means I'm running late. It passed the time and was oddly something to look forward to.

Friday morning changed that dynamic. Then your attempt to tranq me Saturday further changed the dynamic. I watch a lot of old movies and now it was 'that dame is trouble,' but the title Doll still stayed in my head and I was pretty sure that calling you Doll would have the effect it did. There is probably more to it than that but consider that an answer for now because now we are going to have to change up the Doll."

The Doll was studying Doc when her cell phone rang.

"Crap, we also have to get rid of those," Doc said in frustration, "Go ahead and answer it and please put it on speaker."

She unzipped her purse and pulled out her cell,

answering it in speaker mode.

"Doctor Wing?" It was a hesitant female voice. "Where are you? Are you okay? I thought you said you were going to Splashes. One of the security personnel came in and said I should turn on the TV. It's all over the news that there is gunfire at the resort and maybe a hostage situation. Karen ... are you there ... are you okay?"

She looked at Doc, then answered, "We are okay, we're ... on the road."

Doc butted in, "Hi, this is Martin Brensen. I am here with Dr. Wing and we are on our way to San Diego right now. Who is this?"

She looked at Doc again, seemed to make a decision, and continued, "Doc, this is Lindsey; she is my research assistant. Lindsey, Martin's nickname is Doc. We were finishing dinner when the situation, as you called it, started. We ducked out before it escalated and are now heading to San Diego, as Doc said. Lindsey, its late; you're not still at the lab, are you?"

The conversation continued to play out as Lindsey filled them in on what she knew from the news, asked if the Captain was okay, and answered why she was at the lab on a Sunday evening at this late hour.

As far as the news went, the reports indicated that a group of four unknown paramilitary types burst into the restaurant and appeared intent on taking hostages. A security guard challenged them, and in the ensuing gunfight, the guard was killed, as was the leader of the group. The police surrounded the area and the remaining three eventually surrendered and were taken into custody. The news channels were buzzing with speculation. The police and Homeland Security were giving no answers. Nobody had any answers.

Why Lindsey was still at the lab was more informative, since Doc and the Doll knew what had gone down at the restaurant.

Lindsey worked as a research assistant for Dr. Wing. They were part of DARPA's Biological Technologies Offices and worked out of a little-known lab complex on the UCI campus. The thrust of their research was directed at finding new ways to use bio-engineered living materials. The study focused on programming DNA to grow materials to predetermined specifications at sites in a human body. They were developing living materials that were responsive to their environments and could heal when damaged. The secondary thrust of their research was to minimize off-target effects in gene editing. The intended results were to engineer medically feasible, personalized gene therapy.

That answered Doc's question about the focus on his DNA. They were attempting to explain the 'what' factor related to Doc, by using a familiar approach. However, he was sure that DNA testing took days not hours.

He interrupted, "How is it that you have DNA results so fast?"

The Doll dismissed his question with, "We have developed tools to speed up the process."

It was Lindsey who had first questioned what seemed like an anomaly, or possibly just incorrect, confusing results from the tests. The logical answer was that the blood smear on the bullet was somehow tainted. There was no telling what else was on that bullet if, in fact, it had nicked Doc in its travels.

Lindsey now had hair samples from the clean-up at Doc's house yesterday that she had fully processed. She hesitated, however, when asked to describe her conclusions on the open line.

"It's okay," the Doll said without hesitation, "what do believe you are seeing?"

Lindsey was silent for a few long moments, then just spilled out what she thought she was seeing, in a rush, "DNA should be a nucleic acid that consists of two long chains of nucleotides twisted together into a double helix and joined by hydrogen bonds. It carries the cell's genetic information and hereditary characteristics via its nucleotides and their sequence and is capable of self-replication."

She was reciting this like she needed some confirmation or validation of her description, then continued.

"Mr. Brensen ... Doc ... appears to have a partial triple helix ... three unequal long chains of nucleotides twisted together into what appears to be triple helix and joined by what appears to be hydrogen bonds joining some complementary bases I can't identify."

Silence.

Chapter 6

The Doll glared at Doc, sighed, then began," Lindsey, are you sure of your results?"

"I have done the tests three times since I got the new samples from you yesterday. I was reviewing the third run when Andy from security told me to check out the news." She sounded a little indignant, then continued, "There are several aspects and bonds I can't yet identify, but yes, I am sure of what I am seeing and my techniques. I am also sure this is outside of my depth. What do you want me to do?"

The Doll was silent for a minute, looked over at Doc again, then seemed to have decided. "Put all of your results and notes in my private safe, you know the one, and take tomorrow off. I will call you at your place once we get settled in San Diego."

Silence.

"And keep the findings to myself? Right?"

Lindsey was silent for a moment then continued, "I trust you, boss; I do. I will do it. I could use a day off."

But she wasn't done yet.

"Doc, you are the one who rescued Dr. Wing on Friday. Why? You must know you are different, don't you? You had to know this might happen."

The Doll studied Doc as he considered what Lindsey

asked.

"Lindsey," he said, "I have always been what you might consider lucky. My time in the Navy was as a Navy Corpsman; it's where I got the moniker. I was in the field most of the time putting good Marines back together; I have done minor surgery, worked in labs and clinics, but the information you just dumped on me is news I will need to digest."

"I assume your boss was a target because of her work and I was considered collateral damage. Now, I must consider that my becoming part of this picture is going to cause the problem to escalate. Please do take the day off tomorrow and wait for our call."

"Well," she began, then her tone changed to a light-hearted banter, "Oh, hi Andy. Is there more news?"

A faint comment could be heard from a male voice and then back to Lindsey.

"I was leaving a message for Dr. Wing. It is late and I told her I would clean up but asked if I could take the day off tomorrow since I have been here most of today." The call ended.

"We need to work on our communication," the Doll remarked, "Who else knows what Lindsey just discovered about you?"

"Well, Doll, you and Lindsey probably know more than I do. That said, we have a busy few days. And to start with, we need to kill the cell phones and vanish."

"We aren't headed to San Diego, are we?"

"Never were, next stop Lake Elsinore," he said, "I have a plan."

The plan was several plans.

Doc had made some assumptions and considering their previous communication issues; he laid those assumptions out for review.

1) For whatever reason Dr. Karen Wing was the initial target of these abduction attempts and probably had not lost her standing as the primary target.

2) The team at the restaurant had partial, but not full intel. They had been relying on images on a tablet and their operation was probably intended as a snatch and grab only.

3) What Lindsey has uncovered needs to be resolved. However, it was unlikely that those responsible for the abductions had progressed to investigating Doc at that level, yet.

4) With the first kidnapping team dead and the second in custody, whoever was pulling strings had deep pockets and would be planning the next step more carefully.

5) Doc figured that they had at least a few more hours, maybe a day, before things escalated further.

6) He had the loaner, the Jeep, until the end of the following week while his car was in the body shop. Once they dealt with their phones, they would be free to roam untraceable for a while.

The first step was to remove the sim card from the Doll's phone and short out the battery on the Doc's iPhone.

Their next step was to get some cash. Doc and the Doll took the Coast Highway to San Clemente and used two different ATMs to get the maximum money they could withdraw from their accounts. Doc, also, always carried two one-hundred-dollar bills in a hidden pocket of his wallet, so this gave them some working cash. They made sure the Jeep was not visible to any surrounding cameras.

Next, they stopped for gas at a Circle K station on the south side of San Clemente. It was the fourth station they checked and the first where they could cut the camera feeds. They filled up using the Doll's credit card, adding to the electronic bread crumb trail pointing south to San Diego.

Once they had completed these essentials, they backtracked from San Clemente north to Capistrano and took the 74 east to Lake Elsinore.

As he discussed and revised these points with the Doll, he filled her in on the resources he had available. When he was still considering a career as a writer, he had done extensive research on false identities and how to disappear. That research had led him to his current calling in security. A side result of those earlier endeavors was that he had maintained contact with an unusual subset of the population.

As it turned out, some of the close friends, and some unsavory friends, he had made during his time in the service became his best resources. Lucky, aka SPC4 Charlie Rathbone, had been an Army LRRP (Long-Range Reconnaissance Patrol) team lead. On his third tour in country, Lucky's unit had been surrounded and pinned down. Doc was on the Huey sent to evacuate the LRRP. While the door gunner was laying down suppressive fire, Doc was able to pull Lucky and two others out. Lucky lost an arm, but swore it would have been more if Doc hadn't carried him to the chopper. One of the other two was a spook everyone called Spyder.

Lucky retired on a medical discharge when he returned stateside and bought a mini-storage warehouse in Lake Elsinore. Lucky trusted no one, especially the government, mostly California officials, but not exclusively. However, he trusted Doc 110%. So, when Doc need anything related to alternate identities or help hiding resources, Lucky found a way to make anything Doc could dream up happen. Doc called him on a landline as they left Capistrano and headed through the mountain pass to Lake Elsinore.

By the time they got there, it was almost midnight. Lucky had a trailer on the grounds they could stay in and a storage bin large enough to hide the Jeep. After quick introductions, they bedded down for the night. The Doll got the bed and Doc took the couch.

Chapter 7

After the previous day's excitement and despite the noises in the storage warehouse yard, the Doll slept like a baby. When she ventured out from the bedroom at the back of the single wide, the dining/living area of the trailer was populated with various people. More important to her was that she could smell coffee, bacon, and possibly eggs. She was very hungry.

Marian identified herself as Lucky's wife as she handed the Doll a plate with scrambled eggs, and something that smelled a bit like bacon but bore no resemblance, and a cup of coffee. She was a slender, pleasant looking woman in her early to mid-sixties. Doc, Lucky, and a much younger version of Lucky were discussing a box with some trailing wire connections.

"This is it. I've already disabled the GPS and the LoJack that was embedded in the frame. Your Jeep is now invisible to government snoops," said the younger man. "But no worries, Gramps said that you might need to return the Jeep at some point, and I can have it wired back into the system in about 15 minutes. Anyone looking for it will suddenly see it reappear on tracking systems."

At that point, Doc looked over and said, "Good morning Doll. I hope you slept well. Today is going to be a busy day. You met Lucky last night, and I see you have met Marian. The young man eyeing the pieces of fried spam on your plate is Joshua, their grandson."

At that moment, the door to the trailer swung open and

a young, maybe late teens, girl in a crop top, daisy dukes, and short boots stepped in. She had a nice tan, a pierced navel, green fingernails, shoulder-length green hair, and a very colorful dragon tattoo, like a sleeve on her left arm.

"And this is Shadow, Lucky's granddaughter, and your personal stylist."

The Doll was still trying to take this all in. Fried Spam, Shadow's appearance, a reference to Shadow as her personal stylist, and all the simultaneous conversations were pushing her into overload. She tried to focus on Shadow first. As strikingly different from what the Doll considered normal, the look seemed to work on this attractive young girl, but then there was the comment that she was going to be her stylist. And, of course, no one had batted an eye at her being referred to as Doll.

"Spam?"

She said that out loud; it was an odd thing to focus on, but it was something that she could grasp as real.

Her comment must have been taken as an invitation because Joshua neatly plucked one of the two pieces from her plate.

Shadow spoke next, "Hi Doll. Doc tells me we have to make you fit in, so you can hide in plain sight. Easy peasy; I'll cut and style your hair, give it a little color, and while it is drying, I can pick up some outfits for you to try on. Finish your breakfast; I'll go get my scissors and clippers, and I think I have a hair color that will be just what the Doctor ordered."

She chuckled at the pun, winked at Doc, and, as quickly

as she came, she spun and disappeared back outside.

Still not fast enough to enter the conversation, the Doll looked on as Marian addressed Doc.

"Typical man, you haven't told the Doll that she would be getting a makeover, did you? I know that you know better than that. I have some things to attend to in the office and Lucky and Joshua should be helping customers. And ... if she doesn't strangle you first, you might want to update the Doll with your plan."

The trailer door swung closed as the three left, leaving Doc and the Doll alone in the dining/living area of the trailer. The Doll looked down at her plate and realized that, as the previous scene had unfolded, she must have been hungry. She had managed to eat all but one forkful of eggs and a small piece of the Spam. She finished the remainder of her breakfast, picked up her coffee cup with both hands, and glared at Doc as she took a tentative sip. For his part, Doc remained silent and waited.

"I just ate Spam!"

Silence punctuated by a glare.

"Shadow is getting her scissors?"

Doc patiently waited.

"We have to seriously work on our communication." She settled back into the cushions, pulling her legs up under her, "you think I need a makeover and I still have no clue what you are."

He laughed.

"Yup," he began. "Let's shelve what I am for now; it is not a visual marker. You, on the other hand, are. The person I attached the Doll title to wore bright, stylish running suits and it was a pleasure to watch as you jogged along. The scientist and public figure that you present is far less colorful. I Googled you this morning, and every image of you portrays a serious, conservatively dressed, thirty-something, work-obsessed clone. Add to that a thick mane of ebony black, straight, perfect hair. You stick out like a Lexus in a parking lot full of motorcycles.

Even now, you are still in the conservative suit you were wearing for dinner yesterday; the full outfit, including the jacket. Your hair is still pretty much perfect even though you just got up. We have people trying to find us, for whatever nefarious reason, so, we either hide you here, or someplace like this, or we hide you in plain sight. Shadow can do that without breaking a sweat."

Doc studied the Doll for a moment, then asked, "How old do you think Shadow is?"

She took a sip of her coffee, looked down at what Doc had called a conservative pants suit, then brought the image of Shadow back up in her mind's eye.

"She is probably between eighteen and twenty," the Doll replied.

Doc smiled, "Shadow is Joshua's older sister. She has a bachelor's in economics, is working on a master's degree, and is the majority owner in an accredited beauty academy in Riverside. She just turned twenty-nine two weeks ago. It was quite a party. I asked her to blend you in, so we could hide you in plain sight."

"I don't know where my shoes are and I just ate Spam," she started then realized that she was babbling.

A Ph.D. and all she could do was babble. "Focus", she thought to herself. Then looking at Doc, she realized that he had changed subtly. His gray-white close-cropped beard was gone. So was his short gray hair. He now sported a close, buzz cut without any hint of gray and stubble, which looked like a five o'clock shadow with a hint of reddish brown. She had not paid much attention to what he was wearing yesterday or when this whole thing had started, for that matter. But the worn jeans and khaki colored pocket t-shirt were not what she remembered at any time.

Doc was talking again, "I have some new toys and we need to get a couple of them to Lindsey. Do you have her address? I already have someone in Lake Forest who should be close enough to get to her quickly."

He had been busy while she had been sleeping. Doc's friend, as it turned out, was about five miles from Lindsey. This friend just happened to have two burner phones as a surprise gift for her and was in route now. Doc also handed the Doll a burner phone, cautioning her that these were only for emergencies and then needed to be discarded. The next thing she learned was that the Jeep would be on its way to Chula Vista soon where it would have its electronics reconnected and show up on the grid. That was okay because Lucky had picked up a 1984 Volkswagen Vanagon camper some years ago. At the time he told Doc that he should take it on a road trip. A few years back, Doc was considering visiting some more of his special friends, maybe in Texas, possibly

New Mexico or who knows, but had not made up his mind. Now, it was beginning to sound like a good idea.

Then things began happening again. Doc got a call on one of the burner phones. While he was talking to whoever called, Shadow returned to the trailer.

Doc finished the call and commented to no one in particular, "Plans are more like flexible options; you go with the one that works for the situation."

He looked at the Doll and told her there was a surveillance van parked on the same block as Lindsey's townhouse. She wasn't sure how Doc's friend knew that, or why, but all things considered, she accepted the information. Doc then said he would fill her in later when he had more information and left her with Shadow.

Chapter 8

There was a white van parked on the same block as Lindsey's townhouse.

Gunner Anderson and his entire family worked for UPS. His brother flew one of their planes, and his father handled distribution for the Ontario Hub. More important than that, Gunner knew that a generic white panel van with darkened windows and more than three antennas was a pretty sure bet to be a spook surveillance van.

Gunner smiled as he passed the surveillance van. He pulled up and got out of his truck with two packages. He took the first package to one of the townhouses. He knocked, no reply, so he left the package. He continued to the second townhouse with the other package. He knew this one contained a pair of burner phones he was to deliver to Lindsey Miller; whose life was on the way to becoming complicated.

He knocked and, when he heard a noise at the door, said, "I have a package from Doc and the Doll."

An attractive young blond opened the door with a curious look on her face. Gunner smiled and said, "Miss Lindsey, please sign for this package, then use the phone labeled 'Doc' that you find inside. He's expecting your call. Please tell him I'll take care of the surveillance van. Have a good day."

Before getting into his truck, he called his dispatcher and indicated there was a suspicious white van on the street.

He had heard from some of his customers that there had been some recent break-ins and asked her to notify the police that this may be thieves canvassing the neighborhood.

In her townhouse, Lindsey opened the package and found two cell phones, one labeled Doc, the other labeled Doll. She picked up Doc and found a single number in the contact list, which she called.

"Hello Lindsey."

She recognized Doc's voice from the call yesterday evening.

"This is a burner phone and connects directly to me; the other rings directly to your boss. She is preoccupied right now but should be able to take calls in about an hour or so. We sent these phones because you are being watched."

"The UPS driver said to tell you he would take care of that," Lindsey replied. "What should I do, or be doing?"

"Well," Doc continued, "I think we need to arrange a vacation for you. I'm going to plan that right now, and your boss will call you with the details as soon as we have it figured out. Do you have any objections to flying somewhere?"

A short while later, Lindsey was amused when the police cruiser pulled up and hit their siren. The white van took off to escape and was stopped by a second cruiser at the other end of the block. The police took the driver and a passenger away, and, a little later, a tow truck hauled off the van. Lindsey occupied herself with the instructions from Doc as she waited to hear from Karen. The UPS guy had said the package was from Doc and the Doll. Lindsey tried to think of her boss as "the Doll" but couldn't quite make the connection.

Instead, she packed a bag with some old clothes she rarely wore, as instructed, and packed a carry on with essentials she would need for an overnight stay somewhere. She wasn't sure if she should be worried or excited. About two hours later, she got a call from Karen with some of the oddest instructions she had gotten yet, but she promised to follow them exactly.

A little later, her actual cell phone indicated that she had a new email. It was an American Airlines flight confirmation out of John Wayne (SNA) at 4:30 pm. The ticket indicated the flight was to Las Vegas with a layover in Phoenix. The next call was from an Uber driver who was outside, waiting to take her to the airport. She took a deep breath and headed out to the Uber, locking her townhouse. She was still not sure whether to be excited or worried but now she was committed to following through with the plan.

At SNA, she put her personal cell phone in her checked baggage; the phone was on but in airplane mode. She left her iPad home and felt a little odd not having any electronics. The two burner phones in her carry on didn't count, as they were for emergencies only. At the curb, she watched her checked bag disappear wherever checked bags go. Then, she went through security and headed for her gate, arriving just as they started to call for boarding. This had all been part of the plan; the rest of the plan, however, had been a bit sketchy.

An older gentleman, probably in his fifties, walked up and offered to carry her bag.

"Hello Miss Lindsey. Doc and the Doll send their

regards. You can call me Carson. Please follow me. Have you ever flown in a helicopter before?"

She answered "no," and they continued toward an "authorized personnel only" door. Carson passed a card over the lock and the door opened for them. Down some stairs and fifteen minutes later, she was climbing into a helicopter. Lindsey figured she would now be able to answer yes to the previous question if it ever came up again.

Carson was amused by all her questions and smiled at Lindsey's excitement during every part of the short flight to Ontario International airport. She learned that Ontario was a UPS hub, as Carson introduced her to Maverick, who she was told was Gunner's brother. Gunner had been the UPS driver she had met earlier that day. Maverick then directed Lindsey to one of the UPS hangars.

In the hangar sat an old Volkswagen van and two people. They both leaned back against the slab side of the old VDub, arms crossed, watching her approach. It was a young man and a young Asian woman, maybe Korean, based on her outfit. The guy was in jeans and a t-shirt and looked to be in pretty good shape. Lindsey focused on the girl again; she was very attractive.

She was maybe five foot nine, most of her long shapely legs not hidden by her short leather skirt. Part of her height might have been due to the stylish wedge heel short boots. Lindsey really liked the boots. The stylish young woman wore a loose knit tank top and a short vest-like coat. The coat matched her trendy flat top fedora hat, sitting loosely on a short pixie hairdo of rich brown with red highlights. When Lindsey got closer, she was caught by the big eyes boring into her. Her makeup was perfect; not too much, just enough to make them one more feature that popped on this ...

Lindsey almost fell as she stumbled to a stop, a dead stop.

"Lindsey?"

She recognized the voice as Doc.

"Glad to see you made it here; hope the trip wasn't too confusing." This time the voice was coming out of ... the Doll ... Dr. Wing ... Doll.

"Hey Doll," again the Doc's voice, "I'm thinking Shadow might find a redhead hiding in Lindsey.

The Doll smiled, "Breathe, girl. I have a lot to fill you in on during the drive."

Chapter 9

The ride back to Elsinore took under an hour. Doc drove, and the Doll spent the first half of that time, convincing Lindsey that she was really Karen Wing. That was only partly true. The more Lindsey talked to the Doll, the more she began to understand that while this was her old boss, the personality that was visible as the Doll was more real and relaxed. Doc listened in, learning a variety of fun, if useless, facts, as Lindsey posed questions, then carefully watched to see how the Doll answered, to confirm it was her boss.

Then the Doll took charge. She confirmed that Lindsey had followed her orders regarding the information Lindsey had uncovered concerning Doc's DNA, or whatever he had in its place to serve as a physiological building block.

Some months earlier, the Doll noticed citations in obscure papers and journals mirroring the work her team was doing. She was convinced this was plagiarism of the current research. Someone or some group was interested in the work she was doing and had access to what should have been secure government research.

There was a leak. As a precaution, the Doll had opened a personal cloud account with an old credit card. She then arranged access for Lindsey, the only one she trusted implicitly, to this cloud drive; they referred to it as her personal "safe." Any relevant conclusions or research results the two of them produced were only stored in the "safe."

After initiating this protocol, the Doll tracked later

entries in relevant scientific journals and while it was obvious that the direction of the research was still creeping into those journals, none of the Doll or Lindsey's solutions or conclusions were now available.

As they discussed the "safe," their focus drifted. The three began actively debating the cause and effect of the "safe" related to recent events. The "safe" had effectively stopped the leak. Could it have been the lack of access to their findings that had prompted the original kidnapping attempt? This new line of thought kept the three focused for the remainder of the drive to the yard in Elsinore. It was only a little after 7:00 pm when they parked the VDub in one of the larger containers and headed for the trailer.

Lindsey realized that she was so out of her element as she headed toward the trailer. She knew it was a house trailer and she knew she was in a big, sort of open, several acre lot. She was still catching up with the process that brought her here. Yesterday, she was a DARPA researcher with a master's in biomedical sciences, with a boss who was strait-laced to the point of being uptight.

As of today, in no particular order or relevance, she had been given two burner phones, snuck out of an airport to catch a helicopter ride to another airport, and had been reunited with her boss (sort of because this version of her boss went by the name "Doll"). They were driven to this big lot full of trailers and containers by a seventy-year-old man who could have passed for his late thirties, whose blood and DNA made no sense. Now, they were headed into one of those trailers. What next?

Lindsey was still trying to come to terms with the changes in her life when she stepped into the trailer and the door closed behind her. She looked around and the first person she saw was Shadow, all green hair and tattoos. She should have been surprised, but that train left the station when she was in the helicopter.

Ignoring Lindsey, Shadow and Lucky focused on the Doll.

"Well?" Shadow asked with a smug look, "How did it go?"

The Doll tossed her hat toward a hook near the breakfast nook and it landed perfectly. She smiled at that success, then tussled her hair to fix her hat hair. Finally, she looked back, first at Shadow, then at Doc.

"You were both right and, I hate to admit it, but I like my new look."

She then turned to Lindsey, "There will be no discussion; I am still your boss. I want to introduce you to Shadow. Listen to her suggestions; do not argue. You are the next one we need to hide in plain sight. I, for one, have a bet with Doc. He has talked to you, but just recently had the chance to meet you in person. Doc's bias is based on my description of you. I, on the other hand, am familiar with your current look and think I know you pretty well."

Lindsey looked at the Doll, still trying to rationalize that this was her boss, then at Shadow, green hair, piercings, tattoos, and all. She was thinking this must have been how Alice felt when she went down the rabbit hole. She shrugged and listened.

"Lindsey," Doc spoke in a calm, relaxed tone. "You are

among friends. Friends who won't judge you but will be honest with you. I am going to sleep in a shed Lucky set aside for me tonight; I have some things to review. Don't judge Shadow or try to second guess the Doll. Trust them both. You should relax, have a drink, get to know what is going on, and enjoy your make-over. People don't often get the chance to become a new person."

As Doc finished his little speech, Marian appeared like magic, bearing a steaming pot of what turned out to be a perfectly seasoned beef stew made from scratch. Joshua followed her in, dropped off a tray of fresh biscuits, and apologized for not staying, as he had some work to tend to. He disappeared as quickly as he had appeared.

Dinner went well and Lindsey began to realize that she was safe and among friends. She was still a little apprehensive about her impending makeover but was slowly resigning to the fact that it was going to happen regardless. At one point, she spent some time examining the Doll's short hair and how it absolutely fit her. She had never imagined that the Karen she knew would let anyone cut her hair, let alone completely restyle her look. If she had not worked with her for the last two years, she would not have been able to realize that Dr. Wing and the Doll were one in the same. She considered that for a moment and wondered which of the two was the "real," real person.

Shadow, Lindsey realized, was a few years older than her and not at all the person she appeared to be on the surface. Doc and the Doll had disappeared for a while, to download everything from the safe, then clear and close the account. That left Lindsey and Shadow with time to bond. In college, Lindsey had a weak moment and had gotten a tattoo that no one knew about. Shadow managed to get that out of her early on in their discussions. Lindsey was not sure what tomorrow's scheduled makeover would entail, but Shadow seemed to have reached some conclusions by the time they parted that night.

As she drifted off to sleep, she remembered Doc's comment in the UPS hangar. She was pretty sure that he might be right and that she was going to be a redhead, at the very least. She smiled as she drifted off. She was in a safe place and there was no safer place in the world than around the Doc and his friends ... whatever he was. That night she slept better than she had for at least a year or more.

Chapter 10
Near Garrapata State Beach

Ronan Amos Murdock sat at the teak desk, reviewing the reports. He had grown up in Belfast. Ronan was a long way from there now. He had experienced a few reversals in lifestyle, but it all balanced in the end.

The past few days, however, were trying his patience. He didn't traffic in guns, drugs, or anything of that nature. His business was information and people. It was an odd combination, but he kept the two sides of his empire separated. The people side was impossibly simple. He was performing a service, told himself, and he smiled as he thought of it that way. That part of his organization ran like clockwork.

His operatives, worldwide, gathered the homeless, the disenfranchised, the runaways. These abductees were moved through prearranged channels and to a new life. A life, where he had every reason to believe, they were more productive or, at the least, useful. Yes, he was trafficking in living beings, but he thought of it as recycling. The big advantage was, for his part, it was a simple abduction and his clients took care of all the rest. The profit margin was significant, and it allowed him to focus on the other side of his empire.

Every country invested in ongoing research in genetic engineering. That research was split between making better human beings and making super-soldiers. Recently, a small group in an out of the way DARPA lab was making some surprisingly accurate moves forward. The amazing part of this discovery is that they had no idea yet how easily their current path could be diverted. They were working at perfecting genetic tools to allow for faster healing and stronger tissue. Ronan's science teams had begun to project where the DARPA team's research could lead. Of course, Ronan's science teams had an edge, but that was none of his concern, if the profit margin remained.

His team had started by cloning some of the DARPA research and projecting the possibilities. He hoped that it might be possible to merge both parts of his empire as the project moved forward. Suddenly his team was not getting the results of critical tests or changes in biochemical markers. Critical parts of what they were borrowing was now being diverted or hidden. No problem; it appeared that the project was progressing. He was confident they could abduct the principals, turn them over to his clients and have them provide him with a new saleable product.

Unfortunately, the most straightforward solution failed dramatically. The abduction of the lead researcher, Dr. Karen Wing, failed spectacularly. Two skilled operatives had been assigned to abduct the good doctor during her morning jog. Instead, an old man in his 70s had interrupted the abduction, maimed one member of the team, and killed the second outright.

The second attempt had fared worse than the first. This time, a strike team of skilled mercenaries ended up surrounded by local law enforcement, but not before a double tap had dropped the team leader. There were witnesses, but no explanation as to how the scientist and the old man had accomplished this or escaped.

He researched the old man and found that while he

was former military, he was not a combatant, per se. The possibility was that he was a subject in Dr. Wing's ongoing research. If that was the case, they also needed to capture him.

Now, after the failed attempt by the second team, he had information that his targets were headed south to San Diego, maybe even into Mexico. While this information was being followed up on, he decided to have Dr. Wing's research assistant picked up. Instead, she got on a flight headed to Las Vegas via Phoenix but never arrived. Only her phone, which they had been tracking, completed the trip. There was evidence that she boarded the flight in Orange County, and poof, she vanished. Records showed her boarding the second leg of the flight, but no one remembered seeing the young blond woman on board.

Dr. Wing, the research assistant and the retired old man all had a visible social media presence, and quick Google search provided several good headshots. Yet, his operatives could not find them anywhere. They had, in a few days, simply ceased to exist. He needed to broaden his search and search methods.

His clients were not happy with these delays.

──────────── **Lake Elsinore, CA** ────────────

Joshua skidded the motorcycle to a stop near the storage bin where Doc was currently sorting and looking through boxes.

He got off the bike and walked over to Doc, "I'm back from dropping off that Jeep. This is my friend, Amber Rose," he pointed to the passenger sitting on the back of the bike. "Do you need anything more from me today? If not, we're hitting the club."

Doc looked up, first at Joshua, then the bike, a vintage Norton Commander. This model was produced by Norton in the late 60s and was restored beautifully. Doc looked at it as though it was a work of art.

Then he looked over at Amber Rose, also a work of art. She had pulled her helmet off by now, so he could see most of her face. She had a tan complexion with cute freckles across the bridge of her nose. Her eyes, however, were still hidden behind a pair of mirrored aviator sunglasses. Her hair bordered on shoulder length and was a deep, almost maroon red, neatly framing her face. He could see one ear where her hair had been brushed aside as she pulled off the helmet. That ear had a single piercing in the earlobe and three more from the midline of the ear to the top. It was a very appealing look.

She wore a mid-length halter top that did nothing to hide her navel piercing and torn jeans fitting into what looked almost like old combat boots. When she got off the bike, she turned to set her helmet on the back of the seat and he could see the yin-yang tattoo on her lower back. She leaned back against the bike, ostensibly waiting for Joshua, who was peering into some of the open boxes in front of Doc.

"Hi Lindsey," Doc said with a smile, "the look suits you perfectly. I don't remember seeing the freckles before. How did you pull that off?"

She sighed, then smiled, "I used to hate my freckles and covered them with foundation, but now I think they fit in fine. You are not an easy person to fool, maybe something in that "what factor" we are trying to figure out. So, who was closer in their estimation of how I would turn out, you or the Doll?"

Doc smiled, "The Doll, but I don't think she knows you have a tattoo."

Chapter 11

Yesterday had been a long day for all involved in the process of becoming invisible. Joshua shrugged off Doc's easy identification of Amber Rose as Lindsey. In the years he had been around Doc, he had come to realize that nothing seemed to phase the old coot. On the other hand, Shadow had done a great job on Amber and if he hadn't already had a serious girlfriend, he might have considered making a move on this hot nerd.

Amber Rose. Lindsey found the name was growing on her and she was also questioning her identity. She had just experienced her first ride on a motorcycle, as odd as that sounded. Now she was intent on convincing Joshua to let her ride it on her own. At the same time, she was beginning to wonder what else she had missed growing up in a family with a mother and father who both had tenure at Stanford. She had completed her undergrad and gotten her Masters in that same university. Her entire life had been spent in academia. She was not in academia now and, yet, there was so much to learn and experience.

It was now Wednesday and the question on everyone's mind was what would be the next move or plan and, as was the case lately, the plan wrote itself. While Amber Rose was in an animated discussion with Joshua, Lucky came over and pulled Doc to one side.

"Doc," he said without preamble, "we have visitors on the way and they will be here in about an hour. You remember Spyder? His grandson just called to say he was on the way here and is expecting to see you. He said to tell you not to worry; his visit is off the books."

Figuring they had some time to prepare, everyone gathered around one of the large picnic tables. From day one they had discussed options as a group. Any input or insight could be useful in this world where things changed from day to day. There were always options.

"Who is this Spyder you seem to be concerned about?" the Doll asked, looking from Doc to Lucky and back.

"I got this," Lucky began and he filled in the gaps for those around the table.

The short story was this. During the evac in Nam where Doc had pulled Lucky and two others out of a bad situation, a young CIA operative referred to as Spyder had been one of the other two. It seemed, as the story unfolded, that Lucky's unit, had been behind the lines working with the CIA on something unimportant to this discussion.

"You know," Lucky commented to the group while looking directly at Doc, "Spyder always maintained that you took a bullet pulling him out of that ditch, as you drug him to the Huey."

Doc smiled and shrugged. Lucky studied his reaction, and both the Doll and Amber Rose frowned at Doc as he walked off without any further explanation.

Lucky continued. Over the years, Spyder kept in touch. He eventually took a desk job at Langley, married, had a son and a daughter, and eventually a grandson. His kids and grandson stayed in the family business. They were all spooks.

Doc had kept up with the family for several years. The last time he saw them was at Spyder's funeral.

Spyder's grandson grew up loving his grandfather's and Doc's war stories. He graduated from Annapolis a year after Spyder's funeral. Several years had passed since then. Spyder and his grown kids had been responsible for Doc's level of tradecraft, originally for research for books he never penned. Instead, what he had learned made Doc one of the best in the field of identity theft.

The fact that Spyder's grandson figured out that he was here with Lucky amused Doc. Lucky was not amused. Yet, if anyone in the world would randomly have a clue where Doc might be, Spyder's kids would be on the top and possibly the only ones on that list. Doc missed Spyder and some of the shenanigans they had managed to get into. If you wanted to play on the wild side, having a close friend who was a decorated spy was a necessity.

Everyone was in their assigned places and realities when a late model Jetta pulled into the yard. Lucky had produced wireless earwigs from some hidden cache of toys so those not physically at the meeting could listen in.

Doc, Lucky, and Joshua were sitting at the picnic table chatting over a few beers. Several yards away three young women were going through a storage bin pulling clothes out of boxes and sorting what they found. They were far enough away to be ignored.

The driver's door opened and a tall, maybe 6'6," lanky individual unfolded from the front seat and looked over at the table. He was in loose slacks and wore a bright Hawaiian print shirt. Doc had a moment of déjà vu. This was Tommy,

Spyder's grandson.

Doc remembered that on some of their more interesting side trips, Spyder always dressed like a tourist. Spyder once told Doc that this was the perfect outfit to be ignored in. The only thing that would make it better was to be wearing a New York Yankees ball cap. Then you were completely invisible.

By this time, Tommy had looked in their direction and spotted Doc in the group. He turned back to the Jetta, said something, then closed the door. This produced the first surprise of the afternoon for Doc. The passenger door opened, and Captain Thompson climbed out and stood. No Hawaiian shirt, but equally casual attire and, Doc chuckled, he had on a Dodgers' ball cap. Both young men headed to the table as Doc, Lucky, and Josh watched them approach.

"Do you know the other guy in the ball cap?" Doc asked in Lucky's direction and got a negative head shake. "He is the Marine Captain I mentioned. The one assigned to look out for the Doll's welfare."

The identity of the second passenger came through loud and clear to where the Doll and Amber were making a show of sorting outfits; their reactions were fortunately unnoticed. Doc had to give them credit for not storming the castle, the picnic table, looking for answers. That was his job. As the two men approached the table, Doc stood and took a long look at Tommy Conner, then gathered him in for a big bear hug. After a moment, they broke apart and studied each other.

"Hi Doc, it's been a while," said Tommy with a bit of sad smile. "I miss your visits and the craziness you and gramps would get into."

Doc turned and looked at Captain Thompson, who was standing more than a little self-consciously under the combined stare of Doc and Lucky. Joshua was sitting quietly amused. He had heard about the Captain and was certain a few of his new friends were going to make this Marine's life less than happy.

"I suppose you would like that nice little Sig 9mm back, and do you mind if I call you Mike?" Doc said casually.

The young Marine cocked his head for a minute, smiled, and finally replied. "Mike would be fine. As far as the 9mm goes, maybe get rid of it since the authorities have two good samples of the rifling from that piece which they pulled out of the brain case of the guy you double tapped."

Tommy looked at Doc, shook his head, and, with a smile, said, "My guess is that you could use an explanation for our visit."

Chapter 12

Tommy sat down at the table, directly across from Doc. Lucky sat at one end of the long picnic table. Joshua got up, nodded to both newcomers, then left for some reason not apparent. Then the group got interesting.

A rather attractive woman with a short pixie hairdo and short skirt slid in beside Doc. Tommy was enjoying the view, but Mike seemed a bit confused. That was because a cute redhead in a crop top, loose cargo shorts, and aviator sunglasses appeared next. She settled in beside Mike and rested a hand with several rings and finely manicured dark-red finger nails on his arm in a suggestive and possessive manner. When he looked toward her, she smiled directly at him. Tommy looked back at Doc and cocked his head briefly.

"Gentlemen," said Doc, "allow me to introduce you to the Doll, at my right, and Amber Rose, attached to the Captain. They will be joining this conversation."

"I read Mike's report," Tommy nodded toward the Captain, "So I am going to guess that this is the Doll he was supposed to keep an eye on. I can see now how that would be difficult since she is no longer close to the description of the missing Dr. Wing. I am going to go out on a limb with my next guess. That would be that this fetching young lady, screwing with Mike's mind right now, is the demure, bookish research assistant that disappeared on her way to Las Vegas."

The Marine looked like he wanted to say something when Amber Rose touched a finger to his lips and shook her head in a decidedly don't interrupt gesture. A gesture that amused all present. Doc looked at the those around the table, determined they could hold their questions as just suggested, and looked back at Tommy.

"You said you had an explanation. Now would be a good time to roll that out for all of us to enjoy."

Tommy began to fill in the blanks. Some of this Doc knew from visits and watching Tommy grow up. The later years after he was in the Naval Academy were sketchy. So the update was helpful. Tommy had graduated from the Naval Academy and opted for the Marine Corps. When he was going through TBS (The Basic School) at Quantico, he met Mike Thompson. The two hit it off from the start. Tommy already knew that he would be lateraling out of the Marines and over to Langley, following in his family's traditional line of work. Spyder had always told him that when you see talent, seize it. He had tried to convince Mike to make the transition to Langley also, but Mike's family had always been Marines.

Determined to not lose talent, Tommy wrangled Mike a joint position, which allowed him to be a Marine and still work for the Company. This had worked well, and they kept in touch, even though their specific jobs rarely allowed them to work together. That was until recently. Tommy was assigned to see if he could apprehend, or at least derail, a certain Ronan Amos Murdock, an information dealer, possibly involved in human trafficking. Ronan was rumored to be involved in trying to steal research and prototypes or serums for a super-soldier.

Tommy investigated the rumors and found that Mike was in the perfect position to became part of the DARPA research program. It was easy to manipulate the DARPA program into moving to a phase that required a joint operation with the United States Marine Corps Warfighting Laboratory. Their joint investigations had been coming along quite nicely until a few days ago when it all went to hell. The CIA knew about the research leaks and were tracking those leaks. Then, suddenly, the leaks began to slack off.

That was the first indication of a problem. Then Ronan's lackeys tried to kidnap the researcher and the uncontrolled downhill race began. The simple kidnapping failed spectacularly when Doc included himself into the mix. Tommy wasn't initially aware of Doc's intervention. Someone had intervened; he just didn't know it was Doc. By the time he had put the pieces together and realized the cog in the works was the Doc he had grown up around, Doc and the Doll had performed their vanishing act at the restaurant. Then they put a tail on Lindsey, and this also failed. This failure was more mysterious as Lindsey got on a plane and simply ceased to be, anywhere. Finally, Tommy and Captain Mike compared notes. Tommy realized the problem was that pseudo-uncle all kids have somewhere; in his case that was Doc. Having put all the pieces together, he sent a note to Lucky. He was certain that if anyone knew where Doc was it would be Lucky.

Then the story took an unexpected turn. Tommy explained that he was temporarily off the reservation, so to speak. There was a problem concerning the information leaks. They were still not identified and that concerned him. However, the issue Tommy was dealing with was that he had made a promise to Spyder. That last vague comment brought the conversation to a temporary halt.

"Lucky," Tommy started, studying Lucky's face as he continued, "Did my grandfather ask you to hold something for Doc until he, Doc, asked for the package?"

The focus now shifted to Lucky who stared back stoically and said nothing. Lucky always had a good poker face and now all emotion or indication of what might be going on in his mind was missing. He looked like a statue. Doc, who had been listening to the exposé with a look of wry amusement, now stared at Lucky.

Tommy continued, "About a year before he passed, he asked me into his study, swore me to secrecy, then told me some of his exploits and discoveries. He explained that what he was telling me would be important in the future and that I would recognize that point in time. Finally, he told me that he sent a package to you that held proof of what he and I had just discussed."

He was looking directly at Lucky now.

"He said that if Doc hadn't figured it out on his own, that I should get the two of you together and tell you to give the 'Majestic' package to Doc." Tommy looked from Lucky to Doc, then back to Lucky.

Tommy continued, "I listened then and over the years have, let's say, been in a position to verify some of what I learned that night. Before you ask, Doc, I have no clue what is in that package. All I know was that if you hadn't already retrieved it from Lucky, that I was to let you know to pick it up. The part of the meeting with Gramps that always bugged me was his certainty that I would know when that time was at hand."

He paused, looked at both Lucky and Doc, and continued, "That time is now. Lucky, do you still have the package?"

Lucky shrugged, seeming to have made a decision that lifted some sort of weight off his soul. "Yes, I have it. Doc, I am sure I know less than junior here about the box, but considering recent events, I agree. You should open the box and review what Spyder saved for you, in private though."

Doc looked at the five others at the table, "Take me to this box; we can discuss why you kept this to yourself at a later point."

Without another word, Lucky got up and headed for the rows of storage units, leaving the Doll, Amber Rose, Tommy, and Mike to get reacquainted.

Chapter 13

They walked in silence through the warren of storage units into an old warehouse and eventually into a basement. Lucky walked to a door with a rather impressive digital lock that consisted of a palm scanner and a twelve-digit code.

Inside the room were several items which Doc assessed to be high value. Near the back of the room was an average sized footlocker. It looked a little worse for wear but, other than the lock, it appeared normal. The lock consisted of twelve buttons. The first and last buttons were blank; the remaining buttons were numbered one through ten. Doc looked at Lucky and got nothing but a shrug. Then Lucky proceeded to another section of the underground room. There was shelving holding old shoe boxes. Lucky opened one of the shoe boxes and, after rummaging through it for a minute, retrieved a thin plastic case, like those used to hold missile launch codes.

Lucky handed the case to Doc, "I don't need to tell you that while many people thought Spyder was always one card short of a full deck, those of us who really knew him understood that he always had an extra joker in his deck, a wild card, so to speak. I don't know specifically what is in the box, but I do know this plastic case contains the combination."

Doc shook his head in amusement, snapped the card case in half, and pulled out a folded piece of Mylar. He studied the three symbols on the silvery surface and handed it to Lucky.

AπΩ

Lucky looked confused until Doc smiled and said, "The circle of life ... the concept was important to Spyder; the beginning, the circle, and the end."

Before Lucky could react or suggest thinking over what this code might be, Doc punched the first of the two blank buttons, followed by 3141592653, then the last blank button. There was an audible click and the lid of the footlocker raised just a fraction.

"That worked," Doc said with a smile. "Spyder once told me to remember a specific date. Once per century, there is an e-pi-c day, 3.14.15 at 9:26:53; the date/time will correspond to the first ten digits of the mathematical constant pi."

Lucky came over and stood by Doc. "You know," he said, "Spyder had a number of unusual theories about who you are. I know he ran a lot of them by you, but he also ran them by me. Like you, I laughed and told him that he would have to prove it. After a while he tapered off and ... well, he went off on other bizarre tangents."

"About ten years ago, he brought this footlocker to me and told me to hold it for you. He said you might ask for it yourself, but that he had an ace in the hole if you didn't. I guess that was Tommy. What I do know is that this box contains what he thought would be the proof you would need to believe his theory. If that's the case, I hope you'll let us know so we can help you."

Lucky took a deep breath and looked at Doc, "I'm heading back to the group; I hope you'll join us." Then he left.

Doc studied the box. While it looked like a standard issue wooden footlocker, it was not made of wood. It was some form of composite that was cool to the touch and felt vaguely metallic. When he opened the lid, he could see that there were no seams in the material and the hinge mechanism seemed built in. He closed the box and noted that the top joined to the base with no gap. He was relatively certain it produced an airtight seal. He reopened the box and began examining the contents.

It had a removable top tray divided into two sections. Each of the sections had a plastic, or some impervious material, folder. One was labeled documents; the other was labeled photographs. Doc always had considered himself visually oriented, so he opened the photographs folder first. After reviewing the first few photographs, a mixture of 8x10 black & white and color prints, he closed that folder. Before opening the documents folder, he looked around and found a stool to sit on.

He opened the folder and leafed through the contents. Lots of words, there were some redactions, but mostly the documents were clean. They didn't have the visual impact the pictures had, but the headings on the documents were as riveting. He lifted the tray and set it to one side. The remainder of the footlocker contained three metallic devices or tools or ... he did not know what. Each was nestled in a formed cradle of protective cushioning material. He found himself drawn to one of the devices and, as his hand met with the surface of the object, he felt a tingle. He immediately pulled his hand back.

After a moment, he replaced the tray and closed the lid. The lock resealed with an audible click. He had placed the Mylar code sheet in the box before he closed it. There were handles on either side of the footlocker, but he only needed one to carry this unexpectedly light container. He turned off the lights as he left the underground room.

Lucky saw Doc approaching the table first. Tommy was in an animated discussion with the Doll. Mike was talking with Lindsey, aka Amber Rose. It was obvious from the start the previously shy Lindsey was now taking charge. As Doc got closer, all eyes went to him, and what he was carrying.

Doc put the footlocker on the side of the table and sat down beside the Doll. He took a moment to look at each of them without saying a word, then began:

"Doll, please pardon me if I address you last."

"Lucky, thank you for being the friend you were to Spyder and are to me. I might not have dealt well with his gift a few years ago."

"Tommy, I miss hanging out with you and Spyder. I know that we talked about and laughed over many of his theories. I was glad to hear from Lucky that you were on your way here. You hinted that you might be or are considering going off the reservation while this perplexing turn of events is being explored. Hopefully, in the next few hours, we can come to an understanding and whether it may be a real option for you. Regardless, I am glad you're here."

"Captain Michael Thompson, your presence was an enigma until Tommy filled us in. It helped put our first introduction and your subsequent actions in perspective. I am not sure what your status is right now but suspect that it may be partly tied to Tommy. At the same time, I would not want to be part of you having to decide between the Corps and this grand adventure. If you want to stick with us as we try to solve this puzzle, you are welcome to; but I know that you have several masters to serve."

"Amber Rose, you are an important part of this puzzle. Your tenacity has already given us some insight into the issue at hand. I also know the Doll values you and your work. That said, I welcome you as an addition to this odd little group, but you should probably give the good Captain a break."

There was a general snicker around the table and Mike just rolled his eyes.

"Finally, Doll, I did not butt into your kidnapping to cause you problems. It appears, though, that it may have been inevitable that we meet. I don't have all the answers. I believe that each of you around this table have some part of those answers. For some reason, I now feel like I'm in a race I don't understand against opponents whose choices make even less sense."

Everyone at the table was studying Doc, not sure how to reply.

Doc took a deep breath, and spoke again, "Doll, when we first met, face to face at your abduction, and several times since then you have asked what I am. Always what, not who. The who part is simple. I am the being that you have been getting to know over the past few days. The what is that I may not be human."

The silence around the table was epic.

Chapter 14

Suddenly, Doc was holding a fork and shaking his head. Across the table, Tommy was smiling and everyone else looked a little perplexed.

"I thought a demonstration would help speed up the learning curve," Tommy commented.

Everyone seemed to be at a loss, so he asked each of them what they thought had just happened. The responses varied but most seemed to think Doc had produced the fork for some unknown reason by sleight of hand.

The Doll finally commented, "I think that Tommy threw the fork at Doc. I wasn't looking at Tommy at the time, but I know that both Doc's hands were relaxed and on the table. And," she commented a bit self-consciously, "I am sitting close enough to him that I felt him move."

Tommy waved the rest of the comments down and explained, "When I was a kid, Spyder taught me to play a game with Doc."

Doc sighed.

"The game was to see if you could hit him with, well, anything. It was and still is a fun game. I palmed the fork while Doc was speaking to the Doll the first time. When he turned back to the rest of the group, my hand and arm were in optimum throwing position. I let the fork fly right at his forehead."

Everyone looked at Doc.

"It is an annoying game. Please don't pick it up as something to do in your spare time," Doc sighed and continued, "If there is something moving toward me or someone is intent on harming me, I get an uneasy buzz or vibration in my forehead. When the intent or action begins, the vibration turns into a time dilation. In my mind, or to my perception, everything around me slows down dramatically. I didn't see Tommy palm the fork or set up for the throw. An instant before he began the throw, however, I could focus on the issue, and time essentially slowed to a crawl. By the time any of you saw the fork, I had plucked it out of the air, away from my forehead, turned it around, and held it as though I had some purpose for having a fork."

"How many bullets did we find?" The Doll directed her question to Mike.

"Three."

"Yes," Doc replied to the unasked question. "I didn't quite dodge the first but the second and third never got close."

"And the first?" The Doll was staring at him intently, "it grazed you as we speculated?"

"It punched through the right side of my chest in the fleshy area between the third and fourth intercostal rib, apparently missing anything vital," He lifted his shirt.

The Doll investigated what was left of the wound, then sat back quietly.

"Bullet proof, mostly, and hyper fast," She looked at him, "... anything else we should know?"

"I will let you know as soon as I find out myself," he commented as he pointed to the footlocker.

Doc stood and opened the footlocker and removed the tray.

"I may not have all of the answers, but I suspect that the folders in this tray will help shed some light on the subject. The Doll, from the beginning, has asked me 'what' I am. The contents of this box may provide more questions than answers, but let's take a look."

At this point everyone at the table gathered around the container and began leafing through the papers and the photos in the tray. Nobody, however, even remotely made a move to exam the three items nestled in the bottom of the box.

Doc leaned over the footlocker and let his hand hover over the three objects. He could feel something from each of them, a power or hint of power. As his hand closed the gap on any of the three artifacts, there was a hint of symbols on each object. By this time, he again had the attention of the group. He looked, briefly, at his odd collection of friends. His mind was a little cloudy, like waking in an unfamiliar room. He felt certain that he needed to be in a trusted environment when he handled these. He continued to move his hand above the three cylinders. He felt the cylinder on the left side had to be the one he dealt with first.

He slowly reached in, placed his hand around the cylinder and began to lift it out of its padded recess. The symbols became more prominent and he was getting a vibration. It was like the emergency feeling that would normally slow time, yet decidedly different.

Doc suddenly needed to sit; he wasn't steady standing. Between the table and the side of the trailer, there were several worn Adirondack chairs. He let himself ease back into the closest one. He could see concern on the faces of his ... friends.

The world, as he knew it, disappeared.

He saw his parents. How he knew them was a mystery. He saw the ship, several ships, symbols he couldn't understand, planets, other beings, more worlds, family, more beings, formulas for propulsion systems, and environments. The images and concepts continued flooding into him for what must have been days. He needed to get some rest and find his ... friends and share what he was trying to catalog in his mind. He could feel the cylinder still in his left hand and decided to rest it in both of his hands while he ... he needed to do something.

When the Doll and the others saw Doc pick up the cylinder, his eyes closed, and he staggered back and dropped into one of the Adirondack chairs near the trailer. The Doll was the first to him followed by Tommy then the others. Doc seemed to have settled into the chair, eyes closed, the rod or cylinder resting in the palms of both hands. The Doll looked at Tommy then moved to the side of the chair to get close enough to check Doc's pulse and see if she could open his eyes to ... to do something. The total elapsed time had been maybe less than two or three minutes.

She was close to his face, her hand against the carotid trying to find a pulse; her face was where she could see the movement of his eyes behind closed lids.

His eyes snapped open, looking directly into her eyes and he closed the gap. Their lips touched in a gentle but undeniable kiss. She responded before regaining her composure then moved back to study his face.

"Hi," Doc said, "What day is this? Have I missed much? Not that I am complaining, but why did you kiss me?"

Tommy replied to Doc, giving the Doll time to regain her composure, "Welcome back Doc, you picked up the rod that you are still holding, staggered and dropped back into this chair. You have been out for only a few minutes."

"I have a headache," he replied, "I feel like I have been studying some impossible puzzle for days. I am suddenly exhausted. Please put this cyrog back in its space, close and lock the footlocker. Leave the tray out, somewhere safe but available to our group. It was already getting late when I brought the box out. Everyone needs to get some sleep so we can work on this in the morning. I must get some sleep. I have never been this exhausted."

Amber and the Doll helped Doc into the trailer and watched him instantly drop off to sleep when he fell onto the bed. Doc had been sleeping on a cot in his storage bin and nobody felt that was a good place for him tonight.

Chapter 15

Doc lay on his back, eyes closed, trying to decide if he was awake. He was certain this shouldn't be a difficult decision, but it was. He opened his eyes and realized that he was in the bedroom at the back of the trailer, the one the girls currently used. That sent his mind in two different directions. One was to remind him neither Amber nor the Doll were girls. Then he thought, at his age all women under forty-five were girls. But why forty-five?

He blinked as he realized that his thought patterns were all over the place. Besides the concept of girls, he was wondering why he was here and not on his cot, what day it was, was it actually day or night, where was everyone, someone had taken off his shoes, he had an interstellar research vessel, was he still on earth, he needed to get to his ship, humans and others were chasing him, the Doll had kissed him, did he have any pets ...

"Stop!" Doc realized that last thought was verbalized.

If he concentrated, he could divide the questions and confusion into categories and prioritize. He got up and confirmed his shoes were MIA as he headed to the front of the trailer. He had slept there the first night until Amber Rose joined the group, then he had moved to a cot in his storage bin.

There were sounds coming from outside, so he opened the door to take in the scene. The overly large picnic table was surrounded by a collection of beings. The table itself had various stacks of paper, photographs, note pads, dishes with scraps of breakfast, coffee cups, containers with fruit, the table was made of black walnut, the chairs didn't match.

This time he issued the "Stop" in his mind, not out loud. He took a deep breath and forced himself to focus. About that time, the Doll spotted him and made a bee line in his direction. She wore a pair of loose, cartoon patterned, long pajama bottoms, the kind with a drawstring at the waist, well actually at her hips, and a short loose-fitting top. No shoes, no perfect hair just the tussled short 'do' with red streaks. She was a Doll. He smiled.

Doc reminded himself to focus. By this time, the remainder of the group had noticed him, and they all started talking at once. He covered his ears and they must have noticed the grimace on his face because they all fell silent. The Doll had reached him by that time and was looking at him with concern. He lowered his hands, smiled at the Doll, and let out a heavy sigh.

"Please be patient with me for a while. Whatever happened with the cyrog, ah ... the rod, last night has finally stabilized but I have not. I am still sorting information in my consciousness. I need to know what you have found out in your research this morning; and I need to give you some short answers that might help. But mostly I need you to be patient with me for a while. I can only focus on one person's questions at a time for now. I also need to eat something very soon."

He paused, then continued, "While I am eating, there are some things that might help you understand the pile of documents and photos. I was born on Earth in1948. My parents were Dunarian, therefore, am I. I have a ship, they had a ship, that was an advanced survey vessel, I can feel that it is still mine. And we all need each other's help until we find it. I need food."

Doc found that if he let the Doll lead him, he didn't have to focus on where to go. She took him to the table and ... Marion brought him food ... scrambled eggs and ... round ... waffles. This was annoying. He needed to stop identifying every little thing. He focused on the food only and ate. He ate three full plates of eggs, four waffles and was on his second cup of coffee when he realized two things, well three. One, he could look around, without the disorientation of hundreds of thoughts, ideas and plans. Two, his friends, people he valued, were leaving him alone and working on deciphering the pile of information in front of them. Third, the Doll sat patiently across from him waiting.

"Dunarian, huh?" she smiled, "I guess that answers my original 'what' question. My work here is done."

She watched for a reaction. When she didn't get one, she continued.

"Doc," she began, "I have always been a quiet person. My parents died when I was in grade school and I lived with my aunt. I went to Stanford on a full scholarship. From there to George Washington University in DC, then back to Stanford for my doctorate work in Biotechnology and Biophysics. That, by the way, is where I met Lindsey. She was finishing her Masters in Biological and Biomedical Sciences. Finally, I was asked to join DARPA. Now, I have my own facility. I am self-absorbed, self-sufficient, and successful. In short, I am at the top of my game."

She paused, looked at Doc carefully and resumed,

"Last Friday things spiraled out of my immediate control. Yesterday I was kissed by ... and returned the kiss of an alien ... a being from another planet. I am certain that I am in the throes of a full-blown Stockholm Syndrome, and for the first time, in longer than I can remember, I feel alive. So how are things with you? Your turn."

She rested her elbows on the table, hands together under her chin, smiled at Doc and waited for a reply.

Doc looked over at the group working at the other end of the table. He realized that at least a few of them had heard the Doll's comment since he could see some guarded smiles. He got up and wandered down one side of the table then back up to where the Doll sat watching him. He glanced at some of the papers, some with black marks redacting whatever. He noticed the photographs were all older 8 x 10 black & white images. Everyone, including Marion, Lucky, their kids, Amber Rose, and the two spooks that had arrived last to this party now seemed curious to hear his answer.

He smiled, "I feel like I am at some form of sponsored meeting. Hi, I am Doc, and I am an alien."

That got a chuckle from the group and he continued in a more serious tone, "There are human factions and some other species intent on acquiring the Mithrim, my family's survey/research vessel. Not all the players are aware of this yet, but with my confirmed appearance and the Doll's disappearance, people will begin to put the pieces together shortly. Who has any questions?"

From the other side of the table, Tommy responded in an unexpected way, "I think I know where the Mithrim might be located."

Chapter 16

"OK..." Doc replied as all heads turned to look at Tommy

Tommy had a look like the kid with his hand in the cookie jar.

"I didn't mean to blurt that out, at least not like that."

Everyone was focused on Tommy now.

"Tommy," Doc said patiently and loud enough to be heard by all, "I just learned I am not a human being. I have a brain full of information that I am still trying to understand. I know there is a ship, and I feel I know more. I still haven't processed it yet. I need all of you to help me sort this out. There is a larger picture that involves more than me. If you know where the Mithrim is, then I can focus on why this is so important."

"Remember how gramps was always fascinated by aliens, Area 51, Roswell, and every other thing that fit into that mind set?" Tommy asked, looking at Doc then at the rest of the group. "This is why."

Tommy sat back down and began rummaging through one of the stacks of photos as he talked. He stopped when he found a photo and slid it toward the group to look at. The grainy black & white photo showed two groups of people, some in uniforms, some not ... maybe not recognizable human clothing. That got everyone's attention, even Doc's.

Now that he had everyone's attention, Tommy started by telling them Spyder's story, the one not for prime time. After Viet Nam died down, there was a shift of personnel assignments to cover areas the company was involved in. Spyder's known interest in all things science fiction and aliens landed him in Area 51 for a few years. Tommy asked if everyone was familiar with the Men in Black movies. When he got nods around the table, he continued.

He began by insisting the MIB franchise of movies was very definitely farfetched fiction. On the other hand, as hinted at by the photo, there was government knowledge of the interstellar community. The first contact had been during World War II and some of the reference to Foo fighters was, in fact, sightings of observers from some of the species aware of Earth's existence. Spyder had joined that unit in 1976 and was still involved with them when he retired. His son, Tommy's father, showed no interest and at the time of his death from an IED in Afghanistan, was still unaware of that part of the Company.

Tommy, on the other hand, grew up with Sci-Fi, Star Trek and Star Wars. When he graduated from the Farm, as a result of Spyder's posthumous recommendation, he was read into the program. His current assignment was to monitor a crime boss named Ronan Murdock, in part, to ensure the human trafficker and information broker was able to learn of any alien tech or access any resources. Having laid the groundwork, Tommy backtracked.

In 1947 there was an incident outside of Roswell, New Mexico. Contrary to the initial story, later cover-ups and popular myths, there were four ships involved. Two of those were in pursuit of a third ship, the fourth appeared to have been a small drone. The third ship was most likely the Mithrim; and it was theorized to have released the defensive drone. That drone was a small part of the wreckage found at Brazel's ranch. The second and third crashes were the two pursuit ships. The debris field from those two was extensive but was passed off as a single ship to lessen the news media damage control. Company paperwork indicates that both pursuit ships had been heavily armed combat vessels. Very little was known of their target. That targeted ship, however, had trashed its pursuers and escaped the area.

The species that had agreements with the human government agencies could provide very little on the unknown missing ship. They were also reluctant to provide much intel on the attacking vessels. The interstellar community felt it was not something they wanted to share. Tommy conceded that, even now, the information on the entire incident was still sketchy.

Spyder, on the other hand, had located additional information on the 1947 incident and found some inconsistencies that he kept to himself. In the mid-80s, he told Tommy that he had met one of the remaining members of the crew of the mystery ship. Over the next few years, they bonded. When his contact died mysteriously, Spyder was never able to verify what happened. A year later, Spyder discovered that Anexten had placed a cache of documents, photos, and devices in a secure drop. In the event of Anexten's death, a courier service was contracted to deliver a sealed letter to Spyder on the anniversary of his friend's death. Spyder reviewed those notes and then sent the footlocker to Lucky to hold until his friend's son came for it.

"Son?" Doc vocalized what everyone at the table got from that last comment.

"Gramps never forgot your saving him all those years ago," Tommy said, looking at Doc. "The fact that you both keep in touch over the years meant that he had time to study who you were. He put together a timeline and discussed you with your father. He was told that his hunch was correct, and it was important that you discover your lineage on your own. Before you ask, on his deathbed, gramps made me swear that if I was certain that you were that son, I would send you after the Majestic box and not before.

Before that confession to me, he never spoke of you as the 'son.' He did, however, convince me that you weren't human long before I graduated and joined the Company. Growing up, it always made your visits special and exciting. Later, when I had been read in, met other non-humans, and had access to advanced tech, I put my teenage fantasy and my adult reality together. You went from pseudo uncle to an unanswered question."

"We got together last year for your birthday," Doc said to Tommy, "you were in LA for a conference. Why not ask me some questions then?"

Tommy smiled, "I remember that visit. I remember most of your visits. It was my birthday and you took me out for a great dinner at a little place in Korea town. The next day, we toured a train museum and generally chatted about nothing in particular. You were just the same uncle I always knew, older but still lively and interesting, a little grayer than the last time I'd seen you, but otherwise you gave off no super alien vibe. What you didn't know, was that I was in LA to meet with a delegation from Surnastim, a very human-like species interested in aluminum which is rare in their system. So, I was visiting with five-foot-tall, relatively human appearing beings with only three digits on each hand. All three of those digits are opposed, and their dexterity is awesome. On the other hand, no pun intended, I was visiting an old friend who seemed perfectly normal, so you hide well, as you are fond of saying, in plain sight."

"Then at the end of last week, I was reminded why Spyder felt the way he did," Tommy resumed addressing the group. "Someone, possibly non-human, had destroyed two skilled operatives. Early intel indicated they were sent by Ronan's group which raised a red flag for me. I asked Mike to follow up. The next thing I heard was that same unknown could catch tranq darts and there was some irregularity regarding his DNA. Then, like magic, poof, all the players in this puzzle disappeared. Spyder told me that there were three devices in the Majestic box that keyed to DNA, but only the DNA pattern of Anexten's son."

Tommy paused for effect, then continued, grinning at Doc, "You bonded with those devices in the footlocker. I wish gramps had been here to see it. Your father, his name was Anexten, would have been proud. My job finding and confirming your identity is done. Now, Mike and I are at your service."

"At my service?" Doc looked at Tommy then Mike.

"Dude ..." Tommy grinned, "I researched the specs on the crashed ships at Roswell and I have seen current interstellar vessels. The Mithrim is still in New Mexico, and I have a few idea's where. What I also know is that she took out the ships trying to destroy her without taking any appreciable damage herself. Spyder taught me to side with the guy with the best guns."

Chapter 17

Doc looked at those gathered around the table. The group included himself and the two DARPA scientists, Lucky and his family, and the two CIA agents. Others had been involved at some point in getting this group together. Doc felt comfortable that those like Carson, Gunner and his family, and other random contacts were isolated enough that they were not in danger. Doc's immediate concern was that they leave the storage yard in Lake Elsinore for some new location and he wanted to discuss who should go.

Doc began, "I need to decide what we do next based on the information that we have. And if we leave, which seems likely, who leaves and who stays."

Lucky emphatically stated that he and his family would remain behind. After making his blanket statement, he looked at Marion, Shadow, and Joshua. Each in turn agreed with feedback. Marion smiled and agreed that hers was the taxing job of looking after Lucky. Shadow said she had commitments and was sure that her involvement up to now was not known outside of this group. She also went on to say that the makeovers were part of her normal day and no one would find anything unusual about it. Joshua's agreed that he would stay behind to make sure his grandparents had no problems to deal with. In the end, Lucky threw in the comment that once Doc had this under control, he would love a ride on a spaceship.

Doc looked at the two CIA operatives next.

Tommy lead with, "I know where the ship is."

He clarified that statement with a comment that he was pretty sure he knew where it was. On the other hand, his job was keeping track of aliens on Earth. After some eye rolls, he continued and explained that considering the current unknowns and the possibility of leaks in his own agency, he was considering going dark for a while.

"The trick," he explained, "is that by letting the agency know this is my intent, and I can show my rational is valid, I can do so for up to thirty days at a time. This morning I filed such a notification to my senior officers and included that Mike would be working part of this operation. We are officially off the books for the next thirty days."

Mike nodded when Tommy said he was also included. Tommy went on to outline what leeway that allowed them. He and Mike had already disabled their phones while they were still in San Diego the day before. The Jetta was a company vehicle meant for black ops, so it had no tracking devices. When these vehicles were checked out, the operatives created new state license plates and matching registration paperwork. Once done, the memory on the printer and plate maker was erased. So, the Jetta, with its New Mexico plates, was good to go.

Tommy finished by explaining to the group that before getting on the flight to San Diego he had "primed the pump" by hinting to his boss that he might have to go dark.

Mike glanced at the group after Tommy finished, "I'm good with the plan. Tommy has filled me in on his theories and on Doc." He smiled at Doc, then continued, "I have only known Doc for a few short days and in that time, I made up my mind he is the 'Doc' all Marines trust. Trusting and backing him is a no brainer. By the way, Doc, if you still have it, the 9mm Sig is my gift to you."

Doc nodded in acknowledgment, "Thanks, it is a nice sized concealed carry."

Doc continued, this time looking at Amber and the Doll, "Okay, that leaves the two of you. Let's start with the stunning Amber Rose, aka Lindsey."

"Amber will be fine, among friends," she smiled, "I'm not sure I have many options. Based on what I am hearing, if I did reappear as Lindsey, I would end up in some holding facility while someone tried to figure out what I know. And I am not sure if that facility would be good guys, bad guys, or alien guys. I would like access, at some point, to appropriate equipment so I can resume trying to figure out the actual structure of your DNA. In the meantime, I am a quick study, I also a have a minor in languages and someone needs to keep Michael focused."

The last comment almost slid by the group, but not quite and Mike bowed his head in mock defeat.

"Doll?" Doc asked as everyone at the table looked at her in expectation of what she might say.

"Doc ... Doc ... Doc," she said slowly, watching his expression and glancing at the group, who were now very curious to hear what was coming.

"Let's see if I can sum this up. Last Friday, you appeared out of nowhere to rescue me from some unknown kidnappers. Then you stepped up your game. When I came to visit, you tied me to a chair, left and went to a movie. Oh, wait, you also named me Doll. That was okay because the next day we had a relaxing dinner with Mike. Then you, I believe the term is double tapped, a thug, and we ran away to this place."

She paused, smiled and looked at Lucky and his family, "Lucky, Marion, Shadow and Joshua, you have been great hosts. Doc, however, you decided I needed a makeover. While I was getting that done, you arranged to have my assistant hijacked and made her disappear. In the meantime, you began your plan to take over my life. I am approaching forty and my life had been wrapped up in academia and then in running a government research lab. In short, I guess I was a perfect subject for your alien take over scheme."

Doc remained speechless as her dissertation continued to unfold. The rest of the group enjoyed the commentary with ever broadening smiles.

The Doll continued, her expression difficult to read, "Last night you recharged your alien psyche and put your nefarious plan into action. First, you kissed me in front of the group. Second, you have taken that as permission to drag me along on your magical mystery tour, probably in the old VDub micro bus we used on our trip to capture poor Lindsey, who you turned into Amber. Does that about sum it up? Because if you want me to play, we need to discuss a joint plan. In my opinion, your plans could use some refinement."

Doc looked at those around the table and realized he would not be getting help from the grinning crowd.

"My plans have sort of worked," Doc replied more casually than he felt, "Doll, dearest, what are your thoughts?"

Chapter 18

After the laughing, back slapping, high fives, and fist bumps subsided, the group looked at Doc and the Doll. They sat together at the head of the table and began leafing through some of the photos as they waited for the group to regain composure.

"Now that we have resolved the pecking order," Doc's remark set off another round of laughter, "We, yes we, need to come up with a plan of action."

During the next few hours, they used the material from the footlocker to add to the information base they had to work from. Each, in turn, adding their perspective to this puzzle

There were three artifacts in the bottom of the footlocker. Two of those looked like burnished metal cylinders. They were all aware of Doc's interaction with one of the cylinders, so they started with it.

Doc explained that while he had no idea what any of the artifacts were before having touched the first cylinder, once he had touched it, his memory had been refreshed. Last night he had referred to the cylinder as a cyrog and today he could confirm that was the name for this type of device. Cyrogs were, he explained, primarily used for extended interstellar travel that requires a hibernation period. Each cyrog was keyed to the specific individual's genetic pattern, their DNA. These devices were designed to reload memory if the user suffered any memory loss during hibernation. Cyrogs were also tied into the vessel's AI, and anything of importance to the individual was also updated. When a traveler's memory was refreshed, they were brought up to date.

Doc paused for moment, then continued. The cyrog he had chosen first, was not only keyed to his genetic pattern, but it had been designed to draw him to it first. He wasn't sure, but he may not have been able to use the other cyrog or the larger remaining rectangular object, the history panel, had he not connected to the first cyrog. The other cyrog, he was now certain, was full documentation for the Mithrim. What he was painfully aware of was that he was still absorbing the flood of information from the first cyrog. The second cyrog and the history panel would have to wait.

The mental download of information had included everything related to his family, who he was, and who he should have been had circumstances not intervened. The latter part of the brain dump had included an ongoing dialog concerning the time after his separation from his family. His father, he presumed, had used the ships AI interface to update this cyrog remotely so that when Doc finally encountered it, there was no extended gap.

Now curious, each of the group touched, stroked, and handled the two cyrog as well as the history panel to see if they could make any kind of connection. Amber was certain that given the proper resources, she could determine what in Doc's genetic pattern, or DNA, unlocked these devices and she could synthesize it. Doc found that oddly amusing but kept that thought to himself. The Doll took a different approach. She wanted to know if, through the cyrog, he had learned whether he had additional capabilities, other than those he had already demonstrated.

That, of course, prompted a resurgence of the game.

Thanks to Tommy, every member of the group felt obliged to try their hand at playing 'Poke Doc,' the simple name applied to Tommy's childhood game. Tommy explained there were rules to the game. There had to be roughly four feet of open space between whatever you were trying hit Doc with, and, Doc. So, while they read through old documents and looked at photos with magnifying glasses, everyone played several rounds of 'Poke Doc.' Well almost, Lucky and the Doll took a pass. The others, however, tried to toss, throw, or otherwise connect to Doc in any manner they considered might score a hit. Much to everyone's consternation, the success rate was zero.

Lucky had declined to play. He said he was getting slow in his old age, and it was more fun watching the youngsters fail. Through the course of the next four or so hours, random things from food to pencils, coffee to chewed gum, were hurled toward Doc, only to fail connecting. The Doll, on the other hand, chose to study the phenomenon. These were all people that Doc trusted, yet, at the point that any of them committed to hurling, tossing, or splashing anything in his direction, there was a subtle change. The Doll began to change her position so she could see Doc's face, more exactly his eyes.

It didn't matter whether the object in motion was behind, to the side or in front of him, the instant it began its final trip, several things happened. The first few times she had missed it. After some thought, she borrowed Shadow's new cell phone. Unlike Doc, the Doll and the others in their group of pseudo fugitives, Lucky and his family still had regular cell phones and tablets. No one was looking for any of them. Shadow's cell could do video and slow motion. So, the Doll positioned herself and the phone to video the game play. The first few attempts, once she came up with the plan, failed because she hit the button to record well after the microsecond action had concluded.

Up to the challenge, she sent Shadow for her charger. Shadow returned with the charger, some marbles, a dart from the dart board in the house, and other random, soon to be, missiles. Shadow was also on a mission. The Doll made sure that she could see Doc's face and videoed and videoed. After everyone gave up, the Doll watched some of the videos, until she found what she was looking for, well actually more. Doc was unconsciously hyper-focused on the world around him. How was not evident, but the results were. His eyes changed constantly like some device with ever changing lenses. Even using the slow motion, it was still difficult to see, but his eyes cycled through different colors, shapes, and appearance. More precisely, it appeared that the iris and possibly the lens changed, although she was sure that there was more that she couldn't see.

Anyone looking at Doc and studying him would not notice these changes. But the Doll was watching the replay in slow motion, and caught, just barely, the constant changes. He, his eyes, were constantly scanning the world around him. When this constant observation perceived a threat, his eyes locked into a horizontal and vertical slit, forming a four-point star. Then he would turn and pluck whatever out of the air or shift or move to avoid an incoming splash of hot coffee or some other liquid. When the threat had been neutralized, his eyes shifted back into the constantly changing cycle. At one point, she asked him to look at her and risked holding his head in both of her hands as she stared into his eyes. The last time she had made a similar move, he had kissed her, and she was not sure how she might respond again. To her naked eye, his eyes looked normal, maybe a tad hypnotic, but normal.

So, as everyone reviewed and theorized about the documents, she began developing her theories about Doc.

As the morning became afternoon and then early evening, they began to make plans for tomorrow.

Chapter 19

"So, all things considered, I assume we are going after the ship," Doc commented as he looked at the group, then suddenly paused.

He looked at the Doll, then continued, "When this began the issue at hand was someone trying to abduct you. That attempt escalated to an extraordinary level, and we still have no answers. Now we are linked since I butted into your abduction attempts. I don't know why, but I feel that somehow this may be part of a more significant issue. On the other hand, I apologize for hijacking your predicament. "

The Doll rolled her eyes, shook her head, smiled, and commented to the assembled group, "Doc, I have no idea why my world is in such a bizarre state of flux. I know that as a result of your actions, Amber and I are safe, and I suspect off the radar of whoever. In the meantime, I am now part of a bigger story. I am surrounded by caring people, one of them an alien. I am also in a position to return that favor by helping to find your ship."

Then, with a mischievous smile, "Besides, you kissed me, so now I am under your alien spell. That brings us back to you, Tommy. You hinted that you know where Doc's ship is, now would be the time to fill us in."

Once the laughter subsided, Tommy pulled together a few of the documents and photos spread across table. He used these to explain where he was, 90%, sure the Mithrim was. Following the altercation in July of 1947, that included the destruction of a defense drone and the two craft trying to capture her, the ship was rumored to have flown south to the area around Carlsbad Caverns. This prompted questions of why the Mithrim had remained on Earth. Was it damaged, why was it here, why ...?

"I believe that I may have some of those answers," Doc began, "in the jumble of information, I received from the cyrog. Right now, why she is still here is not as important as locating her. This needs to be our immediate focus. That means getting to the area around Carlsbad Caverns in New Mexico where she is hidden. Carlsbad is maybe a thousand miles from here. And, of course, we need to do this while still remaining anonymous."

Joshua chimed in, "Lucky and I figured you would need some new ID's and have been working on them, but that was before Tommy and Mike joined the party."

Tommy smiled, "I am glad I am with you, not chasing you," then continued, "Mike and I have IDs and even credit cards that sort of cover us. The IDs are good enough for now unless we do something major that causes them to be recorded. I'm not sure that I want to use the credit cards, they do draw on company resources and will easily provide a path to us."

And so the evening progressed. Suitable identities, with documentation, were provided for Doc, the Doll, and Amber. Those included Arizona drivers' licenses. The VDub bus also now displayed Arizona plates, and its registration was linked to Doc's new ID.

Joshua handed out the IDs and any needed papers with a grin. First, he gave Amber hers. The picture, of course, matched the new persona that was Amber. Amber's ID showed her to be Amber Rose McConnell. Next, he handed Doc his ID, which he gave a cursory examination. He was now Arthur Anderson, and his birth date had been adjusted so that Arthur was only forty-five. An age that better matched the slow changes apparent in his physical appearance. Next, Joshua handed the Doll her ID. This also matched her new persona but gave her correct age. Her new identity was Catherine Anderson. Joshua continued handing out papers and other random things that the group might need, while the recipients examined their new IDs.

"Ah ... excuse me," the Doll caught everyone's attention. "Who picked the names?"

There wasn't even the hint of hesitation as Joshua and Lucky immediately pointed at Marion. Even Shadow, who had been quietly working with the group, never looked up from what she was doing as she pointed at Marion.

"Marion," the Doll, looked at her with an unreadable expression. "Was your logic that we might look like siblings?"

Doc and Amber looked at their own IDs then at each other. The Doll then passed her ID to Amber, who burst out in laughter as she, in turn, gave the ID to Doc.

"You guys act the part," Marion replied, "more so every day. In any case, it's too late to make new ones now, Mr. and Mrs. Anderson."

When the laughing and congratulations subsided, they continued reviewing identities so that the group was comfortable with who was who. As it turned out, the IDs the CIA had supplied retained both agents' forenames. Tommy

Conner became Thomas Chance, and Michael Thompson became Michael Fisk.

Once the identity issue could be considered resolved, the next topic was travel. The simple solution was to go to Google Maps. That provided them with three primary routes to the area up to and including Carlsbad Caverns National Park. The fastest way was to go through Phoenix, down to Tucson and mostly follow the I-10 West. While probably the quickest route, the group decided that brought them too close to Mexico. Since their original false trail would have taken them toward San Diego and possibly into Mexico, the I-10 route might be one to avoid.

They finally decided to take a northerly path. Initially, the group agreed on a route up the I-15 then along I-40 to Albuquerque and finally down through Roswell to the Carlsbad area. This meant they had to cover roughly 1,000 to 1,100 miles or at least a two-day road trip. They briefly discussed using their UPS connections to fly vs. driving but concluded that would leave them less mobile when they arrived at Carlsbad Caverns National Park.

Over dinner, around the big table, the discussion turned to transport options. Should they all take the classic VDub van or spit the group between it and the Jetta. After some deliberation, the two-vehicle idea seemed to be a more appropriate way to hide the group in plain sight. The original missing players in the adventure were Doc, the Doll and Amber, two women and an older man. So, the final plan was Doc and the Doll in the van, a hot chick and her hubby on vacation. The couple just rolled their eyes. Then two young guys with a sexy girl in the Jetta on a random road trip. It made sense.

To add to the anonymity of the group's travel, the two parties would not travel together. They would take the same route, but one group would go from Elsinore to Flagstaff and stay overnight in Flagstaff. On the second day, they would continue from Flagstaff to Roswell then down to Carlsbad. The other group would take an Elsinore to Gallup to Carlsbad route. They would all meet up in Carlsbad to plan the next step.

Doc and the Doll opted for the Elsinore to Gallup to Carlsbad route. That meant that they had a longer first leg. They planned to leave early, right after breakfast Friday morning. Tommy, Mike, and Amber would leave maybe an hour later. They would have the more extended second leg of the trip. Doc and the Doll to pick a suitably central but not ostentatious place for the group to stay when they arrived in Carlsbad that Saturday. This would be their new base of operations for however long they needed to remain in the Carlsbad area.

The remainder of the evening was taken up with packing the vehicles and taking inventory of their resources. Tommy and Mike had concealed carry permits in their paperwork, so they each carried P938 Sig 9mm's. Doc still had Mike's P938 SAS, and Joshua had included concealed carry paperwork as part of Doc's papers. They had cash. Doc had been putting money in an account in Elsinore listed under Lucky's name. Lucky had been making small withdrawals the past few days, so he could pass $6,000.00 to Doc. This still left a sizable balance in Doc's account should more be needed to cover their costs; however long it took to locate the ship. Doc passed two thousand of the cash to Tommy. Tommy and Mike had also withdrawn money from their accounts before heading to Elsinore, so they had working capital. Since this was the last business of the night as they all headed to their respective beds.

Chapter 20

Lucky and Marion met with Doc and the Doll for breakfast a little after 6:00 am. The Doll came over to the main house from the trailer and was sitting with Marion having coffee when Doc wandered in. Then Lucky showed, and Marion started the eggs and fried Spam. The Doll didn't bat an eye as she added a few slices of Spam to the plate with a sizable portion of eggs.

When Doc looked at her and her plate questioningly, she smiled and said, "I already did my morning run. This is my reward." She looked at Doc, shook her head and finished, "don't judge."

Doc looked at the Doll. No more boring professional on the way to her lab. This was a vibrant woman in loose, worn cargo shorts and a casual smock top that almost made it to the top of the shorts, dressed and ready to travel. He smiled in surrender and joined them for breakfast. He asked about Joshua. Last night he had entrusted the footlocker to him and Lucky. They would scan all the papers and photos. The footlocker would be in the WV Van and the scans would go to the group in the Jetta giving them access to the material during the drive. About that time Joshua and the rest of the extended group wandered in for breakfast. That was the cue for Doc and the Doll to say their goodbyes and head for the Van.

Doc headed for the driver's door when Doll commented, "Let me drive the first stretch. I'm wide awake and I know this part of the road. I used to have some friends in Barstow."

Doc stopped, not sure what to do or say. He had assumed that as the man he would drive. He quickly corrected that line of thought and replied, "Can you drive a stick shift?"

The look he got in response made this a moot issue, so he tossed the keys to the Doll. She smiled, caught the keys and climbed into the driver's side. By 7:25 am they were leaving the yard headed to the I-15. Next stop Barstow. After the first few miles, Doc realized that the Doll was a great driver, again reminding himself that he needed to shed his gender-based concepts.

They made good time to Barstow. Doc answered mission-based questions that the Doll posed by tapping into the cyrog. He discovered, from repeated contact with the cyrog, that the process became second nature. He could refresh his comprehension of the information it contained instantly. They topped off the gas, got coffee and switched drivers for the next leg to Needles. With Doc driving, the conversation switched to each other's lives prior to this current adventure.

They switched drivers again after lunch in Needles but continued exploring each other's previous lives. The one where Doc was just a human and the Doll was just a struggling student rising eventually to her position in DARPA. By the time they cleared Flagstaff, the Doll had heard the real stories about Nam including Doc's reaction to the first time he had been shot and found that he healed on his own. By the time he had retrieved Lucky and Spyder from a failed mission, he had decided that he would take life one day at a time and not worry about the small stuff. He talked about the slump when he retired, and all the difficulties until he settled into consulting. He even told her about Heather, the woman he had thought would be the "one." That relationship had lasted four years, but they had eventually parted ways. Heather had said he was hiding too many secrets from her, and he admitted to himself that was probably true.

Initially, the Doll had listened and asked questions as she tried to understand this man, this alien, that had saved her life twice and now was still looking out for her. The more he talked, the more she also wanted him to know who she was. The miles flew by as they took turns driving. Doc learned that she had been a science nerd and had always been a quiet person. Her parents had died when she was young and she was raised by her aunt. She powered her way through College, Graduate School, her Doctorate and had never looked back. Well, not exactly, she had been engaged to a fellow grad student named Nick while working on her Ph.D. That relationship had lasted almost two years before it became clear her desires and plans were not Nick's. After that, it convinced her she should collect cats, a comment that got a laugh from Doc.

When they crossed into New Mexico, the I-40 joined with historic Route 66 and the conversation shifted focus to the sights of that historic route as they approached Gallup. They got into Gallup a little after 7:00 pm. Doc suggested that they try the El Rancho Hotel. He reasoned this would be a good place to hide in plain sight. The hotel was an elegant, historic structure built in a style from 100 years in the past. In the second floor of the Lobby were pictures on exhibition, of all the western movie stars that stayed here while filming movies in the area. The restaurant also served great steaks.

They booked a king deluxe room whose guests had

included Alan Ladd, Gene Autry, and Rosalind Russell at different times. Today had been a great day, and they had enjoyed a great dinner, then life took a turn. They had checked in as Arthur and Catherine Anderson. Doc's plan was to sleep on the couch. He took his shower first and was in a pair of jersey shorts and T-shirt when he headed for the couch.

"Where are you going?" The Doll asked.

His reply and the conversation that followed was another one of the lose... lose conversations he experienced with the Doll lately. Her point of view was that, while this was a room with a pedigree, the couch did not look that great. In her opinion, they were adults and they could share the bed. If he wanted to put a pillow or two between them that was fine. Then she turned, headed for the shower and the discussion ended. Doc gave up and settled in on his side of the bed.

He must have drifted off to sleep when he felt something tapping on his forehead. That never happened, there was no tingle, no warning. He opened his eyes and looked up to see the Doll in a towel, she must have just come from the shower. Was he on her side of the bed, that seemed a bit much. His night vision had always been flawless, and he realized that the lights were off in the room.
Then the towel dropped.

"Doc," an exquisite, naked Doll whispered, "are you going to move over and make some room for your Doll?"

Chapter 21

During the drive from Gallup to Carlsbad, Doc and the Doll decided not to over-analyze their burgeoning relationship. Therefore, regarding the group, they adopted the mantra of what happens in Gallup stays in Gallup. It was now Saturday evening, and both groups had finally reunited, to review their respective trips, and make plans. They were relaxing at a large table in the back of the Flume Room Restaurant. The waitress left them with menus, and no one was expecting the guest.

"Hi, Tommy."

The greeting took everyone at the table by surprise. A tall, maybe six foot, very athletic, Nordic-looking blond walked up and sat down beside Tommy as though she belonged there. Then, before anyone could react, she leaned against Tommy and appeared to have passed out.

"Hmmm," Doc commented, "That went well, I think. Don't know that I have ever tried that before, but it seemed to work nicely. Tommy, who is your non-human friend?"

Where the group was sitting in the back of the room, the attractive blond looked like she was part of the group and just resting her head on Tommy's shoulder. Tommy seemed a bit embarrassed, confused, flustered, it wasn't clear. He looked like he wanted to be anywhere else.

Doc continued, "I should wake her back up soon before this becomes a scene. Please don't ask me what I just did, it was a reflex reaction to seeing her... species. Not that I can come up with a reason, other than I felt I needed to control the situation. I can wake her back up as easily."

"I take it you never brought one of your dates to visit Doc before," Doll, smiled at Tommy, then looked to Doc, "Really?"

"Her name is Alura, although she prefers Ally for obvious reasons," Tommy seemed to be back in control of his faculties. "She is a Teletin and part of their embassy on Earth. She has no specific title. I think she is my equivalent for her species. She is okay, right?" Tommy looked at Doc.

"Yes," He said, then looked at the group as he finished, "I am hyper concerned about being discovered, apparently something about this young lady set off that odd alarm in my brain. It appears I know how to disable her species. There is more, but for now, please understand her status is temporary. I didn't harm her, and I can awaken her whenever we are ready. I will temper my knee-jerk responses, or at least give the rest of you some warning going forward."

Everyone seemed to mull this over considering how the previous week had started, then nodded, one at a time, in assent to his reawakening the blond amazon. Alura lazily opened her eyes and suddenly snapped to full alert glaring at Doc.

"That," she said sharply, "was uncalled for."

She took a deep breath and continued, "Well, maybe not so uncalled for. I'm sure I could have been more subtle when I approached your group. A group I am certain is trying to maintain a low profile."

She looked at Doc again, smiled, and said, "So, you must be the possible Dunarian rumored to be part of this group. I have some knowledge of your species and have heard rumors of impressive talents, but that caught me off guard."

Ally studied the group for a moment then identified each of them carefully. She started with Tommy and explained that she had partnered with him for over a year working a project. When he suddenly went dark, then Mike also disappeared, Ally began putting the pieces of the puzzle together. Much to Tommy's embarrassed chagrin, she explained that the two of them were exploring a relationship that was a side effect of working together so closely; she was looking forward to exploring that further in the coming weeks. Having finished with Tommy, she moved on and continued identifying members of the group.

Next, she nodded toward Mike, acknowledging him as part of the same ongoing assignment. Mike smiled and nodded back. Then she turned her attention to Amber and the Doll and studied them both for a minute before deciding. First, identifying Amber as the former Lindsey. Then took some additional time to study the Doll. Finally, she smiled and declared her to be Dr. Karen Wing.

Then, as an afterthought, she turned back to Doc and smiled, "I see you two have bonded."

"Are you done?" Doc smiled and asked politely, hoping to divert interest in her last remark, "I would ask you to sit, but we have accomplished that already, albeit the hard way. Just for the sake of clarification, you may refer to me as Doc. Please refer to the young lady at my right as Doll, the Doll or Catherine and the other young woman in our group as Amber Rose. Tommy and Mike have maintained their original forenames."

Doc paused for a moment, studying Ally as she looked at each of the group then back to him.

"Now," Doc said in a calm level voice, "Please fully identify yourself and carefully explain why you are here, now."

Doc watched as Tommy cringed.

"Doc," she nodded her head respectfully and continued, "my given name is Alura Veseranna. If during my brief nap, Tommy didn't tell you, I prefer Ally. I am a Teletin. My species has a small embassy on Earth, and I am, what you would describe as a security or intelligence officer. I work as part of a joint species investigative unit with Tommy and Mike. I am here on my own. Neither my embassy nor your worlds over-site group knows of my interest in this group. Tommy has told me stories of his crazy uncle, and it didn't take much to put that puzzle together. Where Tommy goes, I go, as his partner, I trust his judgment. So, I guess you could say I am here as a friend and additional asset."

She studied Doc, then looked at each of the others around the table before continuing. "My species is, what you would consider, empathic. I can feel or sense some members of this group are unsure whether to trust me. What surprises me is that Doc is emanating absolute trust. Possibly directed more at my species than toward me specifically."

"Doc, while I have a working knowledge of your species, I am still not aware of all your capabilities. Are you able to read me?"

Doc smiled back and replied, "You have the group's attention, convince them why they should trust you."

Before she could begin, their waitress appeared, took the group's orders then disappeared.

Chapter 22

Ally looked around the table then began. She started by explaining that currently, there are very few, if any, considering that a Dunarian might be involved in the attempted DARPA abduction. When she saw or sensed the confusion this statement produced, she stopped and looked at Doc.

"Doc," she asked, "Unless I am very, very wrong in what I am sensing, you are a truly a Dunarian, correct?"

"I am," Doc replied.

Ally started again. Eight recognized species have established treaties with Earth, Dunarians are not in that group. There are many more species, but only eight are physically close enough or could reach Earth. However, one of the earliest recorded species were the Dunarian. No one knows where their planet or system is. The only records are of Dunarian survey vessels. Where records of this species exist, they are said to be peaceful observers.

Regrettably, one such survey vessel appeared in this solar system in early July of 1947, Earth time. Several species were vying for control of Earth at that time. One of the unsanctioned aggressive species attacked that survey vessel. The attacking ships were destroyed, but there is no record of the Dunarian ship ever leaving this solar system. Over the next decade, there were rumors of Dunarians, from that ship, living on Earth.

"I have, what you would consider, advanced degrees in species recognition and studies, so I searched for more information on your species." Ally explained then returned to her story.

I located additional information from rogue studies conducted during that time. That included the earlier accounts of captured Dunarians, describing them as being similar in appearance to a human but possessed unique capabilities. Those theoretical capabilities included increased speed, strength, and the ability regenerate damaged tissue. It was also possible that they had minor psychic and telepathic talents.

There were also rumors of the possibility that the ship was hidden in the area surrounding Roswell or Carlsbad Caverns. However, if it is still on this planet, its actual location is still unknown.

Tommy had frequently alluded to this missing ship and its crew. She indicated that he asked her to let him know of any unknowns appeared to be human but also exhibited non-human traits. Then, a few days ago, she was given access to a transcript of the conversation between the Doll, Lindsey, and Doc as they were supposedly heading to San Diego. One of the unique aspects of Ally's empathic capability was that she could sense and locate anyone she was invested in. She smiled as she intimated that she had an active emotional link to Tommy. Then, when he went dark to his handlers, she began to put the pieces together and tracked Tommy here.

"So," Doc began again, "Are you here in an official capacity? Why the interest in my species? And most important, why should we trust you?"

Ally was quiet for a moment, looked around the table, then focused back on Doc. "I have a borderline manic desire to understand all of the species I have met or studied. When Tommy went rogue, I took a leave of absence. I am fascinated and curious by both humans and Dunarians. Humans don't act consistently, and that drives me crazy. Dunarians, on the other hand, are believed to respond logically and systematically."

"There are pieces of the puzzle that do not fit. Why would the Dunarians remain on Earth, why do we only have vague information on their species? Tommy may have some information that he has hidden from me, and I am concerned that he might be in over his head. Then there is the question of where DARPA fits into this puzzle. The result is too many questions and too few answers. I like answers. ... Oh, and the group can trust me because, well, I can sense that Doc does." She looked at Doc.

Doc looked at the blond Teletin and finally remarked, "Ally is right. I trust what she is saying. I can't say exactly why, but I do. I have made other similar decisions about people in my life and have never been proven wrong. It appears that if I am an alien species, I need to know more about myself and other species. Tommy seems to have some information, but I bet that Ally has more. While we are enjoying dinner, how about if we have an alien Q&A session?"

Doc's remark immediately opened a floodgate of questions.

"Okay," Doc cut into the flood, "Let's keep it simple for now, something we can discuss while we finish dinner, not a conference."

"I have a suggestion," everyone turned as the Doll spoke, "Ally, we are at a disadvantage. We can't identify the players. Doc looks and seems normal unless he is being threatened. You look normal. Neither of you is what I would take to be alien species. Doc is still learning what he is, and you indicate that you aren't sure of what his species capabilities are. So how about telling us what you are. We all see a tall, attractive human appearing female who says she is an alien species known as a Teletin."

"That's fair," Ally replied with a genuine smile, "we are different but the same. Let me see if I can give you a quick overview of my species."

Ally started by explaining that all species that visit the Earth are bi-pedal beings with two arms, two legs, and one head. This got a laugh. She clarified that while there are some variations, most species follow this pattern because it works. Three legs are challenging to coordinate, arms on only one side of the body are not useful. On the other hand, facial features, hair or fur, and skin, those do vary in much the same way as they do among humans.

Ally commented that her species facial features, hair pattern, and body symmetry is closer than some, to human standards, which makes it easier for her to blend in. Then she elaborated on the differences. She is the shortest female in her family, her sister is six foot, six inches tall, and her brother is seven-foot tall. Their planet has slightly lower gravity. She continued by commenting that her fingers and toes had multiple joints. Ally demonstrated this by wrapping her index finger around a straw. The smooth fluid wrap was like observing a tentacle. Yet as she moved her hand and fingers about, they looked human normal.

"I have contact lenses," she commented, "not for vision, but because my pupil and iris are like what you might see in the creatures you call cats."

Ally looked around, the part of the restaurant they were in was near the back, and the waitress had just made a visit, checking drinks. Considering that she was not being watched, she explained that her skin tone and hair color were slightly different than that of a human.

Before demonstrating, she explained that her species had a cellular component in their skin and hair that was like an Earthen chameleon or maybe an octopus. She could change and maintain a different than normal coloration. What those at the table were seeing was a hair, skin color combination that she had developed to match human expectations.

After another quick glance, she shifted to a soft pastel violet skin tone similar to thistle and her blond hair, changed to a deep royal purple at the top of her head to reddish blond at the ends. Her eyes were a deep royal blue and looked like those of a Siamese cat. She briefly indicated this was her normal coloration, then blink, and she was back to human standard. She performed one last transformation. She placed her hand on the white tablecloth with part of her palm covering a blue napkin. Suddenly her hand disappeared or appeared to. Where her hand was, on white material, the skin had changed to match precisely, where the palm of her hand covered part of the blue napkin, that side was now the same blue. If you concentrated, you could see the hand, but only with some effort.

With a dangerously impish grin, Ally commented, "Tommy likes my normal coloration."

Questions continued through the meal and as they all ordered favorite deserts, but it was getting late. Everyone, including Ally, had a lot of information to process. So they left the restaurant as a group and headed back into the hotel.

Chapter 23

Doc had been reviewing the maps, brochures and other flyers he found at the information kiosk in the El Rancho Hotel. The original plan was to go to White's City, a tourist gathering point a few miles from the Carlsbad Caverns State Park entrance. Instead, after recommendations from the staff at the El Rancho, he had changed their destination to the Stevens Inn. It was a little over 25 miles from the Cavern Park Entrance, but a much better choice for several reasons.

The Flume Room Restaurant, where they had just eaten, was part of that Inn complex. He then made reservations using a pay as you go credit/debit card. So as they left the Flume Room, the group, now six individuals, headed to a suite Doc had reserved as a central meeting place. It was also the suite he and the Doll would occupy. Doc explained he and the Doll's suite had two separate rooms, but by the time the group headed up to the rooms, all had dismissed that ruse. Doc also reserved two smaller suites, one for Mike and Tommy, and the other for Amber. With Ally's addition to the group, the plan was changed to allow Ally to share with Amber. It was a good plan and made sense.

Now, away from observation, the group settled down to planning the next few days. Ally, as was hoped, turned out to be an excellent resource. The group had assumed that this trip was for two reasons. One was to keep the Doll and Amber from the reach of some unsavory individuals. They had theories, but nothing regarding why they were a target. The second issue was a little more tenuous. In the process of being saved, the Doll had acquired an alien benefactor, Doc, and that alien had knowledge of the location of a missing interstellar ship. And, the group now included a new alien, Ally.

Content to observe, Doc sat back as the Doll explained her observations. She and Amber were heading a research program to primarily provide the tools to improve humans. Now, in retrospect, if she stopped looking at the goals altruistically, she was providing the tools to build super-soldiers. That seemed to coincide with Tommy's investigation of this Ronan character who was an information broker and also appeared involved in human trafficking. A super-soldier would be something he might like to market, and if he had abducted humans, he had a captive audience to experiment on. Tommy not only pinpointed the Ronan issue but then outed Doc. The fact that Doc was an alien was most likely not an issue, yet. Outwardly he may have appeared to be a successful application of their research. There were some murmurs in the group of agreement.

Then Ally gave a heavy sigh and added additional input. She had been working with Tommy and other agencies to try and make a case against Ronan. Yes, he was a significant dealer, but it was becoming more apparent that he also had ties with some of the splinter alien groups that were known to be on Earth. Some of these were part of the coalition, but others were not. Proving this had turned out to be a monumental task. Then the whole incident with the Doc and the Doll appeared, changing the focus.

Ally then spun that focus. She asked who remembered seeing Doc and the Doll's escape on the news and social media. Despite the sensational aspects of the story, followed with the report of Lindsey's disappearance, the story had vanished. This type of news tended to grow a life of its own.

Instead, suddenly, there was nothing. The story didn't taper off. It ceased to exist. Tommy's agency had no answers. Ally's group and her network also had nothing. In Ally's experience, that meant that the human and alien underground was on the move.

This prompted Ally to locate Tommy because she was sure he was following some part of this puzzle. She based that on the fact that she found out that Mike was involved, and Ally was aware of his connection to the Doll. She studied all of the accounts and information available, factored the Dolls research and the possibility of a super-soldier. What didn't add up was Doc. Therefore, this Doc person had to be a species that had stayed below the council's radar.

She went back through all her research and studies and found a species rumored to have regenerative tissue and possessed superior speed and strength. She got access to Doc's service records and concluded he was a Dunarian. The only firm documents of that species had surfaced around the time Doc would have been born. These reports were mostly unsubstantiated and were treated as myths. There were also rumors that this species had an all-powerful ship hidden somewhere on Earth.

Ally smiled her engaging smile and announced, "So Doc had to be a Dunarian, doing what they were rumored to do, intercede in conflicts, and if I could figure that out, so could others on both sides, human and alien."

"So, the human scientists and the lumbering alien are both the targets," Doc commented wryly, "but nobody is looking for us anymore?"

"That's the problem," this time Tommy and Ally were

speaking simultaneously, "nobody is acknowledging they are looking for you, so that they, one or more groups can go about their search with having to explain to the authorities."

Doc laughed and said that it was time for all of them to get a good night's sleep, meet for breakfast no earlier than 8 am, and after breakfast, make some real plans.

Tommy and Mike left first and headed out to their room. Doc watched as Ally said something to the Doll. In turn, the Doll came over to speak to Doc as Amber and Ally headed out.

"Doc?" She said, "I'm going to accompany the girls to their room. Ally has something she wants to talk to me about. I don't get the impression she is trying to hide anything; she just seems to want to talk to me."

"Okay," he replied, after studying her face to see if she was trying to hide any concerns, "I want to spend some more time with the artifacts to see if any of the fog will clear in my induced memories. Don't hesitate to call me or either of the guys if there are any problems".

That remark got him a nod and an eye roll.

Chapter 24

Doc wasn't sure when the Doll returned. He didn't think it had been that long but realized that each prolonged session with the cyrog left him mentally drained and in need of sleep to refresh. He had been holding it when he fell asleep. He was aware when the Doll slid into bed beside him, she gently took it and placed on the nightstand.

The next morning Doc woke to someone tickling, more like tweaking, his ear. He rolled over, and as he saw the Doll realized this is not going to be the start of the day, he had just drowsily imagined.

Yesterday they had stopped at a Walmart on the outskirts of Roswell, at the Doll's insistence. She realized as she packed hastily for this adventure, she had forgotten a few things. This resulted in a shopping trip for jogging shorts, tops, new cross trainers and other paraphernalia. That had not been the extent of the madness. She also insisted that Doc get the equivalent gear. Doc's metabolism, triggered by recent events and his exposure to the cyrog, was that of a younger man in his mid-forties. The Doll intended to keep him in prime shape.

This morning the pest tweaking his ear was already suited up and tapping one foot in an indication he should get up and get ready.

"What time is it?" Doc asked.

"5:20 am, and there is a treadmill in the gym down on

the first floor with your name on it," She replied, then sealed the deal with "you promised."

After 15 minutes on the treadmill, he was awake and feeling pretty good. The Doll ran them both through a series of repetitions on the various machines before they headed back to the room. On the way, they ran into a tall woman with a mass of curly red hair, and a milky complexion that made her look like she was an Irish model. She was also in running attire but appeared to have come from outside the building.

"Ally?" Doc and the Doll both asked as the redhead stopped directly in front of them.

"We may have a problem," she remarked in a low, conspiratorial tone.

Ally walked them near the entrance to the Stevens Inn and pointed to a small device over the door. Doc studied it for a moment and said it was a CCTV (Closed Circuit TV) unit and there were two cameras. It was not unusual for a hotel to have cameras at building access points. Ally smiled, pointing out and identifying the third device. It was pointed down to catch someone entering the hotel.

Ally identified this as alien tech designed to pick up the aura of an unknown, or non-human. While most alien-detection devices focus on chemical signatures, these newer designs also focus on molecular movement. Vibrations. These nanomechanical oscillators were sensitive devices and were deployed to areas where governments and the council want to track non-human activity.

Ally continued by admitting that she would have expected them in White's City and the entrance to the

Carlsbad National Park and some of the caverns. Apparently, at least three hotels she had checked this morning were also so equipped. How actively the agencies were monitoring these devices and the fact that this group didn't match the specific pattern may be working in their favor. On the other hand, the unidentified splinter groups that were also tracking them may be putting the pieces of this puzzle together. Right now, their group included a species type not necessarily in the database and one other non-human, Ally. The organizations hunting them were looking for a different grouping. One that contained two humans and an unknown. With Ally now part of their group of three couples they might fly under the radar for a while longer.

In any case, they should be cautious and recognize that their time to find the ship may be limited. This was one more factor to consider when planning out the day. Ally confirmed she would meet Doc, the Doll, and the others at breakfast, as initially planned, and update the rest of the group on her findings.

"By the way, this latest look is pretty hot," The Doll commented to Ally as they got into the elevator.

Ally smiled and replied, "It drives Tommy a little crazy when I leave some location in one form and return as another, but he is getting used to it. Next to my natural form, this is the one he particularly likes."

As they headed back to the room, the Doll updated Doc on the room assignment changes the night before. He knew the Doll had gone to meet with Amber and Ally to answer some questions. Ally wanted to switch from sharing a room with Amber to sharing with Tommy, but she was unsure of Mike and Amber's status or arrangement. She was new to the group and didn't want to cause any issues.

The Doll filled Doc in, concerning her assistant and the Marine Corps officer's status, just in case he hadn't already figured it out. Lindsey, now Amber, had developed a crush on Mike from the point he was assigned to their project. Mike had noticed. He would have had to be blind not to, but he had been the model of professional propriety. Once the adventure, as they referred to this, had begun and Amber had assumed her hot little persona, Mike had tried but mostly failed to not be affected. The new assertive persona of Amber was all it took to sway his resolve.

Doc looked at the Doll and commented that this explained Ally's comment about returning to Tommy. Tommy and Ally now had one suite, and Mike and Amber shared the other.

As he was getting out of his running gear, he remarked, "So this whole trip is now turning into a couples retreat?"

He got a non-verbal answer as he was pulled into the shower. They managed to finish their shower and dress presentably a few minutes before 8:00 am. As they were headed to the elevator, Doc remembered something he needed to do. The Doll guessed he had forgotten the small pack which contained the three artifacts from the ship. He was, she considered, rightly concerned that they did not fall into the wrong hands, even though they had determined that no one else could do a thing with any of these devices.

When he caught back up to her at the elevator, Doc had the small shoulder pack but had both cyrogs out. That wasn't exactly true. He held what appeared to be the two cyrogs joined together. Instead of a cylinder about 12 inches long,

Doc held a seamless rod twice that length.

Doc saw the look on her face and replied to her unasked question. "While you were gone last night, I experimented with the two cyrogs and found that they could be joined together. I also learned a few things I am still trying to sort out, so I thought I should bring them and explain."

Even though they thought they were running late, they still beat Amber and Mike. The group again took over the large table near the back. They all opted for the buffet without hesitation. Once everyone had food and coffee, they focused on planning the day's activities.

Ally led off the discussion in pure tour guide mode. She had remained in the Irish lass persona, and to Doc's amusement, no one seemed concerned. Ally explained the Carlsbad Caverns National Park area encompassed a little over 73 square miles. That was a large area to cover, and the ship was only rumored to be in this area. That was where Doc interrupted.

"The ship is about 30.5 miles from here," Doc said in a calm matter of fact voice.

Chapter 25

Everyone at the table was silent as they stared at Doc. Well, not all, the Doll did a facepalm, then looked back at Doc, "Really ... you could have said something."

Everybody was still looking at him, so he explained. Last night while the group was sorting out the accommodations, Doc had been experimenting with the two cyrogs. He was testing them based on the pieces of memory that had already surfaced. He knew that the second cyrog was related to the ship, but he could not get anything meaningful from it. A fragment of memory suggested that he put the two together. To his surprise, they instantly fused into a single unit. He was concerned at first but determined he could still separate them. However, when they were united, he got impressions of the ship. Similar to his experience with the first cyrog, he was immediately flooded with information. As before he needed time to assimilate what he was being fed.

This morning when he joined the two rods as he grabbed the pack to catch up with the Doll, there was a distinct impression he was holding them wrong. As Doc walked through the lobby, that earlier impression began to make sense. He needed to point them in the direction of the ship.

The Doll remarked, "That helps, I was beginning to think you had taken up baton twirling."

Doc continued after the laughter died down. He discovered that when the paired cyrogs were oriented with the ship, he received mental feedback that she was waiting. He knew the physical direction as well as the distance in miles, kilometers, and some dimension he did not recognize.

"We need some maps," everyone replied in unison.

"We also need to not do this in a restaurant with more diners coming in," Doc commented, gesturing toward a family of four headed for a table near them.

The group managed to calm down, finish their breakfast in an orderly manner and head up to Doc and the Doll's suite. Mike and Amber broke from the group and left to find a small convenience store where they hoped to pick up a variety of maps.

Once everyone had returned, they spread out the maps. One of those included a GPS coordinate grid. Doc explained that while he had a set of coordinates, they weren't in the standard format, and they included a third coordinate point that might have been ... who knows.

Then they attempted to orient the maps using compass lines until they realized that none of them had a compass. Mike was about to head back to the store when Amber rolled her eyes and opened the compass app on her phone. Finally, they got organized and found a map they could all agree on. With the cyrog vector and the compass orientation, they were able to draw a straight line to a point 30.5 miles from their current position. They marked a big red X on that spot.

The big red X was in the Guadalupe Mountains and the Lincoln National Forest. The next step was to figure out how to get there. The 30.5-mile distance was based on how the proverbial crow flew, or whatever the Dunarian equivalent of a crow was. They discovered that they could take the 137 to the 258, also known as the Queen's Highway, for 54 miles and then they would have to leave the paved surface and cover several miles overland.

Now, with a precise target location, the discussion shifted to how to get there. The off-road stretch was the issue. Mike and Tommy reviewed the terrain map and estimated it was between five to eight miles, depending on where they left the road. This spawned a very brief discussion on who would go. No one was willing to stay behind and wait while the others found a ship that had remained hidden for nearly seventy years. Their next hurdle was how to transport six individuals several miles off-road including a growing list of what everyone felt necessary to unearth the ship.

The discussion ranged from one large vehicle to dirt bikes, and quad runners. Mike, however, was the first to present a reasonable option. While he and Amber had been out getting the pizzas they had for lunch, they had picked up a local paper and a copy of Auto Trader. Mike had come from a large family that liked to take camping trips, and he found the ideal solution in the local paper.

That solution was listed as a 2000 Ford Excursion 4WD Limited, and the private party was asking $12,800. Mike assured them that this would be the perfect option. It could handle the off-road part of the trip. It could carry the six members of the group as well as haul anything, including tools, shovels, or tents if they needed to stay overnight. The next problem was their current combined cash resources were a little over $4000.00. They couldn't sell their two existing vehicles in any reasonable time frame. Besides, Doc was not a fan of getting rid of the Van that Lucky and Joshua had worked so hard to restore. And Tommy didn't think the agency would appreciate it if he sold the Jetta. They needed the cash or some financial leverage soon. Doc was able to address that issue, so they planned the next steps.

Mike, Amber, Tommy, and Ally called the owner of the Excursion and arranged to go check it out. Doc called Lucky and arranged for a Western Union cash transfer of $21,000 from the sizable resources he had acquired over the years. Lucky knew Doc might need to tap into his hidden resources, and had pre-arranged the easiest way to move a chunk of cash if needed. Doc had all of the credentials required to pick up the transfer, so he and the Doll made the pickup at a Western Union in town. They would have these extra resources even if the vehicle didn't pass Mike's inspection.

When they all met back at the Inn for dinner, they had the cash and Mike confirmed that the Excursion, while in need of paint job, had suitable tires for the terrain and ran well. They could meet again tomorrow with the owner and make the deal. The rest of the evening was lost in planning what they would take. That produced the last minor surprise of the day. It came from Ally.

"I'll be right back, I need to go down to the hotel safe and get the weapons I stashed there," Ally said casually as she left the room.

Chapter 26

After their morning jog, Doc and the Doll met with the rest of the group for breakfast. They decided that since Mike found the Excursion and was already known to the owner, he and Amber should complete the purchase and the paperwork. Doc and the Doll made the rounds of some of the local shops to pick up additional supplies. Tommy and Ally were responsible for sleeping bags and other items they might need to stay in the area of the ship overnight.

The Excursion was an olive drab, lightly rusted huge SUV that Amber immediately nicknamed The Tank. They all agreed with the name when they saw it. The Tank, despite her appearance, ran well and was comfortable with her six passengers and their gear. The group left the next morning after breakfast.

Just outside of Carlsbad, on a barren stretch of road, The Tank made her first off-road excursion to confirm she was up to the trip ahead and to give the group a chance to test-fire Ally's contribution. Ally had a small aluminum case, about the size of a standard briefcase with locking latches. Inside this innocuous case were small rose gold "dove" soap bar-shaped and sized devices.

Tommy let a gasp escape when he saw them and looked directly at Ally, who calmly replied, "I requisitioned them for field testing. These are the new smaller snappers."

Tommy looked like he wanted to take that a little farther, but finally shrugged and said to no one in particular,

"I guess we all better get familiar with them."

The snappers turned out to be small personal defense weapons on steroids. They were designed for concealment and maximum impact in a limited hostile engagement. Ally was glad that they had a full set of eight.

They could test and practice with two units without depleting the effective capacity of the remaining six snappers. Each snapper stored sufficient resources for 50 to 100 shots, depending on the setting. Ally explained that the snappers were plasma pulse personal defense systems with two parameters, tight or broad pulse. They were designed to be easily hidden and simple to use. She demonstrated where the safety was, recessed so it would not accidentally be released. Then she explained the two studs with Teletin symbols for a tight and a broad pulse and a central stud marked as the trigger.

Once they got comfortable holding the snapper in a manner that allowed them access to the trigger, all the members of the group took turns firing at boulders and tree trunks. The broad pulse produced a 12 to 18-inch diameter hole in the target. The tight beam produced a 1/4-inch hole. When fired, they emitted a sound like a finger snap followed by a yellow-orange teardrop of plasma hitting the target. The results were quite satisfying as the members of the group defended themselves against tree trunks, boulders and anything else they could point at.

Tommy put the excitement of shooting the snappers into perspective as he explained that a few years ago he had been part of an action where two members of the team he was with had been hit by the earlier versions of this weapon. Before they all piled back into The Tank, they discussed the reason for carrying the snappers. Tommy, Ally, and Mike were confident that while they had been cautious, the likelihood that their whereabouts was known now was maybe 50/50. And they were, most likely, being hunted by human and alien groups, either separately or as a group. Finally, they would be away from any population center so neither group would have any problem with open hostility.

This put a damper on the excitement and brought the group back to a semblance of reality as they resumed their road trip. The night before they had estimated the approximate location they would need to reach before beginning the off-road portion of the journey. They calculated the GPS coordinates for the cutoff and used that information with their phones to determine the physical spot. Once near the position, they looked for the most accessible entry point, all the while having Doc use the joined cyrog staff to point the way. Having arrived at that entry point, they pulled into the brush and had lunch before continuing the next leg of the adventure.

The banter over lunch was light-hearted and included questioning Doc about the impressions he was getting from the cyrog staff, as they had taken to calling the two joined cylinders. Doc noticed that as they got closer that it felt like the ship itself was trying to communicate with him. He was getting impressions, like visions, that it was aware and had started some process that he could only describe as waking up. None of the group, including Ally as the only one who had been on an interstellar craft, were quite sure what that meant. Doc helped ease any apprehension by explaining that the ship was welcoming the visitors.

The Tank as it turned out was more than capable of covering the ground from the paved road to where Doc smiled and said, "Stop, we are here!"

It had only taken them just under an hour to cover the six miles to a spot that looked like it had once been a riverbed, or a channel cut into the surrounding landscape. The place that Doc called "here" put them in a flat area that bordered along a wall that looked as though it was the result of gully erosion. This had produced a cliff face of several hundred feet with the plateau on the top. When Doc oriented the cyrog staff on the ship's location, it pointed directly at the cliff face.

"Marxten has finally come home, they call him Doc," said Wyik as he studied the readouts.

Araime smiled, "All ship systems online. Shifting from standby to full combat-ready status."

The Mithrim had brought Araime and Wyik out of stasis yesterday when Anexten's son had identified himself through the joined cyrogs. Mithrim added American Standard English to their cyrogs so that the refresh provided them a working knowledge of the language. Wyik was scanning the group, now, and determined there were five individuals with Marxten. Four were human, and one appeared to be a species known as the Teletin. They all appeared to be speaking English. Araime nodded and set the ship systems to use that language for the immediate future.

Wyik and Araime settled in to watch the group as the Mithrim methodically brought all systems online to full combat status. The holographic readout indicated systems at seventeen percent and climbing.

Chapter 27

"So ... do we start digging or what?" Said the Doll with a chuckle.

Doc had a studious look on his face then answered, "Until a moment ago I have been getting, for lack of a better word, impressions from the cyrog staff. Much of what I was getting was in Dunarian which I seem to understand but not fluently. As we have been walking around and looking at the cliff face, something changed just as you asked your question."

The Doll smiled, "Of course." And the rest of the group laughed defusing some of the tension.

All of the attention shifted back to Doc as he tried to explain, "Suddenly it's like everything shifted to English. The ship, Mithrim, has been in standby mode and is now coming to full power. She is currently at eighteen percent and climbing rapidly."

"And ... so ... is there a door or tunnel or is it going to beam us up?" Tommy asked as Ally punched him in the arm.

"You have been watching too much Star Trek or whatever show they beam people up in," said Ally as she rolled her eyes.

Doc had wandered away from the group and was studying the cliff wall. To no one, in particular, he commented that there once had been a secure tunnel opening where he was standing, but he was now sensing that had been sealed twenty-five years ago. Suddenly, he stopped and turned to the group.

"We have a problem!" he said emphatically.

The group was spread out between the cliff wall and The Tank, where Tommy and Ally had just opened the rear to get out some shovels.

"Snappers and find cover!" was all Doc said as he wrapped his arm around the Doll's waist and used his speed to get them to The Tank in an instant.

Ally heard Doc and shifted, also in hi-speed mode, from what she had been doing to pulling out the snapper case. She, Tommy, Doc, and the Doll, already had their snappers when Amber and Mike got to The Tank. Mike spun a fraction after Doc and looked to the south.

"Choppers."

They all looked around for cover. The group was on a semi-flat area in the deep gully. The area at the top of either cliff face was not suitable for a chopper to put down and was at least two hundred feet above the group's current position. The helicopter or choppers would need to land near the group. The group, on the other hand, needed some defensible position. There was a cul-de-sac area with large boulders and smaller rock features that seemed to be their best option. Mike saw the same thing and nodded to Doc and Tommy as he jumped in The Tank moving it forward to add its bulk to the boulders and other features of the cul-de-sac as a barricade.

"We will be boxed in," said Tommy as he and the

others headed for cover.

"The ship is going to free herself and help us," Doc replied with an odd look on his face as he considered the report, he was somehow receiving from the Mithrim. "She is at thirty-eight percent."

In the distance, the rest of the group heard one or more helicopters. After another minute, a vintage Huey and a newer Ranger came into view. Both choppers flared to reduce both vertical and horizontal speed and to allow a near zero-speed touchdown. The Huey was closer to Doc's group and sitting with its door gunner clear and present. Their group was well back from the downwash from either of the two helicopters and at Mike and Doc's insistence, they kept behind cover until each bird appeared to be at ground idle, controls locked. Finally, after an annoying pause, the door on the Ranger opened and out hopped a man that Doc did not recognize.

From somewhere near his left shoulder, Doc heard Tommy, "That is Ambrose Cobb, one of Ronan's Lieutenants."

Figuring that if he took the lead, he could buy more time, Doc stepped out from the side of The Tank, "Hello, what brings you and your friends to our quiet little camping trip?" He said in a voice loud enough to be heard over the pair of idling helicopters.

Cobb stopped in his tracks and considered for a moment, "I am here to escort Dr. Karen Wing, her assistant Lindsey Miller and an older gentleman named Martin Brensen to my boss who would like a word with them," he also replied with enough force behind his voice to be heard.

"I am sure you have some valid reason to believe we might know the people you are looking for. Do you have any photos or a description of these individuals?" Doc commented casually, "Our little camping group is composed of Mike and Amber Fisk, Tommy and Ally Fenton, my wife and I. My name is Arthur, and this is Catherine."

Each couple stepped out from cover for a moment and back as they were identified by Doc. Doc had represented the other two couples as married to further muddy the waters. While Doc had been talking, a second man, with a folding stock AR-15, emerged from the Ranger and stepped to Cobb's side. Cobb said something to this man who disappeared back into the Ranger, looking none too happy about ducking under the slowing spinning rotors more times than necessary. After a moment, he returned with a large manila envelope. Cobb pulled out, what Doc assumed were photos and studied them for a moment. He was not having an easy time handling the full-page images due to the downwash.

Through the cyrog lance Doc received a clear message. "Mithrim will emerge in thirty-four seconds, please be prepared to leave this area. You are in danger."

Both choppers were still idling, the rotors turning slowly making enough noise that Doc could, in a low voice, say, "If the gunner in the closer chopper starts to fire that 50 cal, ladies, please use your snappers on the gun itself, gentlemen, please use your snappers on the engines."

There was no verbal reply, just nods.

Cobb had looked back at Doc and continued, "While your group numbers and makeup do not match who I am here to retrieve, I was specifically told I would find the group

I initially described. Please come out from cover and allow my crew to inspect your vehicle or I will have my gunner open fire."

There was a rumble behind the group, and some smaller rocks and debris fell free from the cliffside. Suddenly, it got dark, and they realized that something was blocking the late afternoon sun. Next, the 50 cal on the Huey fired, but before the group could return fire with their snappers, they realized that rounds from the 50 cal were being stopped by some form of force field.

Chapter 28

Behind them, they heard a lyrical female voice with an odd accent, "Please use the ramp behind you and follow me to the command deck, time is of the essence as there is an incoming hostile." They had no problem hearing her soft voice, it seemed that all outside sound was being suppressed by whatever had stopped the 50 caliber rounds.

They looked to Doc and saw that he had taken the Doll's hand and was heading to the ramp. The ramp had what looked like gradient steps leading up into the dark surface above their heads. As they each reached the ramp, they could see a humanoid shape in the distance, backlit by a soft blue light. When the last two of the group, Tommy and Ally, climbed onto the bottom step of the ramp it began to retract and raise up into the ship. They hustled to keep up with the female leading the way, first along a short corridor then up a ladder, sort of, it was like steep open stairs with a railing. It reminded Doc of what were called ladders on Navy ships.

"I apologize for the less than ... gracious ... path to the command center, we took an ... emergency... route. Please pardon my use of your language I am still puzzled about some of the ... irregularities" said their guide.

They finally had a moment to catch a glimpse of her, the command center, and a male companion. She was still speaking as she began doing something on a panel in front of her.

"Please place yourself into any of the couches, we need

to depart immediately," said the young female as she settled into a seat in front of the panel she had been manipulating.

The group dropped into similar seats they found in the spacious command center, trying to avoid any that looked like it had control surfaces. They appeared to be in what looked like a command bridge with several view screens, or maybe windows, they weren't sure. Through one of them, they could see the smoking ruins of the Huey. Cobb and some companions, in tactical attire, huddled by the Ranger. It also did not look operational, but wasn't a smoking ruin, yet.

Suddenly, as a large, dark, triangular-shaped craft appeared approaching the area as the other being on the ship spoke, "We need to clear from this place, please pardon my focusing on that for now."

For a fraction of a second, the view windows, or whatever they were, appeared to show them beginning to rise, then the movement became a blur. The ship now seemed to be maneuvering, and they could see Earth below filling half of one of the viewports. The excitement and thrill vanished as the next thing they saw was the dark triangular vessel reappear on one of the screens.

One of, what they had assumed were windows, was a screen. On it was the image of a bulky, unpleasant, somewhat human appearing being. This being looked like it wanted to, or was trying to, address someone in the command center. As it turned its head from side to side, it appeared that it was looking for the female member of the Mithrim crew who had initially guided them here.

Before the conversation could begin, the male crew member quickly said, to the group, "The Thurog Commander, is trying to identify this ship's commander, Araime has narrowed his view to only see her station. Earlier, we set all incoming communications to be in your language, so you should understand what is being said. Please refrain from any remarks or noise as Araime deals with him."

"I am Massrten, commander of this security vessel, you will stand down and allow a boarding party," said the massive being in a heavily accented voice.

"Why should I allow such a rude overture, it borders on being a hostile act?" They all recognized the lyrical voice of the crew member now identified as Araime.

"I am a representative of this planet's security forces. Your vessel has violated our Sovereign space," The Thurog Commander replied with what might have passed for a sneer.

Araime smiled and looked around until she located Ally, "Is his claim true?"

A little startled at the focused question, Ally replied that his species was not part of the confederation.

As she was responding the other crew member on their bridge commented to no one in particular, "They are arming weapons and targeting us." Both Mithrim crew seemed unconcerned.

Araime responded, "I have a Confederation representative on board who states you are incorrect."

Suddenly, the forward view screen lit briefly with an incandescent reddish-white glow, then it appeared that some filter was in place as the Thurog ship remained in sight but was some distance away. They could see it begin moving forward toward the Mithrim. Everyone turned and looked at Araime, who seemed unconcerned. She did, however, have her left index finger hovering over at a point on the console.

"Commander Massrten, I suggest you resist hostilities," she said in the same calm, lyrical voice.

The Thurog ship closed the gap, then discharged some form of energy weapon again. The viewport darkened. It was like looking through eclipse glasses or a welder's mask. The incoming weapon beams appeared as small bright lines. Smiling, Araime jabbed her poised finger at the unseen point on the console. Two, noticeably thicker, blue-white beams focused on the central bulge of the triangular vessel. The central bulge ruptured at the point of contact. The blue-white beams ceased, and the contents of the bulging section of the ship burst outward. Even with the dark filter, hundreds of colors were terrifyingly beautiful as they exploded outward like fireworks. The Thurog ship ceased moving. Seconds later, small craft were visible making haste to get away from the hulk of the now derelict ship.

Keeping his voice calmer than he felt, Doc asked, "Araime, Wyik, what just happened?"

The two crew members looked at Doc then glanced at the rest of the group for a moment. Araime replied, "I, we, are sorry for the abruptness of our actions. Wyik is tracking three more hostiles headed to our location so I will be brief, I hope you understand and can be patient for a few more minutes. Once safe, we can elaborate."

She cocked her head to one side, looking at her console, took a cleansing breath and continued, "Two of the three hostiles headed our way are unknown. Seventy years ago, we lost the first three of our crew in that earlier engagement. It will not happen again. There will be a moment of disorientation as we jump."

For a moment, the reality surrounding them suddenly became ... vague.

Chapter 29

The view from the screens or viewports was extremely dark. They could make out very little other than a barren, bleak landscape. Then the portal dissolved to nothing and the area presently appeared to be part of the bulkhead as the ship settled.

"Clear," came a single comment from Wyik. He had been standing and now settled back into the seat facing his console.

"Please follow me," said Araime, more a suggestion than an outright order.

Wyik shrugged and got back up. They all followed her down a corridor and eventually into an open conference room with a round table and possibly thirty or so comfortable looking chairs.

Wyik studied the room for a moment and commented, "Please allow me a short period of time to make this more ... comfortable for a smaller group."

His command of English was good, but it was evident that both ship's crew were still getting used to the language

Araime smiled and sat on the arm of one of the chairs while Wyik apparently performed a magic act, or what seemed like one. The chairs moved to the perimeter of the room in an orderly manner. Then the table downsized, that was the only way to describe it. Finally, seven of the chairs made their way back to surround the table, leaving a place for the one Araime had anchored with her presence.

While this was going on, the group took a moment to study their hosts.

Both Dunarians were of medium build, not stocky, just robust. In retrospect, both had the same solid physical build that Doc had somehow reverted to in the past few days. Both were approximately six feet tall, and despite their solid frame and height, moved like cats. Their movements never seemed to include any wasted motion, each action or movement was swift, but fluid. The group was watching two, relatively human appearing beings, with uncanny speed, agility, and possibly superior strength. If the Dunarians were predators, they would most decidedly be at the top of the food chain. While the two appeared neither aggressive nor domineering, their recent reaction to the attack on this ship demonstrated they didn't appreciate being bullied.

Both wore what appeared to be ship jumpsuits. The material was some form of microfiber that was not tight but not loose. No matter how they moved, the suits shifted in a semi-elastic action so as not to restrict movement. That described their similarities.

Araime and Wyik, however, were two very different individuals. The ship jumpsuits they wore, while identical in design, varied in the number of pockets and color. Araime's jumpsuit was bright forest green. It suited her long, auburn hair and almost matched the green in her eyes. Her facial features were delicate, with a cute smallish nose and almost elven shaped face. The group had already seen her smile. It was warming and put you at ease even if you could see a hint of mischief.

Wyik, on the other hand, had facial features like Doc, with an almost square jaw and piercing blue eyes. His hair was a jumbled mass of almost blue-black curls that framed his face, and he didn't appear to have any facial hair. His jumpsuit was navy blue replete with several extra pockets on the thighs and the sleeves. Wyik's voice was smooth, with no noticeable accent and lacked the lyrical overtones of Araime's. It also appeared that he might have some vocal control over whatever allowed him to reconfigure the room.

Once they were all seated, Araime again took charge of the discussion or perhaps the dissertation. She explained that as they brought the Mithrim back to full operational status, they had split the tasks and functions. She oversaw all command and control functions, and Wyik oversaw all engineering and power functions.

"It is vital that we get to know each other and that you feel comfortable and safe here in Mithrim," she began, "but while it may not seem so, it has been a long few days for us, and I assume for you. We were released from stasis when Marxten, you know him as Doc, linked the two cyrog yesterday. Yesterday is a subjective concept. For us, a normal day is the equivalent of thirty hours of earth time. Before entering stasis, we had been on this planet long enough to adapt to your shorter days."

She paused, took a deep breath, smiled, and continued.

"I digress because I am tired, please forgive me if I cover topics more than once," she began again, "We began the evening before yesterday, I have no clue how you would refer to that time frame, but we have had only about six Earth hours of sleep since then. It is currently what you would refer to as 7:00 pm. I would propose that we all adjourn to our quarters and get some sleep. I will answer some of your immediate questions now, but that is all."

Over the next hour, she and Wyik patiently gave the group an overview of what had occurred to this point. Doc's action with the cyrogs had started the process. It took about four hours for Araime and Wyik to be functional after they had woken. It took another two hours to get brought up to date by their cyrogs and to begin to adapt to the English language. The Mithrim had been in standby and moved from five percent standby status to an active crew level of fifteen percent throughout the previous day, as they tended to the ship. By 4:00 am, the Mithrim was stable and autonomous.

It remained at fifteen percent, but all systems were tested and primed so Mithrim could rapidly transition to a minimum combat readiness level of fifty percent should it be required. Araime and Wyik managed to take some small rest periods but mostly monitored the progress of Doc's group. The intent was to welcome the group and acclimate them before Mithrim left her secure resting place in a large cavern. That, of course, did not happen, instead they pushed Mithrim from fifteen percent to her now full readiness level for all systems.

Their current location was the group's foremost question. The answer was not one any had expected. Araime explained that they were in a crater on the dark side of Earth's moon, the result of an advanced methodology devised by Doc's father. They executed a wormhole jump the short distance from Earth's orbit to the dark side of the moon. Wyik patiently explained that wormhole jumps, in general, move a ship from one point in space and time to another.

Jumps are always carefully selected outside of a solar system. This is to prevent a vessel from returning to real space inside a planet or object moving between stations. Jumps are also in the range of light-years. This jump, on the other hand, had been a tiny 242,103 miles to a point on the dark side of the moon where a monitoring beacon had been set in place seven decades earlier.

Wyik interjected, "When that beacon was placed there was nothing on the moon at all. Over the intervening years, a Russian base was setup but is no longer active, and a Teletin base was established. That Teletin base is active, but this crater is in a different hemisphere, and we can mask ... hide our activity."

Everyone looked at Ally, who shrugged, "Nobody told me we would be hiding out on the back of your moon. I have been to that base. It is a sophisticated monitoring station. Are you sure they do not know we are here? They have a myriad of stealth satellites relaying information."

Wyik worked at suppressing a smile, unsuccessfully, "We are in a crater and hidden by the beacon we used as the target jump point. That beacon, sentinel might be a better human word, monitors all activity on this dark side. We knew when the Russian station was established and later when it failed. We observed the operation of the Teletin surveys and biased their results to the other hemisphere. We have, since then, continued to monitor their station.

Today they reported our departure from the Guadalupe Mountains to your headquarters in Dulce, New Mexico. They have also reported the destruction of the Thurog ship, and the movement of the other three vessels. The station's last report was concerning our portal jump outside of this solar system. They are trying to figure out where that jump might have taken us."

Araime just smiled, as did Wyik. Ally was unreadable, and the rest of the group just seemed to take it as one more incredible piece of information.

There were more questions, but those were mostly related to the ship accommodations, where would they be quartered, what should they know about their accommodations. Food. Food was a big question as all, including Araime and Wyik, suddenly realized they had not eaten for a while. Wyik did more of his magic with the layout of the room, and some panels opened to reveal what looked like chafing dishes, plates, tall containers like glasses, and recognizable utensils.

"For the immediate future, we will all take meals in this place, it is easier. We refer to this area as the common room. The covered containers contain slices of a protein substance similar to a meat patty and a puréed vegetable substance. There is also a sauce to put on both. It is not unpleasant and, until we can work together on the food synthesizer, I hope it will be okay. We will, of course, be eating with you. There is also a flavored liquid, again this is just temporary."

Everyone tried some of the meal, and no one seemed to find any real fault, or maybe they were all just tired and hungry. There were a few additional questions, but mostly they all just ate. After "dinner" they were shown three separate quarters, one for each of the pairs and everyone retired for the night.

Doc and the Doll looked around their room for a moment, located the bed and were asleep in minutes. It had been a long day.

Chapter 30

Doc woke to a gentle touch on his shoulder. He remembered throwing off his clothes and slipping under the covers and into bed. Seconds later, if that long, he felt the Doll cuddle into him like a cat shifting to gain the maximum contact. It had been a long day. They began the day closing in on where the Mithrim might be and ended up in her on the far side of the moon.

He woke refreshed and smiled to himself, at least he wouldn't have to run this morning, maybe. When he opened his eyes and located the Doll, she was sitting in some form of hovering egg-shaped chair. It wasn't precisely an egg or even half an egg since it provided support for her long legs. It was more like a wrap-a-round floating lounger. The Doll and her chair were gently swaying side to side, and she was smiling. She was beautiful, and not at all concerned that she did not appear to be wearing anything but that smile. Then he focused on her face. It had only been a little over a week, and he already could recognize her many smiles. This smile was broadcasting, "I know something you will never guess."

She seemed content for the moment, inwardly enjoying whatever was responsible for that smile. Doc took advantage of the pause to glance around the room. The part of his brain that was continually updated via the cyrog supplied the term "cabin." He was amused that it had provided "cabin," not, the Dunarian title "figaw." He decided that figuring out the dual language thing was for another time and resumed glancing around the cabin.

The cyrog continued overlaying what he saw with Dunarian subtitles. He took a moment to examine his surroundings before whatever the Doll was amused with caught up to him. They were currently in the sleeping chamber of this cabin. To one side was an entrance to the refresher or bathroom. Several built-ins were part of the headboard of this king-sized bed. These expanded to the right and left of the bed forming built-in nightstands. Beyond the bed itself, there was a couch-like piece of furniture, a small low table, and an additional hovering lounger.

The walls, bulkheads, held panels that, his memory supplied, were hiding storage and other compartments. There was an opening, a hatchway, to the main living area of the quarters. He realized that last night, they had headed straight to the bedroom and sleep.

Doc had once won a Carnival Cruise to the Bahamas that included first-class accommodations in what the cruise line referred to as a Grand Suite. From what he could glimpse through the hatchway, their quarters in the Mithrim made those accommodations look small.

"So, when you are done looking around, would you like a cup of coffee to start off your morning?" said the bemused naked Doll.

Refocused and still wondering what he was missing, Doc replied, "Yes, please."

"Jeeves, please bring Doc a cup of coffee, then get me a refill," the Doll said with that same odd little smile.

Coming around the edge of the bed, Doc saw a cup of coffee appear to float at the same level as the bed. The floating vessel approached the side of the bed nearest to him and began to rise. The cup was now hovering about an inch above the top of a bowling pin. Again, memory supplied that this was the cabin attendant, sort of a majordomo.

It looked like a slightly overweight bowling pin, off-white with a color band around the neck, but otherwise featureless. Doc noticed that any feature accents in the bedroom were a pleasant maroon color, unobtrusive but there. Jeeves' neckband was that same color. He began to wonder what real bowling pins had been patterned after, then decided that was not important now.

Doc took the coffee. Jeeves cruised away and immediately brought a second cup to the Doll who took it without taking her eyes from Doc. She was still smiling and waiting for a reaction.

"You named it Jeeves?" Doc asked, smiling back.

"Yup, it appeared from nowhere when I was coming out of the bathroom. Introduced itself, in English, as the room attendant. Then it asked me, it called me Doll, how you and I would like to address it. I said Jeeves. It repeated the name and asked me to confirm which I did. Jeeves asked me if there was anything it could get for me, I said coffee, and we have spent the last half hour or so getting to know each other while you snoozed."

Doc asked the Doll to elaborate, so she continued. Her first question to Jeeves, after asking for coffee, had been where her clothes were. While Doc appreciated her current attire or lack thereof, he had figured that they would need to meet with the rest of the group soon and he was relatively sure the ship's crew would not be naked.

The Doll had continued, while Doc's mind had taken a side trip.

On-planet clothing was scanned, then recycled. The replicator could then reproduce it and variations in minutes, less than five minutes per person, including footwear. The replicator also provided standard and varieties of the ship jumpsuits matched to the occupants' size and perceived taste. In one of the compartments behind the bulkheads in the sleeping area, was today's ship-wear. This included undergarments and footwear.

Doc decided to focus less on the Doll's current attire and instead inquired about the status of the other two couples in their group. The Doll continued, she had woken early and gone through introduction, naming, and understanding Jeeves when she had the same thought. Jeeves, when asked, confirmed he could interface with the other attendants. Both other couples in their group were still sleeping soundly, even now. Now turned out to be the equivalent of 6:00 am. The attendants in those quarters were supposed to notify Jeeves when their charges woke so Doc and the Doll could ease the adjustment.

"So, there is a shower-like compartment in the bathroom, more than large enough for two," The Doll remarked, conversationally, as she slid from the floating lounger and padded into the bathroom area. "Jeeves tells me it uses sonic jets of something and is soothing, restorative, and he assures me relaxing. You are going to help me through this first experience of spaceship living, right?"

"What is this fascination with showers?" Doc asked idly as he headed to the refresher.

"It's the company," came the simple reply, then an afterthought, "and I like having my back washed."

They took some time experimenting with the settings in the refresher, then got dressed in the shipboard jumpsuit clothing. The jumpsuits seemed simple enough, like putting on, well, a jumpsuit. This proved to be more of a mental than a real challenge. The conundrum was the undergarment. It should have been, and turned out to be, simple. It just stymied them both until the Doll got hers on. These undergarments looked like a pillowcase, and they would have ignored them had Jeeves not butted in and told them that they had to wear undergarments. The Doll finally gave up and braved one of them. When she stepped in, her feet instantly emerged from some apparent hole in the bottom, one hole for each leg. As she continued to pull it up, she found a place for her arms and that signaled the rest.

She found herself in a one-piece covering that blanketed from just above mid-thigh, covering her whole torso with a short, maybe an inch-long sleeve and a V-neck. When she moved, stretched, jumped or any variation of movement, the sheath changed. More than that, it adjusted and appeared as if it had been spray-painted on her. As Doc was marveling and enjoying the skin-tight clinging garment on the Doll, she held up one finger in the universal wait a minute pose. She then stepped into the refresher area and was back out in a flash with an odd little smile.

"Try it scaredy-cat," she said with an amused look, "I just checked, it allows access to ... then closes back up."

They were relaxing and enjoying another coffee when they got the alert that Ally was the first one up, in her and

Tommy's cabin. Through the attendant in Ally's cabin, the Doll explained its function. Ally took in the information and then named their attendant Siri. She said that Tommy had an iPhone and was obsessed with Siri, so this should be fun. She also explained this to the attendant, Siri, and let it get a voice pattern sample from Tommy's phone. Finally, Ally examined the rooms in the cabin, the clothing and decided she liked the Doll's approach to waking up Doc and figured that would also work with Tommy.

Fifteen minutes after leaving Ally to mess with Tommy's mind, they got the alert that Mike and Amber were both up. They went through the same explanation with the two of them. Mike suggested Widget for a name, and Amber agreed. They left the two of them to get organized and arranged to meet them in the ship's common room with the crew at 9:00 am for a late breakfast and planning session.

Chapter 31

Doc and the Doll were greeted by the smell of sausage and eggs as they entered the common room and immediately noticed Ally and Tommy. The couple was digging into what looked like scrambled eggs, sausage patties, and something that resembled an English muffin. They looked up, nodded, and returned to eating breakfast. Araime and Wyik were at a sideboard preparing their plates and looked up with a smile.

"Your father liked to try different foods wherever we were," Wyik said casually as he moved toward the table with a full plate of eggs and at least a half dozen sausage patties, "If he liked something, he analyzed, then programmed it into the food processor. This is a combination we all like, and, I am still getting my strength back after about thirty or so stasis cycles." Araime just nodded and attacked her eggs.

Amber and Mike appeared shortly after, gave everyone a nod then headed for the eggs. The assembled couples settled back after cleaning their plates, found coffee, some odd but refreshing juices, and then took in their surroundings. The chaffing dishes disappeared, and now the colorful array of jumpsuits grabbed their attention. Everyone was in a ship's uniform, but it was the lack of uniformity that caught the eye. There were four couples and a total of eight different variations of suit colors and accessories. Well, seven distinct hues. Ally apparently could control the fabric component of her jumpsuit in much the same as she could her own skin. She was amusing herself and the group in general, as she shifted to an almost invisible state, depending on where she sat or moved.

"Now that we all appear to be rested and in a good mood," Araime said casually, "We should probably consider some plan, any random plan would be a good start. We, your current hosts, have some topics on our agenda and I am sure that you have similar agendas. I suspect or hope that all these agendas can work together. If you don't mind, Wyik and I will start by explaining our current objectives."

Araime and Wyik patiently explained their current status and immediate hopes and plans. They glossed over the initial landing on Earth, the conflicts and the ultimate loss of several crew members. They touched briefly on Thracen's pregnancy and the birth of Marxten, now known as Doc. All this aside, they explained the Dunarian initiative.

Dunar no longer existed as a planet. Despite the best minds and over a century of warning and planning, they could not prevent their sun from going supernovae or the projected catastrophic results. When they could arrive at no reasonable solution, they focused their energy toward finding a way to move their population, since they couldn't move their planet. Dunar was an earth size planet with over 60 percent of its surface covered by vast oceans. The population centers were spread across small island nations under a single government. The total population at the point of departure was just under 1.5 billion.

They developed massive ark ships, 261 to be exact and exactly 1,000 Seeker Class Star cruisers. The Mithrim was one of those. The population on each of the Ark ships were under 5.8 million with a rotating crew of 1,200. That crew would regularly rotate with those in stasis as the Arks looked for a new home. The Arks and the Seekers maintained loose but consistent communication. When the Mithrim returned to full power yesterday, she received an update. So far, no new home had been found. As this odyssey continued, they had lost two of the Arks, and there were now less the 600 of the Seeker class remaining

The full story of the Dunarians and their odyssey was not crucial at this point. Araime indicated that it was important that they rebuild the Mithrim's crew back to at least eight or ten members. With a full crew compliment, they could leave Earth's solar system and contribute to seeking a potential home for their species. Araime turned to Doc and the Doll.

"Marxten ... Doc," Araime said as she looked at Doc, "why are you and your group here, now? Based on our observations, and the updates from the Mithrim, your group represents six very different personalities. You are four humans and two non-human species, one of those being Dunarian. While I suspect that your cyrog enhanced memories have answered some questions, it is apparent you all sought the Mithrim for different reasons from those I just explained. We need to know where or if those disparate desires can be melded together."

"You refer to me as Marxten," Doc began, "from the pieces coming together in my racial memory, I understand the reference. For the immediate future, however, I would prefer to be addressed as Doc. I am still sorting out those memories as they overlay my years of experience as a human. For now, I would be interested in feedback from my original group as defined by our joining the Mithrim yesterday."

He looked to his right and simply said, "Doll, please?"

The Doll looked at the group, back at Doc then to the

two Dunarians, "Three weeks ago I was a respected scientist heading up a government research facility. Then hired goons tried to kidnap me for my research. Since then, I have been attacked again, gone into hiding, abandoned all I knew, changed my appearance, even my persona from Karen to the Doll. I have learned about a world of espionage and alien interaction I had not even dreamed existed. I learned that a being I have developed a strong emotional attachment to is not human. Then we added another non-human to our group, our family, of six. My world is more than a little off-kilter."

"This morning, I woke up as though it was normal to be on a powerful interstellar combat vessel parked on the dark side of the moon. I chatted with a bowling pin named Jeeves and had a relaxing breakfast of scrambled eggs, sausage, toast, that was not derived from either a chicken or pig. I am relaxing with a cup of coffee that, also, was never once a bean. What I do know is that I trust the six members of my family group and see no reason to not include the two crew of this amazing vessel in that trust."

She paused for a moment, then resumed, "I would like to put this Ronan character and his organization out of business permanently. And maybe deal with the alien group that tried to attack us. Yup, right now that will work for me."

All present were absorbing the Doll's comments when Amber cleared her throat and began, "I am not sure who is supposed to go next, but I volunteer Mike and I. We had a similar discussion this morning, which is why we were last to arrive for breakfast. Mike, do you mind if I speak for both of us?"

Mike smiled, "Go for it."

Amber resumed, "Like the Doll, I have undergone a personal adjustment. I am very comfortable as Amber. I have several degrees in biosciences and will get back to that in a moment. Mike's background is in engineering. We are still exploring our relationship, one that we avoided due to the constraints of our previous lives. We joined our current family, an excellent description for our group, to help the Doll and Doc unravel where their lives were going. That is what families do. We need to put this Ronan character out of business, and then deal with these Thurog characters that tried to attack the Mithrim. Once those two issues are resolved, the concept of traveling the stars and visiting other worlds seems like a challenge we both would love to be part of if you will have us as part of the crew of the Mithrim."

Araime and Wyik both had broad smiles as they looked from the couple to Doc who shrugged with a smile. Everyone turned and looked at Ally and Tommy.

Chapter 32

"Wow, no pressure," remarked Tommy as Ally elbowed him with a smile.

The group was aware that Tommy and Ally had worked together in the past. It was no surprise that they had an ongoing personal relationship that they had kept below the radar. Now they both contributed to the discussion in a manner where they sometimes completed each other's sentences.

The group knew that Tommy was CIA and linked to a unit that worked with a consortium of eight extraterrestrial species that had a secret agreement allowing them to be on Earth. Ally was also connected to that unit in her capacity as an enforcer. A significant part of her job was to prevent unauthorized actions by any of the aliens allowed on Earth. Both Ally and Tommy filled in the gaps as they explained that they were both stationed in a secret base below a small southwestern town in Dulce, New Mexico. The complex was a several story compound including embassies, housing, and research. So, unlike Amber and Mike, they were a bit conflicted. Both had worked to stop Ronan's arms deals which had somehow included some alien hardware and were equally involved with dealing with unauthorized non-human incursions.

Before realizing Doc's lineage, they had both been aware of the initial historical appearance of the Mithrim in the late '40s. They knew of an attack against the ship by Thurog cruisers that resulted in the famed Roswell incident. What they didn't know was what had really happened. In the years following the Roswell incident, there were also rumors of a captured Dunarian or Dunarians. They had looked to Araime and Wyik and got very closed looks in return.

Ally commented, "We want, no, need to understand what happened and is happening. Both of us have had misgivings about some of the information we were fed in Dulce."

Tommy nodded and continued, "When I began to put together what I had learned from my grandfather and then joined up with Doc last week, I knew that some of the information I had was not right. When I asked Mike to join me, we went dark so even the Dulce operations can't be sure where we are. Although, they would have to be blind to not put the pieces together now. Though, of course, guessing we are on the far side of the moon might be a stretch."

Ally took over, "I tracked Tommy because I can," she smiled at him, and just shook his head in resignation, then she continued, "my species is what would be considered very family-oriented. When I joined this group, I was welcomed like family, something that is and will always be significant to me. As for not knowing all the facts, my species is also ... less gullible... I would like to suggest that we contact the Teletin base hidden here. My brother is currently stationed there. I believe that with their help we can gather some additional needed information."

Ally and Tommy turned back to Doc, then Tommy grinned and said," So ... what's up, Doc?"

Five beings groaned in unison, two Dunarians looked confused, and Doc just shook his head.

"It seems to me," Doc said after a minute, "that we have three issues. The first being the resumption of Mithrim's part as a Seeker. That requires a minimum crew compliment. The six of us could, with training, possibly be that crew, but we also have other issues we need to resolve first. Part of our group has become targets for an international criminal element. The third issue seems to encompass all eight of us. The Mithrim is a prize sought by one or more rogue species and possibly sanctioned species. If we consider the Mithrim's return to mission the most important of the three issues and that we are all willing to leave with her, then we need to only tackle the other two issues."

Doc looked at the group. He already knew how Amber and Mike felt.

"I love my family, but want to explore this new family relationship," Ally offered as she looked at Tommy.

"When Spyder passed, Doc, you were the family that was most important to me, the extended family that was important," Tommy said, then looked at Ally as he continued," Ally is my family going forward. I am willing to go where my family goes."

The Doll, rolled her eyes, "Araime, Wyik, is there a need for a biomedical scientist on the Mithrim's crew?"

The Dunarians nodded.

"Doc," she stared directly at him, "I supposed that had you not butted in to start with I would have been kidnapped by Ronan and his group and that would not have gone well. Your rescue of me spun us into this current interstellar conundrum. In the meantime, you have grown on me, so help me put Ronan out of business and I will wander the stars with you and this crew."

Doc laughed at that, paused for a second, shrugged and finally commented, "you have grown on me too." He looked at Ally, "explain to me why you feel that working with the Teletin base will help us resolve any of the issues?"

Ally was quiet for a moment then explained why she felt her species, as represented by the station on the moon would not only be a useful asset but would help to even the odds, whatever they might be.

The Teletin were a new species as far as the council on Earth was concerned. Not new as a species, but new as a partner. This was in part because the Teletin generally didn't play well with others. They were, as Ally indicated, very family-oriented, that meant biological family, and they had a general mistrust of other species. The feeling appeared to be mutual. It seems none of the species were fond of individuals that could blend in so well that they practically disappeared. However, over time, the Teletin were invited to join the council on a trial basis. That trial basis meant that they were assigned every clandestine or questionable operation wherever their unique traits were needed. What the authorities, initially, failed to grasp was that the Teletin now had free reign to gather information. As a result of this first oversight, several attempts had been made to bug the Teletin consulate. That never works and those doing the bugging are spoon-fed worthless, and sometimes comical intel.

Ally absently commented, "This funny little family group we are part of is so ... Teletin-like that I forget it is composed of humans and a Dunarian, or three."

About a decade ago, the current head of the Teletin consulate made a big show of the creating a regular rotation from the consular duties to returning home. This involved visiting dignitaries and a week-long celebration during which time some of the those, departing for home, ended up at a newly established, ultra-stealth station on the far side of the moon. Any Teletin posted to Earth now rotates through three postings. First, the moon, to acclimate to the culture they would soon be involved with. Then Earth, where they end up with all the odd clandestine assignments the council is currently engaged in. Finally, back to the moon to detox and refine their skills. Ally smiled and let that sink in, to the group and Tommy.

Doc spoke up first, "Okay ... so how do we approach the base without getting our asses handed to us?"

Chapter 33

Ally had done a short tour of duty at the surveillance base when she was first posted to Earth. That had been eight years ago. Dezir, Ally's brother, had transferred to the station six months earlier, and it would be at least another six months before he was posted to Earth as her replacement. That last comment netted a curious look from Tommy.

The base, designated Geray complex, had an average occupancy of thirty-six individuals. There were core staff with an indefinite rotation period as well as those who rotated home after a three-year tour. There were also transient personnel moving through to an Earth posting then back to the complex for detox before going home. Part of this permanent staff included a trusted Alution, the only non-Teletin, and a valued researcher. Besides the clandestine unit, there were also four flight crews for the two gunships kept at the station. These deadly ships required three trained and dedicate crewmembers, a pilot, a weapons officer, and an electronics officer. A pair of these gunships could take on a Thurog cruiser. Ally admitted that it would not be as decisive an action as when the Mithrim took on the Thurog cruiser, but they could do the job.

The base also had advanced counterintelligence equipment. Again, Ally admitted that she was more than a little surprised that the Mithrim's presence had remained entirely unnoticed.

"Can we offer a suggestion?" This from Araime, who was sitting relaxed in one of the chairs around the table.

"Please hear me out before making your decision. You are all aware that Doc grows more comfortable with his heritage as each day progresses. You are also correct if you assume this change is due to his interaction with the cyrogs. These devices augmented his memory. I assume you have encountered these devices and arrived at the assumption that they only aid a member of our species. That last assumption is not entirely true."

There was a palatable silence as the group now focused on Araime as she continued to explain her proposal.

"When we left to search for a new homeworld, we understood we also had to preserve our heritage and memories during the long gaps of time where individuals would be in stasis. When a Dunarian child is born, they are bonded to a cyrog. That cyrog also includes a link to their family history and more. When the Mithrim brought us out of stasis, we had no clue why. We had no frame of reference. No idea why we were being brought out or what had occurred throughout our absence. During the first hour, as we gained strength, we were updated on world events, and anything relevant to assisting Marxten, including that Doc, is his current name. One of the two cyrog Doc has, was bonded to him at birth, the other was an emergency training and command sequencer for the Mithrim. Doc's action of combining the two devices was the trigger to wake us from stasis and prep Mithrim for departure."

Wyik took over the discussion for a moment as Araime responded to some signal from the bridge.

Addressing Doc, he began, "Your father was, in terms all here will understand, an engineer and geneticist, an unusual but effective dual discipline. From what we remember and what we have since learned, before his demise, he made several modifications to the cyrogs on the Mithrim. He was building a library of sorts. All of this group can access those cyrogs, with some assistance."

Araime returned, "The Geray complex is on alert, but not due to our presence."

With no further comment, she returned to discussing the cyrogs. Araime explained that, if any of the group were willing, Wyik could set up a blank cyrog to permanently pair with that volunteer. Based on what they had learned of Anexten's work, once paired to their own cyrog, any of the group could then access the library Anexten had been preparing. She suggested this might prove useful moving forward. Two members of the group replied immediately.

"We would like to volunteer," was the simultaneous reply from Mike and Amber.

Mike continued, "We've already indicated that we would like to be part of this crew. This opportunity would give us the tools to be an effective addition to the Mithrim."

The chamber was silent as all present considered the offer. Finally, Doc spoke up as he looked at the group. Initially, he discussed the devices themselves. He confirmed being drawn to these devices and could have no sooner ignored them than he could ignore water in the desert. He explained that while the information dump had been almost overwhelming, his ability to interpret that information was an ongoing process. Even the information he had processed was not working knowledge. Instead, presented with a situation, he could draw on pertinent information related to the issue. He couldn't just browse topics as though he was in a library.

His immediate concern was that the process that Araime was suggesting would be different than an infant being bonded at birth.

Wyik confirmed that there would be a difference. Any of this group willing to undergo the bonding would undertake a two-step process. The first step would be to establish a link to their personal cyrog. That process would be initiated using one of the stasis pods present in all the crew cabins. Once the link and the memories of that group member were transferred to their cyrog, Mithrim would create a pathway that would allow the cyrog, the individual, and the Mithrim to continually update. Once this had occurred, the second step would be a limited transfer of ship systems information suitable for a crew member as well as a preselected topic. This would be like choosing a major in college. The discussion continued, but the consensus was that knowledge is power. No one attempted to dissuade Mike or Amber from taking this step toward becoming a contributing member of the Mithrim crew.

As the discussion continued, Ally's patience finally ran out.

"Excuse me," she said with a hint of an edge to her voice, "could someone please tell me what the Geray complex is on alert means. I have family there."

Chapter 34

Araime smiled apologetically, "I am sorry, Ally, my intent was not to ignore the situation, but it was not one that poses a danger to either that complex or the Mithrim. If you could be patient just a few minutes longer, I will go with Mike and Amber and get their process started."

"Can we all go to show our support?" The Doll asked, looking back at the group who all nodded.

"They will be fine. I give you my assurance." Araime continued, "For the first link, they will need to enter their own status pods sans clothing. It is up to them, but they might prefer some privacy."

Michael blushed a bit, but Amber just smiled and replied to the group, "We appreciate the gesture, but we'll be fine. Use the time to figure out our next move." Her last comment was directed at Doc.

Amber, Mike, and Araime departed. So, the group turned to Doc. Doc, in turn, looked at Wyik who, in turn, glanced at Ally then began to fill the group in.

While Araime had responded to the initial alert, he had continued to monitor the Teletin complex. Wyik explained that due to the diverse background of the remainder of the group, he would keep his explanations basic. He started with the ship.

The Mithrim was equipped with a stealth unit that

effectively deflected any electronic and hyperspatial based systems. While this system was actively cloaking Mithrim, her own sensors could actively monitor signal traffic across the expanse where they had earlier staged sensors. These sensors and relays allowed the Mithrim to track signals originating or returning from any point on Earth, the Moon, Venus, and Mars. The ship was currently in a crater. Listed in Earth records, as the Stevinus crater, this was a lunar impact crater located in the southeast part of the moon. It had a depth of over 9,800 feet. Where they sat, near the inner wall of this 246,000-foot diameter crater, even a well-equipped surveillance vessel traversing the area would not notice them.

Wyik continued his commentary with an odd mischievous smile as he discussed the Geray complex. It was in a crater known as the Plato crater; the lava-filled remains of a lunar impact crater located on the northeastern shore of the Mare Imbrium. Plato was more extensive, but not as deep as the Stevinus crater due to the lava fill. Still smiling, he intimated that the Teletin had an excellent security unit, but there were human government reports that indicated there might be a secret base in the crater. Wyik waited as that sank in. He continued by explaining this crater had been used well before the first contact. As early as the late 1800s there had been reports of ships, and lights had been reported there by ancient Earth astronomers. The crater had been initially abandoned as a base for just that reason. The Teletin took this into account and assumed that hiding in plain sight would work in their favor. So far, they have been successful in that respect.

Ally grinned, "Doc, you have to appreciate the hide in plain sight concept. When the location was being researched, there were still ongoing contemporary UFO reports concerning that crater. Even though the Alution or Gray aliens had abandoned the base several decades earlier, the continued and repeated rumors of sightings worked as an easy reason to excuse any real sightings."

Doc looked at Wyik then Ally, "So how do we contact this advanced, stealth, Teletin stronghold? Or as I put it earlier, how do we approach the base without getting our asses handed to us?"

Ally chimed in, "And why are you so sure that they are on alert, but that it doesn't concern us at this point?"

Wyik addressed Ally's concerns first. The communications tools on Mithrim were extensive. They were designed to allow the Seeker crews to gain some understanding of the inhabitants of populated worlds as they looked for a new home. The Dunarians, it appeared, had previous experience with the several species that composed the council and were aware of the Thurog. As such, the Mithrim was able to intercept incoming and outgoing message traffic to the Geray complex.

After Mithrim had pulled her vanishing act, the three ships, heading to join the Thurog cruiser, continued to try and determine where the Dunarian vessel had gone. Those three ships had extended their search to include a full circuit of the moon. That search produced no results. The Geray complex, however, has been put on alert for a different reason. Two of those three ships are still unclassified. The Teletin intelligence unit had not been able to identify those vessels as they passed over the Plato crater.

About an hour later, Araime returned as Wyik was wrapping up their options for contacting the Teletin complex. They had discussed several options as well as contemplating how to determine the origin of the two mystery craft.

"Amber and Mike will be out of stasis in about three hours. Each has chosen a specific discipline from the library.

"We need more information," Ally remarked with an exasperated harrumph, "You said the Doc's father had filled a library with information that might be useful to a mixed crew. I know the active cycles at the complex. The main crew will be going off duty about the time that Amber and Mike are back. I can assure you that we are better off dealing with the main station compliment than freaking out the night duty crew. I think that the rest of us should get cyroged so we all can actively use the information available."

She looked around and saw no apparent objections, so she continued, "If we get ... scanned and adjusted now, we can then get a good night's sleep, and maybe have the information we need to proceed. I know my species' communication protocols but not Dunarian. Knowing both protocols will give us an edge. I sense that the remaining human members of our group trust Doc and, as a result, trust the process will not harm them."

The Doll was relaxing in one of the chairs, and gave a casual nod of agreement, checking first to see if Doc was going to provide any additional insight. Tommy also looked at Doc, then back at Ally with a shrug and nod of agreement.

Doc smiled and looked at Ally, "This is a good plan, but something has you spooked?"

After a moment, Ally replied, "We, as a species, aren't very trusting of other species. I am not sure why I find myself trusting all of you. However, to me, you feel like family. It is a good idea, but now I must consider if this process works on humans but not my species. I am still a little taken aback by Doc's casual trick of putting me to sleep. What if I can't bond with a cyrog?"

Araime cleared her throat to get the group's attention, "One of Anexten's closest friends, from what we have learned was a Teletin. Whatever Doc was able to do to you was based on his interaction with that friend and companion. They worked together on the library, which is why the idea of all of you having access is an excellent plan. The only side effect that the process might befall you, as a Teletin, according to the notes, is minor. Something about your skin turning a permanent shade of orange, and your hair turning a brilliant green."

Ally turned literally white, both skin and hair.

Doc frowned at Araime, then chuckled, "My species, as I am learning, has a twisted sense of humor."

Chapter 35

Color slowly began to return to Ally, she leveled a glare at Araime and Doc that was, well, just short of flames.

Doc, still smiling, began, "With each passing day I have more access to memories and information. As with all these memories, until I experience a triggering event, it is useless information. I have realized that the Dunarians had a definite sense of humor early on. Now I am aware there is a counterpoint to balance the odd sense of humor. All Dunarians also have a unique tell when spinning a tale or setting up a joke. The tell, while unique, is centered anatomically. A little twisted joke like Araime just targeted you with must be released into the wild before the tell is visible. I think it would be a welcoming family gesture for Araime to share with Ally."

Araime had always seemed graceful, courteous, and generally a smiling, welcoming personality. So, when she wrinkled her nose and stuck her tongue out at Doc, it was a surprise. Well almost, Wyik burst into laughter.

Ally studied the group then a slow but decidedly dangerous little smile replaced her previous frown. Araime shrugged and casually shook her head from side to side, her medium length hair almost hiding her ears. Wyik snickered. Araime and Wyik looked as human as Doc, Tommy or the Doll.

"It's the ears. They twitch right before the punchline," remarked Doc, "I had always wondered what caused that sensation in my own ears, now I know, or maybe remember. Sadly, with that memory comes other memories."

"Those memories are of family, of friends and of loss. Memories of my mother, father, and others have begun to integrate with my existing memories. These memories are bittersweet because they are memories of my family. A family I will never meet."

"I am going to tell you all a short story, then, unless there are objections, I think the Doll, Tommy, and Ally need to head to their stasis pods for integration before we tackle the Geray complex."

The story was not what any of them expected. Doc began by explaining that, for unknown reasons, the increased memories were overlapping his day to day memories. When this happened, it was generally in response to some current action triggering the dormant memories as a reference. Today was one of those days. Oddly, it was the memory of the tell that brought back specific memories of his father and his close friend and companion, a Teletin. That memory was of their final day together. Doc related parts of that last day. The two of them had been tracking the group responsible for the initial attack on Mithrim. The vessels involved appeared to be of the same type as the two unidentified ships discussed earlier today. In an expected final confrontation, his companion had been killed, and Anexten was severely wounded. Both had forced the last upload to their cyrogs as the conflict escalated. The Teletin succumbed to his wounds first. Then aware that he could not survive his own injuries, Anexten set off a rhunsan, an explosive device that would incinerate anything in a thirty-meter diameter area to prevent their bodies from being scavenged.

Doc made a point, confirmed by Araime and Wyik. One is that part of the bonding with a cyrog included a bio cellular implant that allowed the Mithrim to keep the cyrog updated with its host.

Doc now felt that he needed to review that last upload thoroughly. Then he also insisted that Ally review the cyrog once bonded to Anexten's long-time friend and companion.

Doc focused on Ally as he continued to speak of his father's friend. When he divulged the Teletin's name, Ruvator Kalach, Ally turned white again.

Doc asked Ally to explain who Ruvator Kalach was. After assuring her that he was positive about the identity of the Teletin.

Ally, having regained some of her composure, explained that Ruvator had been a senior science officer and ruling member of the Earth-side Teletin command team. Then at some point in time in the 1980s, he had disappeared. There was speculation but no real explanations. Ruvator had, besides the titles she had indicated, been a master in counterintelligence. Then, with an odd look on her face, she concluded with the admission that he had been her maternal grandfather.

Doc resumed his comments. He felt that the final thoughts of the two, Anexten and Ruvator would be critical in solving the puzzles they were faced with. The personal cyrogs could only be accessed by immediate family members. Doc was confident that Ally would be to able access her grandfather's memories; Ally was a genetic match.

Ally slowly got her normal coloration back as she

listened to Doc. She was silent for a few minutes before turning to the rest of the group, "Let's get this done before I figure out an excuse why I should back out of the process."

The decisions made, Ally, Tommy, and the Doll proceeded to their respective stasis pods. The Doll smiled, kissed Doc, then relaxed into her pod.

"Are you sure?" he asked her as Araime made some adjustments.

"My life has been twisted, turned, rebuilt and otherwise remained in a state of dynamic flux the past few weeks," she began, "the only constant is you. You have been honest with me and answered my questions, regardless of the outcome. My constant companion now is an alien trying to rationalize how he got here. I am glad I can help when I do, and I intend to see this, whatever, to the end."

Doc smiled, nodded to Araime to continue then relaxed in one of the egg chairs prodding and reviewing his father's cyrog. It was not like reading a book or listening to a lecture. It was a bit like standing on a cliff overlooking the ocean on a quiet evening. The sun was setting, and a seabird was winging its way somewhere. As you figuratively stood and watched the scene, your view would slowly split between what you were physically seeing and an overlay of the bird's perspective. Sometimes the pieces fit to provide a cohesive look into the distance. Sometimes the bird's view was replaced by a squirrel on the branch of a tree near your shoulder. Then the question of view became squirrel vs. bird or maybe a combination. He was sure those in stasis were enjoying their own squirrels.

The next few days would prove interesting.

Chapter 36
Geray complex - Pluto Crater – Moon

The day shift had just taken over. Day shift was a relative term in this crater on the backside of Earth's moon. The night shift had given their reports and had withdrawn to their quarters or to the recreation areas. The morning meal had occurred between the two shifts, so all present were relaxed and beginning to settle into the day to day routine.

Total darkness ... no klaxons ... no flickering of lighting systems ... no explosions suggesting an attack ... nothing. Commander Arisate Lovan, base commander for the Geray complex, was sitting in the command chair. There was no panic. This was one of the best crews he had served with over the years. His eyesight, like all Teletin, was excellent in low light levels but not so good in no light levels.

"All stations report," Arisate said in a level commanding voice.

The reports coming back were unusual. Most of the power systems were offline. The exception was the life support systems. Reports indicated that all pressure, external system doors, and hatches remained secure.

As they were checking to find any active systems, a light appeared on the central communications console. This was followed by a moderate level of lighting in the Command Center. In the passageways Arisate could see from his position, emergency lighting had come back online.

"Greetings Commander Lovan, to you and your crew. I am the commanding officer on the bridge of the Mithrim. We are a Seeker class research vessel." The voice was female, with an odd accent and a neutral but friendly tone. "We would like to meet with you and your staff to discuss some recent issues."

The command center staff turned to their Commander. His hands were in constant motion signaling for the launch of the two gunships and to determine what of the command center was under their immediate control.

"Commander," the female voice again, "my weapons officer has suggested that you inform her brother and the pilot of the second gunship that their propulsion systems will remain offline for the immediate future."

The transparent forward section of the Command Center ordinarily displayed a view across the crater. That scene was usually unremarkable, providing a glimpse of the crater wall. The defense batteries, as well as the launchpad for the two gunships, were also visible if the ground lighting was active. Then low-level lighting came back up slowly showing the familiar scene with the addition of an impressive view of the Mithrim holding station ten meters above the surface.

"Your vessel resembles the rumored Dunarian ship that recently destroyed a Thurog heavy cruiser," Lovan stood as he spoke, "Identify yourself please."

"You may refer to me as Doll, I am the Commander of this vessel. Our crew includes four humans, three Dunarians, and one Teletin. You know that Teletin as Alura Veseranna," the Doll replied, "we would like to meet with you concerning the two vessels that appeared during that previous confrontation. Our ultimate intent is to draw them out, identify, and destroy them."

The silence was palatable. Lovan's fingers were rapidly signaling as he stared at the Mithrim. A holographic image appeared between him and the view outside, then a second and a third. The first was a strikingly attractive woman, even for a human. He was confident that the voice he had heard moments ago fit this human female who appeared relaxed and in charge of this seemingly untenable situation. To her right side was a male human, with a muscular, robust build and like the Doll exhibited a casual indifference to the severity of the situation. Finally, on the Commander's left stood Ally. He recognized her immediately from her previous assignment at this very station. She was not hiding her Teletin ancestry as her soft pastel violet skin tone and her deep royal purple to reddish-blond hair was a visible accent to the additional statement made by her holster, visibly absent of a weapon. The next sound came from the holographic group.

"You know," said Ally, in her native tongue, "Doc, the Dunarian on the Doll's right can understand your hand language as well as I can. He learned from Ruvator, my grandfather, your mentor."

"We are currently cloaked to any observer outside of this crater, and could keep up this ruse forever," this from Doc, in flawless Teletin, "We can provide an atmospheric bubble passage from our ramp to your outer pressure hatch. If you'll allow the three of us into your station complex, we could meet with you and your advisers in person. We request an hour of your time to present our findings. After that meeting, if you decide to help us, we will extend our visit. If not, then we will depart the area and proceed on our own."

As Doc completed his sentence, the three holograms vanished, and in the crater, a ramp lowered from the massive ship. The three figures that had appeared as holograms strode down the ramp and casually approached. While still visible from the observation area, they stopped and looked up, then looked forward to where the airlock would be.

Lovan sighed then signaled to his head of security. The two proceeded down to the surface level, where the primary airlock was located. As they approached that airlock, they were joined by Dezir and one of his pilots, Astir. Both were armed.

Lovan turned to his security chief and signaled, "Are the defense batteries operational?"

He saw the hand signal for no and continued, "Do you believe internal communications are secure?"

Again no. Lovan smiled and looked at Dezir as he signaled, "Are the weapons systems in your gunships active?"

Again no. "How about the Mess, does it have any refreshments to offer our guests?"

This time he got a non-committal shrug.

Lovan then addressed Dezir verbally, "Did you see the hologram of our visitors and/or note their physical appearance through the view plate where they are waiting for us by this hatch?"

Dezir replied verbally, "A one-third size version of the hologram appeared at all areas with view screens. When it vanished, those screens showed the ramp lowering and this group approach."

Lovan thought for a moment, smiled then continued again, "I assume all other systems are still offline or non-responsive." He didn't wait for a reply. He was sure he knew the answer as he continued, "Tell me, Dezir, about their stance, their physical positioning."

Dezir was caught off guard, but considered a moment before replying, "They are...in a Family stance, equal status, each able to reply as part of the family, or that would be the case if they were Teletin."

Lovan smiled, "Send your weapon with Astir. Keep the weapons belt. Then, like your sister, you will be signaling that we are also unarmed and not an aggressor."

Before Astir could leave, Lovan directed him," Please, find some suitable refreshments and have them brought to the conference room where we will be welcoming our guests," He added, "I suspect much of Geray's systems will be back online shortly."

Chapter 37

The airlock opened, Doc, the Doll, and Ally crossed into the Teletin complex. They were cautious about maintaining a 'Family' pattern that Ally had coached them on. As the group leader, the Doll stepped through first; then Ally and Doc followed. Once inside, they regrouped to stand side by side as they met with their host and followed him to a conference room directly under the command deck.

When the group was planning this excursion, they were working from Ally's knowledge of the complex. Doc had been concerned then, about what he felt was a foolish way to expose the command deck to unscrupulous guests. Ally explained that things were not as they appeared, playing to Doc's pet theory of life. The chamber itself was practically indestructible and would vent outward, never allowing any subversive blast or attempt to damage the deck above. The room also contained several blast deterrent shields and drops to protect the Teletin members of any meeting in this safe room. This discussion had been part of the planning session that involved the now evolved Mithrim crew. After the bonding process, the new cyrog adoptees had been allowed a day to rest and adjust. The following day had been spent planning this meeting with the staff of the Geray complex.

When Amber and Mike came out of stasis, they learned that the Doll, Ally, and Tommy had entered stasis. While the other three were undergoing the process, Mike and Amber took the time to rest then proceeded to review the Mithrim from their new perspective. When they had been joined later by the remaining members of the crew, they all eased into their new roles. Where they had already begun to function as a cohesive group, they now formed one large family. All of the personalities and quirks remained; they had not been transformed into some new species. Instead, they now just seemed to fit together in a new, yet to be defined, way.

Three of that Mithrim crew were now sitting opposite Lovan and his team, which included Ally's brother. Doc, the Doll, and Ally knew precisely what they hoped to accomplish here today and were relaxed. Lovan's team were still in the dark, so they played at being polite hosts. Once all were seated, refreshments were brought in. That included coffee, a beverage popular with all species that visited Earth.

While the others were selecting their cups and condiments, Dezir glared at his sister.

Finally, when he got no response, he began, "Alura, what is going on here, and why are you forming a family unit with two other species?"

Lovan did not look pleased, but before he could intercede, the Doll took the lead. "My given human name is Karen, but you may refer to me as Doll or the Doll, an appellation I have grown to appreciate. Our crew is, as I previously indicated, composed of human, Teletin, and Dunarian. The Mithrim, sitting at rest in your crater is a Dunarian Seeker class cruiser and is now back to full crew strength with those previously mentioned. We will leave Earth and this system once we have resolved a few minor issues that affect each of us, your species, others in the council, and Earth itself. We could most likely resolve these issues on our own, but it will be faster with your assistance."

Lovan considered this for a moment, giving Dezir a

hand signal that indicated he was to remain silent, then responded, "How is it that you believe we can be of assistance?"

Over the next hour, and more coffee, the Mithrim crew members each added their perspectives. Doc explained his heritage and how he fit into the puzzle that was being presented to the Teletin. He recounted the recent realization of his status and was still sorting information thrust into his conscious memory. He explained that his father had been the mission commander and that authority had been passed to him.

Doc explained that each member of the Mithrim crew had been tested and had assumed roles defined by the mission. The Doll had a combination of skills and personality that made her the logical choice for command of the Mithrim. While the overall objective was Doc's responsibility, the Doll was command and control for the vessel itself.

The mission of the Mithrim, simplified, was to assist in finding a suitable home for Dunarians and the Arcs that carried them. Mithrim's dalliance on Earth was the direct result of an unprovoked attack some seventy years earlier. During that attack, their fuel cells had been damaged. Subsequent interference, by those the Dunarians had believed to be part of the alliance, eventually cost them all but two crew members. Doc had been born on Earth. His father had been the mission commander and his mother, the command and control officer at that time. She had died when Doc was six months old. That had occurred during one of the many confrontations with the race from the unknown ships.

Ally then took point in the discussion, calmly continuing the exposé. Shortly before his mother's death,

Doc's father had, during his hunt for answers, met and befriended Ruvator Kalach. This was Ally's and Dazir's maternal grandfather. It was Ruvator who helped find a safe home for Doc with a human family. He and Doc's father spent several years trying to resolve the puzzle of the initial and subsequent attacks. Ruvator, a highly regarded diplomat in the council, at that time, suddenly disappeared without a trace. Ally was now aware that Ruvator had spent time on the Mithrim when he was associated with Anexten, Doc's father. She knew this because she was now in tune with the ship and felt it through her grandfather's memories.

Ally referred to cyrogs most simply, by explaining that they stored the memories of those paired with them and that direct blood relatives could, under certain circumstances, access that information. She made it clear that she did not see a formed picture like a video, she only experienced the impressions of the other. Simply put it was like having never seen a strawberry yet the first time you smell or bite into one you recognize it and how that distant relative felt about strawberries.

Despite a request from the Teletin side of the table to pursue this farther, Ally ignored them and continued. She explained what she had learned, including what had led to Anexten and Ruvator's death. They had died during an ambush by the Others, the species that the Mithrim crew now sought. Ally's next comment drove that home.

"As I was able to see some of Ruvator's memories in those final hours," Ally explained, "there was something related to that ambush that kept niggling at the back of my own memories. Finally, I realized that there were matches in my own memories to what Ruvator had seen. I recognized the underground passages that are, even today, used to access the lower levels of the Dulce compound."

Chapter 38

The six current inhabitants of the conference group sat opposite each other. Lovan was flanked on his right by a Teletin named Harec who was head of security for the complex, and Dezir on his left. Opposite the Teletin group, the Doll was flanked on her left by Doc and on her right by Ally. In the command center above, and throughout the station, live feeds were streaming from the conference room.

This is what that audience saw.

Lovan and Dezir slumped forward, face down on the table, while Harec stood for a moment then froze. He appeared to be vibrating or at least fighting against something. Doc suddenly appeared standing near Harec. The Doll had not moved; instead, she sat motionless, both hands palm up on the table and with her thumb in the center of each palm. Ally seemed to waver for a moment.

Those viewing the stream throughout the complex were in shock as all view screens were plunged into darkness.

Trained to react in an emergency, those in the command center turned to their consoles trying to coax some response from systems that had been remotely shut down for the second time today. One of the communications techs opened a panel, depressed a button, closed the console and headed out of the command center. When the watch officer questioned this move to leave, the tech produced a snapper and shot the watch officer. The tech was gone before anyone else could respond. The button he depressed launched a small pencil-thin projectile. It was the second of four such missiles to head away from the station where they could broadcast an emergency signal to a remote listening station.

In the conference room, Doc had delivered a punch to Harec's face that dropped the younger being, apparently out cold. Ally arrived next, checked Harec to confirm Doc's action was not permanent then turned to Lovan and her brother. Her nod to Doc, as he headed back to the Doll, resulted in the two Teletin's return to consciousness.

"Good shooting!" Doc smiled at the Doll.

She smiled back and relaxed, wiggling the fingers on both hands. She had not questioned Doc or Ally when both felt, based on their parental memories, that there might be one or more spies in the complex. As with the entire Mithrim crew, besides memory enhancements via their respective cyrogs, each had undergone minor species-specific improvements. In an emergency, the Doll's reaction time was now close to Ally's. In the palm of her right hand, she had a sensor that could act as a trigger for the equivalent of a stun gun on steroids, twin electrodes fired from the stylized earrings she wore. She also wore contacts with a reticule that placed the electrodes wherever she was focused on when she triggered them. Ally confirmed that the electric stun effect would not harm a Teletin if used on them. In her left palm, the Doll had a second sensor that currently established a link to the Mithrim, a single tap would blackout the station systems, like the Mithrim's initial action. A double tap would restore all system functions.

Ally, during discussions post cyrog, learned that the ability to blank out a Teletin, as Doc had done to her, was a species' anomaly. Both Anexten and Ruvator were concerned that other species might also be able to exploit this Teletin flaw. As a safeguard, they developed a way to block this odd anomaly. In the Mithrim's library, Amber found their joint research. Ally, therefore, wore small, simple earrings that worked as a shield against this genetic knockout punch.

What occurred in the few seconds that all external observers missed in the conference room was?

Harec had reacted to the news that the Dulce compound was involved or at least compromised, by reaching for his snapper in a concealed compartment. His move to action triggered Doc's early warning system, and Doc began to move towards Harec. Doc's movement set the Doll on alert. Ally felt the hint of the knockout wave as it incapacitated Lovan and Dezir. The Doll touched the sensor in her left palm. The Mithrim locked down the stations' systems, again. The Doll had also discharged her stunner at Harec, even as he began to bring the snapper up. Doc reached Harec as the electrodes lit him up, sending a perfectly placed punch to knock out the vibrating spy. Ally approached from the other side of the table as a backup.

Doc released Lovan and Dezir from their momentary daze then examined Harec as Ally filled the two Teletin in on what had just happened. The punch had not killed Harec but had dislodged a contact lens covering one of his multifaceted eyes. This was enough to answer Lovan's initial questions, and Lovan asked the Doll if she would restore communications.

The Doll complied, resetting communications, and those in the conference room found that both the Mithrim crew and the Teletin contingent had alarming news. Each group tried to make themselves heard first. Out of courtesy to their hosts, the Doll signaled to Lovan to get updated first.

The reports were grim. The watch officer in the control center was not the only casualty. Three other independent actions had resulted in a total of five victims, three dead and two in the med bay. More alarming was the fact the unknown agents had escaped. They, apparently, had a shuttle or escape craft hidden in the hanger and, after a quick firefight, escaped, damaging the hanger pressure doors. Dezir's weapons and electronics officers had been two of the casualties in this engagement. Both had been caught unprotected when the pressure doors were blown to allow the escaping shuttle. While this turn of events was being digested, the Mithrim's crew added their report.

The Mithrim's information proved enlightening. Four micro-stealth communications drones had been launched from different parts of the complex, presumably by the escaping Others. The Mithrim had not been able to spot or intercept the drones immediately, this resulted in one of the four being able to transmit a partial signal. While tracking the drones, the Mithrim's sensors also picked up the fleeing escape craft. It was hugging the moon's surface, presumably to avoid being targeted by the complex's defense batteries.

Dezir interrupted, "Can I have control of my gunship?"

"Done!" responded the Doll, she and Ally shared a quick nod.

Ally announced, "I will handle your weapons, can you do without someone in the electronics seat?"

Dezir looked like he was going to say something then just nodded assent as he and Ally raced out of the conference room.

"Good hunting," said the Doll as they left, then followed up with, "Mithrim, what is the status on the drone that did succeed in broadcasting a signal?"

The report was brief and to the point. A cruiser level, or possibly more capable vessel had jumped into the solar system from an unidentified location. That vessel was now headed toward the moon and the Geray complex. Mithrim's current crew had discussed the likelihood of a confrontation. Mithrim's original compliment had been reduced, eventually to two members, as the result of an initial attack by this unknown species. Ally had lost her grandfather, and now people she had known in the complex, to this homicidal species. The Doll was being hunted, presumably by the human element that had joined with this unknown antagonist. Then there was Doc. Doc had no love for this incoming combatant. During the years he had been growing up, and before Araime and Wyik had gone into stasis, every effort had gone into making sure the Mithrim would not have any issue in the future with the Other's vessels. The Mithrim was ready.

The Doll smiled, nodded to Doc then simply said, "Mithrim, you are Weapons Free."

Mithrim's departure shook to the complex.

Chapter 39
~ Weapons Free ~

To those in the complex Control Center, the Mithrim simply vanished with an explosive backlash.

Mithrim's crew had been prepping for launch as they gave their report. The Doll's declaration of clear intent was all they needed. In nanoseconds, an energy shield, like that used to protect Mithrim in combat, formed to enclose a rupture in space. From within that bubble, she shattered space and executed a jump.

Even though this cataclysmic abuse of space and time was contained within the shield, the Teletin complex experienced, what on Earth would have been a direct hit by a category three hurricane.

In the days' post cyrog enhancement, the Mithrim crew expanded from two to eight highly training and motivated crew members. These were not automatons slaved to a ship. These were the same individuals with the same personalities and now in possession of additional skills and enhancements. Mithrim could function with only two crew members; in an emergency, each member of the crew able to cover multiple positions. Her ideal crew was twelve, but the current crew of eight easily covered all functions and was an excellent fit. With three of her crew on the station, the shipboard breakdown included Araime as command and control, Amber as pilot and navigation, Wyik and Mike covered engineering and propulsion. Wyik also managed defense systems and shields while Tommy was on weapons systems.

Mithrim's initial departure jump brought them to one of her specific sentinels. From there, she jumped directly into the line of flight for the Other's ship, coming to a full stop three miles from the approaching vessel. They watched as it powered back. At about one mile, they could make out the particulars of the oncoming vessel. Tommy and Wyik reviewed all existing diagrams and could not find a match. The vessel itself was obviously intended as an interstellar. The stacked and plate structure assured that it would never do well in any form of atmosphere. By her conspicuous armament and size, they estimated that she was at least the equivalent of a heavy cruiser. When the enemy vessel closed to about a half mile, the show started.

Araime and Wyik had been present the first time the Mithrim had encountered the Other's, so they were prepared for the next move. Mithrim began broadcasting a challenge, not aggressive, a simple we are ... who are you and what are your intentions. Without any prelude or answer to the broadcasts, the cruiser launched four gunships. Two of them moved into a forward attack position, two angled to bring themselves in on Mithrim's flanks. Seven decades earlier, a similar tactic had resulted in damage to Mithrim's fuel system. Subsequent changes made that approach no longer effective, something the gunships were not aware of.

Mithrim released four drones to engage the gunships. The drones took out the two flanking gunships immediately. Tommy fired a short burst from one of Mithrim's particle beam weapons, bisecting the two-remaining craft before Mithrim jumped. Plasma blasts tore through space where she had just been.

This jump positioned Mithrim about 1000 yards above

and slightly behind the Other's plasma cannon batteries. From this position, Tommy released four hi-yield torpedoes that detonated in the gully that separated the lead plasma cannon from the weapon platform above and behind it. Based on the positioning of the two batteries, Tommy felt this was an optimal position for the feed plasma for both weapons systems. The result was a spectacular display of unconfined plasma. The dramatic results were wasted on the Mithrim crew. They had already jumped again and were now roughly 1500 yards to the rear of the Other's now faltering cruiser.

The cruiser, trying to find and target the Mithrim opened the rear hanger doors to launch more gunships. Space battles, if ship to ship, tended to be head-on engagements. Mithrim's crew had reviewed and decided to use their ability to make repeated micro-jumps to even the odds. Thus, as three more gunships launched through the aft hangar doors of the damaged cruiser, Mithrim sent a single anti-matter torpedo in return, then jumped to a safe distance.

From a mile away they watched as the Other's warship imploded forming a momentary tiny black hole. Not about to miss an opportunity, they directed two of their original drones to tag the fleeing gunships. As the drones approached, the gunships returned fire apparently destroying the drones. The drones, however, had exploded into hundreds of tiny tracking nodules that adhered to the three fleeing gunships as they traversed the debris field.

On the bridge of the Mithrim, there was no cheering, no high-fives. The five crew members remained at their stations while they reviewed the action. They destroyed a capital level combatant and had taken no damage. They did not consider the gunships as survivors since now they were playing the role of snitches. At no time during the engagement had they been able to raise the Others via any communications method. The limited knowledge they had of the spy captured at the Geray complex was that he was bipedal. They had more questions than they had answers.

Dezir and Ally raced across the surface of the moon at a height fewer than three feet. They were closing on the much slower escape craft the Others had used when leaving the complex. They had been able to pick up the escaping shuttle on the gunship's sensors. It was hugging the surface to avoid detection and to remain below the threshold of the complex's defensive and offensive batteries. Even as they watched the sensor array, it appeared that the fleeing craft had ducked into a crater.

They reached that crater in under ten minutes and approached with caution. They knew the escape craft had angled into this crater and was now off their sensors. Considering its previous actions, they had no idea what to expect. They were aware the escaping shuttle had not been armed, but the crater was an unknown. As they circumvented the crater perimeter, there was a flash of light and the blast of an explosion. In the moon's lesser gravity and the stillness, it was more of a matter of bright inconsistent lighting and debris. This was followed by a Scorus class tactical assault ship climbing out of the crater.

Dezir jinked the gunship to the right as a pulsed blast passed through the point they had just occupied. Ally instinctively targeted the fleeing craft, firing her laser cannons for a direct hit. The crippled vessel lost altitude and plummeted back toward the inferno brewing in the crater. Dezir leveled the gunship, and they climbed to get a better view. The inferno in the crater had already been extinguished by a lack of combustible material. The assault ship was a scattered debris field where it had exploded on impact. The remains of the original escape craft was a twisted, discarded shell, where it sat to the side of a small habitat. The shattered ruins of the habitat and the escape craft had been the earlier explosion

Chapter 40

Dezir and Ally finally had a chance to talk during their return to the Plato Crater. It began with a round of compliments on Dezir's piloting and Ally's targeting but soon devolved into family matters. Dezir, as the older brother, was concerned that Ally was considering leaving Earth aboard the Mithrim. Ally countered with her commitment to the Mithrim and the feeling of a family it evoked in her. After some prodding, she also admitted her relationship with Tommy was also a deciding factor.

Eventually, the discussion focused on their recent action or encounter.

Dezir, and Ally, clearly recognized the vessel they had destroyed as a Scorus class tactical assault craft. These were heavily armored craft used to carry soldiers into combat. They could transport up to twelve armored warriors, their equipment, and typically included a pilot, co-pilot, and two weapons officers. The additional wreckage in the crater included the unknown shelter and remains of the escape craft, nothing more.

The disturbing implication was that this smaller crater may have been a staging area for the spies in the Geray complex. How long had this been going on? How had these spies infiltrated the complex? Were there more? They had questions, but no answers.

The Plato crater was bustling with activity when Dezir's gunship and the Mithrim both settled quietly to one side. As he staged for a landing Dezir took his time to study the Mithrim. During the return flight, they had seen images of the one-sided exchange between the unknown cruiser and the delicate, graceful appearing Mithrim. All those present, in the station, stole glances at the unusual vessel coming to rest, complacently, near the complex. Dezir, in turn, settled his gunship a respectable distance from the Dunarian ship. A pressure enclosure extended from a temporary environmental dome, allowing them to leave the gunship and proceed to the temporary structure near the complex that had once been a mess hall.

The complex, when first conceived, had been a partially completed orbital station. Now it was well on its way to being deconstructed to the base module initially delivered. In fact, the basic module was now about 10 feet off the surface being held aloft by a series of repulsors. Some of the structures once mated to the complex now stood as separate outbuildings. In the makeshift command structure or mess hall, plans were already in motion.

The complex, with its usual crew complement of thirty-six, had lost three, and two more were in medical. Four additional members were missing and identified as the spies having fled in the escape craft. They now had one prisoner to deal with, locked in a stasis chamber. That left a working complement of twenty-seven able-bodied staff. Two of those, in turn, had been assigned a rotating shift to watch over the prisoner.

Lovan expressed his concern that there may be additional spies. The Teletin, as a species, were fond of hiding things in plain sight. Doc explained he could sense the brainwave pattern from the prisoner and was able to quickly clear the remainder of the base staff. He wasn't entirely sure what he was sensing, but the mental emanations given off by Harec were very different than those of any of the other species present in the complex.

The final plan was simple, move as much of the complex as immediately required and destroy the rest. That included one of the gunships that had been sabotaged by the spies and the two defensive batteries. The strategy was to have it appear the base had been destroyed by sabotage, while the remaining viable components would be moved to the larger, and still secure Stevinus crater. The sections that would go to their new home were secured by a tractor beam to the Mithrim. The Mithrim would return and dress the stage for anyone curious about the Plato crater.

The plan progressed as the complex was stabilized and anchored near one of the steep walls of their new home. A temporary environmental bubble was in place, allowing the staff to quickly anchor the outbuildings and other structures that would compose the new Teletin complex.

Doc, the Doll, and Ally had stayed with the complex and helped to settle it into the new location. The Mithrim remained on alert until the installation was stable then settled gently into its previous nest. Wyik drew the first watch, and the others headed to what was already being referred to as Geray 2

Everyone assembled in the mess hall waiting for answers, and there were many questions. Those included the Mithrim, the spies, the space battle, and finally the relocation to the Stevinus crater.

They began with the Mithrim.

After a brief clamor for attention, Lovan settled the Geray group, and they looked at the seven members of the Mithrim crew who relaxed behind a long table facing the assembly.

Lovan began, "All of us, at some point, heard of a brief battle between a Dunarian ship and rogue elements in 1947. For the most part, it became an urban Earth legend. There was additional speculation the mystery ship remained on Earth with its crew. Then you appeared in our crater. None of us had the time to verify or explain a vessel of this ... "

Lovan stopped, apparently at a loss for words, then continued, "The design is unusual, yet oddly familiar, the resources it appears to have are unexplained."

There was a viewport in one of the walls of the mess hall, and the Mithrim could be seen, unobstructed where it rested on three extended struts. Its physical design was counter to that of any interstellar cruiser, any known combatant, or research vessel. There were no external weapons systems, no easily identified engine pods, no prominent bridge. Instead, there was an almost surrealistic graceful, semi-triangular shape with no intersecting lines. A fluid form that almost appeared to have wings curved downward. It might have been considered delicate were in not for the fact that the span across the gently curved upper surface was more than four hundred feet.

The silence was shattered when Amber explosively announced, "She's a Martian War Machine!"

While everyone was staring at the petite human, Dezir made a very human face-palm gesture and added, "without the heat ray neck, but yes, and bigger, much bigger."

Chapter 41

The entire group, Teletin, human, and the Dunarians turned like they were watching some variety of sporting match. First to Amber, then to Dezir, next out through view panel at the Mithrim. Wyik, on duty in the Mithrim and known for his odd sense of humor, lifted the Mithrim an additional ten feet from the surface, dipped the nose then set her back down. With a touch of finality, the group then stared at Doc and Araime as the only Dunarians present.

Doc looked at Araime, who sighed, "Mithrim is not a Martian War Machine."

Apparently fascinated by human vintage Sci-Fi, Dezir, somewhat smugly replied, "The vintage human movie called the War of the Worlds was first shown in the year 1953, by the human calendar. The Mithrim was first seen in 1947, same calendar. There is no other interstellar warship or even commercial vessel with the profile of the Mithrim that I have ever seen or studied. Yet a human portrayed it in a visual medium at a time when this planet still thought of rocket ships as interstellar vessels."

Dezir seemed rather proud of his conclusion, and apparently several of the Teletin had heard rumors of the mystical Dunarian vessel. Some it seemed, had also seen the 1953 movie.

Doc shrugged; this was his first real good view of the Mithrim sitting quietly on display in the crater. Only Araime and Wyik were familiar with Mithrim's atypical design. The rest of her new crew had spent time getting to know her from the inside, in environments where taking a walk outside to check out their ride wasn't an option.

"Ahmmmm," Araime cleared her throat. There was a hint of mischief in her bright green eyes, "If I answer your Martian War Machine fixation, can we move forward with solving the bigger issue?"

The nods were unanimous. Araime began by giving those in the group a quick summary of the Dunarian migration. She described the Arcs, the Seeker ships, and that they could maintain long-range communication. These communications protocols, though not perfect, provided updated packets of data. This included where the Seeker ships have been, and anything of importance to the overall mission. The Seeker Dopplim left message packets that the Mithrim retrieved when she entered this solar system as she approached Earth. The Dopplim had passed through this solar system years earlier, in 1942.

During the years the Mithrim was interred in the Guadalupe Mountains and the crew, including Doc's parents, had dwindled down, the appearance of what resembled a Seeker class ship in a 1953 Sci-Fi movie was a puzzle. Doc's father had managed to put the pieces of the puzzle together.

The Martian War Machines were designed by an art director named Albert Nozaki. On Wednesday, February 25, 1942, at 3:06 AM the 1942 Battle of Los Angeles took place in the sky over Baldwin Hills eventually passing over Redondo Beach. To turn back the large invader or invaders in the air over Los Angeles, more than 1440 rounds of anti-aircraft munitions were expended. That same night Al Nozaki was helping guard a friend's field against vandals. When interviewed later, Nozaki described what he saw in the early morning hours:

"Approaching him well above the fields from the west, silhouetted against the slightly lighter night sky, was a fairly huge dark airborne object coming straight toward him at a fairly quick pace. ... It was huge, dark, very long, and wide with no lights or signs of windows. Although it did not have protruding wings like an airplane, the object's outside edges ominously curved down..."

"Nozaki later went on to be an Oscar-nominated art director. Drawing upon his experiences, that morning in 1942, he designed the terrifying Martian War Machines seen in the 1953 movie War of the Worlds. During a one-on-one interview, Nozaki indicated that he had incorporated some of the ominous aspects of the object he saw, such as the down curving contours, into his War Machines. He had wanted to capture some of the fear he felt as the real-life dark object passed over him."

"What he saw was the Dopplim. That Seeker class vessel had descended into the atmosphere in the hope of avoiding two smaller interstellar frigate class vessels that had begun to chase her. Dopplim's crew felt that the frigates would not be suitable for atmospheric entry. Descending would give them time to assess the situation, lose their pursuers, and maybe determine why they were being hunted. Their approach, as they slowed and reduced altitude, produced a dark atmospheric cloud-like anomaly. The frigates chose not to pursue and instead released smaller gunships to continue the pursuit. Based on other reports from the time these gunships were referred to as Foo Fighters by WWII fighter and bomber pilots. So, with Foo Fighters closing in and anti-aircraft fire from Los Angeles, Dopplim slipped out over the ocean, then back out of Earth's atmosphere, jumping as she cleared the lower atmosphere. It was a short jump, and she dropped off some of her sentinels before departing the solar system. The Mithrim, even now, is using and maintaining those sentinels."

Araime thought she was finished, but Dezir, other Teletin pilots, and random other members of Geray station, still had questions. Those questions ranged from why the completely atypical design and what exactly was she, a survey vessel or a warship. Araime looked to Doc, the Doll, and the rest of her new crewmates then gave in.

She sighed, "I will give a short overview. Then we need to get some answers from our prisoner and review the data from the trackers we put on the fleeing gunships."

She began with the design. All the Dunarian ships, including the Arks, were designed with graceful, pleasing lines. Araime took a moment to indicate that she and the previous crew could never grasp why the ships they encountered on their quest were so ... angular. The Dunarian designers knew that they would have to deal with interstellar space, atmosphere, and even aquatic environments. The Seeker class were designed to complete the mission assigned them by the Dunarian World Congress, regardless of the location. While interstellar space would not hinder a cube, entering an atmosphere required a less aggressive shape. The same was true if they were to come to an aquatic environment. Dunar had been mostly oceanic, and the Seeker class were more than capable of traversing a fluid environment.

The size was next. Mithrim was designed to support a crew of twelve in a family environment. The quarters were designed to accommodate twelve paired adults and any family that was the result of the travel. She made a point of pointing out the pairing of the current crew, with mixed reactions from that crew. In addition to the primary crew compliment, the Mithrim could comfortably carry or accommodate thirty additional crew, more if circumstances made that necessary. She had three decks, and all quarters were in the tight oval that circumscribed the central core. Engines and equipment were outside of the oval and extended into the down curve wing sections.

She continued with her explanation. The lower deck contained supplies and some of the laboratory facilities, other research sections were aft of the command center.

She waited patiently for someone to crack the silence.

It was Lovan who spoke in a measured tone, "You have indicated nothing of the Mithrim's offensive capabilities. While remote, we witnessed you decimate an unknown class of interstellar warship."

She smiled an almost angelic smile and replied, "We are not an aggressor, but we are not a soft target. Our shields can withstand anything we have encountered to date, and our ability to prevent further aggressive actions towards us are adequate to the task."

The Doll stepped forward, "While I understand that the Mithrim is a point of interest, maybe even of concern, we need to divert this discussion for now. Our current priority is the Earth. You must understand we are only remaining in this solar system until we can help you resolve your current issues."

Chapter 42

The hall was quiet for a moment as the Doll's statement appeared to convey different connotations to those grouped in the Geray complex. Several questions required answers. The group looked around, trying to determine what direction they needed to move in. Finally, Lovan stepped forward again.

"Let me first thank you for answering some of our questions concerning the Mithrim." Lovan began, then continued, "Those of us here have no idea what is going on or the issues at hand. You, the Mithrim and your crew, approached us in the early morning. We met with three representatives of your crew. That short meeting was in the conference room. For reasons, still unclear, suddenly all present were attacked by our own security officer. That escalated as several of our personnel launched beacons identifying our previous location. That was followed by an attack on the complex itself. I have lost several members of my team. I have an unknown species as a prisoner. And my entire secret complex has been moved to the other side of this moon's equator."

Finally, and apologetically, he looked around and said in a severe but cautious tone," I, for one, am not even sure that all of the unrealized radicals are gone."

Doc interjected, "When Ally returned, I asked her to accompany me to visit the prisoner. We were able to detect where his neural pattern differs from other Teletin. Together, we have casually wandered through those assembled here and are certain all remaining are Teletin, Gray, human, or

Dunarian."

Lovan looked around the assembled group, sighed, and appeared to be resigned or maybe relieved, "So, can we start with what happened in the conference room. Harec has been here for over four years and had worked his way to being head of Security. While we were not close, I considered him a friend and someone I could trust. At the very least, his actions earlier today took me by complete surprise."

Araime, Doc, and the Doll teamed up to fill in the gaps. They hoped to address the critical issues the Teletin needed to understand

Araime began. The Mithrim approached Earth in 1947. After reviewing the information left by the Dopplim, they were curious to see if the war existing in 1942 had ceased and what remained. On the initial approach, they were hailed, then fired upon without provocation. That attack and the tactics used resulted in a rupture to part of the fuel system. Mithrim dispatched the attackers, then jumped to this crater to assess the extent of the damage. Besides a loss of fuel, the unprovoked attack resulted in the loss of three of their crew. Mithrim was repaired and made several micro jumps to points on Earth. During one of these sorties, they were able to locate a raw, unrefined fuel rod source. They relocated to replenish their fuel reserves. The Mithrin remained at that location until emerging to retrieve Doc, the Doll, and those that would become Mithrim's new crew.

Since Dunarians appeared physiologically similar to humans, several surveys and exploratory missions were conducted while new fuel was processed and refined. During that time, they attempted to discover why they had initially been attacked without provocation. Those attempts to understand the issues cost three more Dunarian lives. To protect the Mithrim and her mission, one paired couple was chosen to go into stasis, controlled by Mithrim. In the event they were the only crew remaining, they would be revived and leave this solar system. There were other directives and plans, and at least twice during their stasis, they were awoken, and plans were adjusted. Because Araime had partially fragmented information due to the stasis gaps, Doc stepped in to help fill in some of what he had learned.

Doc's information was the result of his interaction with the cyrogs keyed to his biological markers. He was one of three children born between 1948 and 1950. The couples had integrated into human society and away from the Mithrim. During that time, efforts had been made to contact scientists or leaders in the hope of getting answers. It was during this time that Anexten and Thracen, Doc's father and mother, met and were befriended by Ruvator, Ally and Dezir's grandfather. Without going into details, Doc explained that the couples had been discovered, and only three individual Dunarians managed to escape a raid by forces stationed at the Dulce Base. Doc's mother, Thracen had died during that attack trying to defend the other two Dunarians born on Earth and their parents.

The three that escaped had been Anexten, Ruvator, and Marxten (Doc's birth name). Ruvator had some human friends he could trust and unknown to anyone in the Dulce Base, Mary and Tom Brensen raised the infant Marxten, renamed Martin, as their own. Both passed away peacefully, six months apart, in 1988 without ever revealing the truth to Doc.

This evidence that the Dulce Base was compromised was unknown outside of the remaining crew and Ruvator. Now, during the process of updating Doc's memories and giving Ally access to Ruvator's, they learned that the Dulce Base was compromised. Doc made a point of emphasizing that it was this revelation, during their meeting, that triggered Harec and the others with him to spring into action. Once the group calmed back down, Araime continued.

She explained that when Doc had been turned over to the Brensens, it was the last time she and Wyik had been temporarily brought out of stasis. Working with Anexten, they had prepared all of the links to the cyrogs, and other items eventually passed to Doc. New directives were put in force before the two returned to stasis for the last time. If only Araime and Wyik remained, Mithrim would revive them when Marxten appeared, with the cyrogs, as he had, and they were to assist him in any way possible to answer any questions he may have, then leave this solar system and resume their mission. If Doc had not returned in an unspecified time, the original directive would be followed.

Doc continued his explanation, drawing on the information from the cyrogs up to the final entry when Anexten and Ruvator had died in the tunnels trying to get some answers. Then Doc passed the discussion to the Doll to continue.

The Doll smiled at the group and took a moment to explain why she, a human, was helping define the issues.

She briefly explained the current status of the Mithrim's crew mixture. And, of course, why she held that position of command and control. On Dunar, an individual's place in their society was based on abilities. Those abilities were identified from birth through adulthood and were a range of inherent and acquired traits. The humans were prepped and bonded to their cyrogs. During the process, they were assessed as though they were Dunarian. Their abilities and capabilities were openly reviewed with each new crew member as the process developed. Where it was considered viable, they were also given the option of augmentation.

The Doll avoided any discussion of augmentation and explained who she was. Before becoming part of this team, she was a preeminent expert in the field of genetics. She was what might have been described in human terms as a Type A personality, with a strong tendency to quickly analyze any situation. Without missing a figurative beat, she could always evaluate information and formulate a concise plan of action.

In her view of reality, Dulce Base was the figurative patient zero for what was interstellar trafficking of humans and other species. The base was run by human and several other species. Obviously, not all of the inhabitants were part of the problem, and that was going to be one of the more challenging pieces of this puzzle. They were confident, however, that this mixed human and non-human group had a base on Mars for transport and combat support, as well as additional human support for planet-side ventures. Once these organizations had been dealt with, the Mithrim and her crew could and would leave.

Still holding the attention of those assembled in the complex, she finished by saying, "This has been a very long and eventful day. The prisoner is secure in a stasis pod on the Mithrim. This complex has, for all practical appearances, vanished. I would suggest we all get some sleep and start making plans tomorrow."

With that said, she smiled, the Mithrim crew smiled, and everyone went their own way.

As they headed to an airlock, that would allow access to the Mithrim, Doc commented, "So that went well. I know that I hung the title Doll on you for, well my own reasons, but If you would rather assume a more appropriate title like Commander let me know and ..." He didn't seem to have an end to his sentence.

The Doll smiled, shook her head and considered before replying, "I'm still the Doll you hung that rather non-politically correct label on, you're just getting soft in your old age."

The rest of the crew had been listening to the conversation and just laughed at both party's comments.

Chapter 43

Back home, in the Mithrim, the crew relaxed and reviewed over dinner. They worked through the days' events in reverse order. The review began with Ally and Dezir's chase across the dark side of the moon. They had not expected to come face to face with the armored assault vehicle as it climbed out of the crater at the end of the pursuit. That encounter resulted in their destroying the escaping vehicle without gaining any additional insight. What little they discovered in the ruins of the camp was that it might have been active as long as the Geray complex itself.

Dezir was new and had only been at Geray for six months. Ally, on the other hand, had cycled through the complex years earlier. Neither had any reasonable insight into who or what Harec was. Dezir had met him a few times and, of course, had been interviewed by the Security Chief when he checked in to begin his rotation through Geray. Ally vaguely remembered that Harec had been on the station when she had rotated through but didn't recognize him holding any position of authority at that time. Other than Harec's rise through the ranks, not unusual among the changing crew at the complex, neither of the siblings could pinpoint anything uncommon about the spy.

The next topic was the attack on the complex itself and the ramifications. For the immediate future Commander Lovan had replied to the Teletin Expeditionary Force headquarters that the complex was experiencing some temporary communications issues. This, in response to the headquarters concern when the compound had gone dark.

Lovan knew he would eventually have to give a full account of this ongoing incident. He personal experience was causing him to question recent events, and he needed some answers before showing his hand. He was aware that having a strike force of Teletin cruisers in the solar system might not be the best immediate response. Lovan had confided all his concerns to Doc and the Doll before they headed back to the Mithrim.

The Mithrim crew understood that there was more to the unrest in the complex. Currently, the crater was completely hidden from all sensors and still dark except for the faux message to Expeditionary Force HQ. It was also evident that they had been host to a small but unhealthy infestation of spies. This, Ally informed the Mithrim crew, was not generally a big deal since all the non-indigenous species spied on each other. The issue was the lethal response from the spies and the fact that they had been so well hidden.

While they were discussing the spies, Mithrim interrupted them with the simple statement that the prisoner had expired. None of them gave much thought to the descriptive term, as they proceeded to the stasis chamber area. On the short trip, they fired questions at Mithrim ranging from, can you revive him to how the stasis had failed to keep him, well, in stasis. Mithrim continued to reply stoically that the prisoner had expired.

Doc stopped as they entered the stasis chamber and addressed the disembodied voice of Mithrim, "Explain why you continue to use the precise term, expired?"

"The being contained a bio-electronic implant. I did not identify the device until it activated," replied the voice of Mithrim. "The device had a countdown timer. It was attempting to contact some unknown source, requesting input. I was not able to determine the point of reference it was attempting to contact. Had I identified that point, I would have allowed access and notified this crew. When the device did not receive a handshake reply, it expired, sending a surge through the prisoner's brain. The prisoner, in turn, expired. Elapse time of the incident, fifty-eight seconds."

As the crew considered this, Mithrim forwarded a message from Lovan. One of the complex's maintenance team had just dropped dead. She had told coworkers she needed to check a circuit on the air scrubbers. As she rose to leave, she grabbed her head then fell over dead. Doc asked Lovan to check and make sure this crew member was the only recent loss. After a few minutes, he responded that every one of the remaining staff was healthy and alive. Doc and the Doll gave Lovan a quick thumbnail overview. The secure isolation in the crater was blocking some timing signal. When it could not reach out to whatever guardian system, the spies were automatically terminated. This provided a reasonable confirmation that all the spies had now been identified. It didn't, however, help those in the crater with any answers.

They opened the stasis chamber and studied the prone body lying there. Harec had been unconscious when he was put into the stasis chamber, before that he had been in a holding cell in the complex. Harec had been given a cursory examination, but nothing more and he had remained steadfastly silent since his capture.

Amber had removed the damaged covering that had initially allowed those present to see the faceted one eye or eyes. She peeled away the tissue on the other side of his face to expose the other eye. Now, expired, there was no visible difference, there was no closing of the eyes. No empty stare, just the same amber faceted orbs. To the eight members of the crew, observing him now, it was one more mystery they would have to resolve.

Wyik and Mike reviewed and set up some routines for the Mithrim to use to determine the signal path that might have been blocked, thus allowing the other spies to be terminated. Then the crew of the Mithrim went to their separate quarters get some much-needed rest, it had been a busy day.

Chapter 44

In the cabin Doc and the Doll shared, the mood was somber, not depressed, just thoughtful. This was the first night that Doc could remember, since they had paired up, that the seriousness of their situation had not resulted in an amorous release of tension. When the Doll joined him in bed she had moved as close as possible, yet despite that closeness, they both just fell asleep.

The same scenario played out in the other four cabins. It appeared that letting this day draw to quiet end was the common desire.

The following morning, however, was far from tranquil. Mithrim woke the crew with a gentle but insistent warning alert.

Several things seemed to be happening at once. The normally peaceful and undisturbed far side of the moon was a flurry of mixed fleet activity and potential hostility. Unsure of what had happened, the Teletin war council had sent ships to investigate the apparent absence of the Geray complex. This did not bode well with the combined council headquarters in Dulce. Several of the species that were part of the council also had notified their home worlds and the resulting cacophony of communications traffic made it almost impossible to determine who was who. It appeared that while the Teletin had believed they had been discreet concerning the Geray complex, most, if not all, the combined species were aware of its existence.

Compounding the confusion was the fact that, despite a request from Commander Lovan, Mithrim still effectively masked the existence of their new installation in the Stevinus crater.

The Doll opened a communications link with Commander Lovan and asked him for a suggestion as to a course of action. Before he could reply, she offered the following observations: If they dropped the current cloaking, Mithrim would be evident, as a previously described "War Machine." That might, at the least, provoke an incident. She left the possible outcome of such an incident to Lovan's imagination. She also reminded him that there was a distinct possibility that some of the current searchers might, in fact, be part of the reason they were in this situation. .

While Lovan deliberated, she looked to Doc and the rest of the crew, "Suggestions?"

Araime, also part of the link with Lovan, offered her input. She had been following the situation and had a possible solution. "The cloaking device, that is masking our presence, is a hard device and does not require the Mithrim to continue masking the installation. We could jump out and do one of two things. We could make our presence known and tip our hand, or we could take one of the small emergency launches from the complex and release it with a select crew of ..."

She hesitated as she searched for a word, then smiled and continued, "a hand-picked party of misinformation experts."

She had explained her idea to the Mithrim crew earlier. There was very little hesitation as the options were passed on to Lovan and explained to those in the complex. In short order it became a contest to determine who in the complex were the best, most believable, liars. Within an hour both groups met in the complex to devise a plan. Time was of the essence as the ships scouring the surface of the moon were not letting up with their relentless search. Those in the complex wanted to diffuse the situation as quickly as possible so they could get back to looking for answers. Having some of their own back at Dulce would allow them more flexibility, since they were assured that the Mithrim would be able to maintain communications.

There were some concerns with the implementation of the plan itself. Could the Mithrim perform one of her magical short jumps and not be discovered as she released a theoretically escaping emergency launch. The answer to that was a simple yes, not only could the Mithrim make impossibly short precise jumps, she was able to emerge cloaked in much the same manner as the entire complex in the crater was now hidden. As most of the current Teletin crew of the complex were technophiles, this answer was followed by a series of pointed questions.

To those present, a jump represented a transition from normal space through a rift in space or what was considered a worm hole, to the opposite end of the worm hole. Disregarding the energy and mathematics required to perform this feat of instantaneous travel was the question of the short distance and required accuracy. These jumps were a method of overcoming the vast distances in space by moving from a point in one universe to a point several or several hundred light years distant. The Dunarian ship, on the other hand could tunnel through a rift in space and reappear as close as a thousand meters. This generated several new discussions, or possibly disagreements, but Araime dismissed them as not relevant to the task at hand.

The escapees and their shuttle were readied. Minor blast marks were added to the shuttle as evidence of a battle, then twelve of the remaining staff packed into the cramped vessel to play out this subterfuge. The small emergency shuttle normally would have accommodated eight personnel but cramming the extra four would help sell the escape scenario. Dezir was one of those chosen to escape, not only because he was a trained pilot, but he could also explain what he had seen in the crater where he and Ally had followed the escaping spies. They also brought along the body of the recently terminated female tech. This was to see who might claim the body or offer some insight. Sadly, a cursory examination had confirmed she was Teletin.

The escapee's stories varied, and they made every effort to add enough confused comments to sell the differences. The overall impression was that some unknown spies, led by Harec had tried to take over the base. A ship (they described the ship the Mithrim destroyed) had opened fire on the base and they had all fought to stay together. An unknown ship (they gave a sketchy description of the Mithrim) had appeared, destroyed the attacking vessel, then vanished. There was more and each of the escapees had been chosen for their ability to weave realistic non-conflicting stories. They were also trained observers and hoped to gather additional intel from this ruse.

A little over two hours elapsed from inception to the application of this plan. Mithrim jumped to an area a few hundred kilometers from the original Plato crater location, released the escapees, and popped back into the Stevinus crater. Now the waiting game began to see what their red herring could produce.

Chapter 45

The Mithrim settled back down in the crater, and the crew headed over to the Geray 2 complex to plan their next move. The complex was down to thirteen Teletin and one Alution or Gray. Sally had been, until recently, the only known non-Teletin staff member at the complex. At over 100 years of age, using Earth as a point of reference, she also had a unique perspective. When the Mithrim crew entered Geray 2, Sally approached their group. They had met her earlier during general introductions, but other than recognizing her species, there had been little interaction.

Recognizing her species was a wow moment for some of the crew. Doc, the Doll, Amber, and Mike were meeting the first Gray that was not part of some "B" movie cast. The fact that, except for Sally, the entire crew of the Geray complex were all Teletin made her stand out even more.

Grays are typically depicted as small, generally from two to four-foot-tall humanoid beings with medium to dark gray skin. They are also referred to as human size or taller, so their physical size could be whatever a script called for. They are portrayed as androgynous beings with minimal, if any, external differentiating characteristics. Sally was defiantly a Gray, or Alution as the humans were told, but was far from the stereotypical being seen in the Roswell depictions. She was a little over five-foot-tall and while slight of build, yet possessed a definite female form. Again, though entirely hairless, as far as could be seen, there was also something very feminine in her facial features. When Doc had asked, he had been told she was, in Earth years, about one hundred and fifty years old.

Sally was, for lack of a better job description, a xeno-biologist with a specialty in xeno-genetics. She had worked for several years at the Dulce base complex but had asked for a transfer and had convinced the Teletin contingent she would be useful at the Geray complex. She had been at Geray since the mid-seventies.

Now, making a beeline for Doc, Sally found herself suddenly facing the Doll, Tommy, Mike, and Amber as they moved into her path.

Sally paused for a moment, smiled and with a decided British aristocratic accent, commented, "Aren't you all just adorable. You know that even among his own kind, he stands out and certainly does not need your protection?"

She paused for a moment and looked at the four humans, then looked over at Ally, "Wow," she commented. "None of you are aware of his ..."

She paused for a minute, looked at Araime and Wyik, then seemed to consider something before looking back at the remaining Geray staff, thought again, then responded. "Not my place to comment."

To Doc, she smiled and said, "I met your father twice, once in the company of Ruvator, and once in a private meeting where your mother was also present. I believe I may have some information that will help us all to put a stop to the poaching."

Doc stepped forward, Tommy moved to one side, giving him room to approach Sally while the Doll moved close to Doc, at his left shoulder. Doc glanced back and noticed that Araime and Wyik appeared as though they wanted to be transparent. When Sally moved to stand in front of him, he motioned for her to pause. Doc studied the gathered individuals from both groups before continuing.

"Sally," Doc said in a matter of fact voice. "Is anything you are going to tell me, not relevant to all of those remaining here?

Sally looked at the assembled group, Teletin, Humans, Dunarians and seemed to ponder the question for a moment before answering, "Nope, this little group might be able to get something done. Gather around, I have a history lesson for all. Let me begin with this young man, his ship, and companions."

Now she looked to Araime and Wyik. The two, ordinarily calm, relaxed and in charge pair suddenly looked like two kids caught raiding the refrigerator when they thought their parents were asleep.

"So," she began, clearly addressing Araime and Wyik, "I take it that you helped Marxten aka Doc learn his history, probably using one or more cyrogs. I also guess that you left out a few important pieces of information."

The Dunarian pair, shrugged and nodded, but did not offer a reply.

"Doc, if I may also refer to you in that manner," Sally resumed her comments looking directly at him. "Let me fill in some gaps in your knowledge that I am sure your older sister and her companion omitted for some good reason."

The momentary silence was palatable.

Doc looked at Araime. She looked back at him with an odd, somewhat resigned smile, nodded, shrugged then looked at Sally to see what the Gray was going to say next.

Sally began by describing her first meeting with Ruvator and Anexten near the end of 1948. The Roswell UFO crash was no longer news. That incident, however, posed several unanswered questions in the Dulce complex. During that time frame, the Mithrim had settled into a deep cavern on the periphery of Carlsbad Caverns, where she had remained until a few days ago.

Araime politely contributed information to Sally's description of events, to fill in some gaps. Mithrim's crew, after the Roswell incident, numbered nine well ten if you considered Thracen was with child and beginning to show. Three of the original crew had been lost in the initial aerial conflict over Corona.

Dunarian crew makeup was always intended to have complementary pairings. As the Mithrim was approaching this solar system, Anexten and Thracen announced that they were expecting a new addition to the family. The following day, Araime and Wyik had both lost their partner as had another member of the crew. Eventually, the crew would be reduced to Araime and Wyik who had made a pair bond by the time Marxten was born. They had already explained the directives that had placed the two in stasis and later released them.

Sally continued, acknowledging the input from the two surviving crew and began to fill in the gaps. She knew the Araime and Wyik would have been updated to some degree by their cyrogs, but now she felt that the story needed her own flesh and blood observations to give it more life.

Chapter 46

Sally had been one of Ruvator's friends, a confidant, and she explained they had known each other before his posting to Earth. Both had been sent by their own species to ferret out rumors of cosmogenon (multi-species) trafficking occurring on Earth. In the past century, an increasing number of humans had begun to appear as part of the underground slave traffic, on nearby solar systems. In the past few decades, this trafficking had expanded beyond the nearest solar systems. It was always tricky to pin down the smuggling of beings from any underdeveloped planets, but the increasing supply of humans was disturbing.

The confused look on the faces of the humans prompted Sally to add, "The genetic makeup of the human species is such that many species can produce hybrid offspring with humans."

None of those present missed her glance at the Doll, before continuing with an explanation of her initial remarks.

Ruvator had begun actively perusing all leads related to the mystery ship that had vanished after reducing its attackers to a debris field near Roswell. He was sure that ship was still on the planet, and its design was fraught with rumors. In the interim, the Mithrim's crew had been making repairs, mourning their loses and studying the world they were temporarily stranded on. Anexten and Thracen's initial concern was that she was already with child and whether she should go into stasis until the issues at hand were resolved. That decision was a hard one, but after doing some preliminary neonatal tests, they decided it would be better for the child to be birthed on the planet. After his birth, there would be further decisions to make. One month before Doc's birth, Ruvator and Sally finally established contact with the Mithrim crew, or vise versa, as Sally indicated, she was never sure who had made the initial contact.

Sally paused for a moment then continued, she had begun this as a preamble to exposing the trafficking issue and had digressed to explaining Doc. She looked at Araime, got a return nod, and gave a simplistic explanation for her earlier remarks about Doc.

As with all species, Dunarians had some differentiating characteristics. Some were visible, some not. Speed, strength, and endurance were among the Dunarians' common traits. In a statistically minuscule part of the population, there is a bio-molecular anomaly.

She looked at the Doll and Amber and said, "I believe your sciences refer to this as an anomaly in the DNA?"

When Amber nodded, Sally continued to explain that the crew makeup of each of the searcher ships contained one, and where possible, a bonded pair that possessed this anomaly. Doc and Araime's parents both had this DNA variant.

Araime nodded silently, then took over this part of the explanation. She explained that in the females, this was most often expressed as telepathic capabilities. That sent a ripple through the group, and she acknowledged that she possessed that trait. She pointed out that she had not violated the privacy of any of those present, nor would she. In the male Dunarian, the feature most often was expressed as the ability to heal from injuries that would otherwise be fatal. In rare cases, however, a male or female Dunarian possessed both traits as well as a few undocumented but speculated traits.

"My brother," Araime commented with a wry smile, "is one of those exceptions. Although he has not used it fully, his telepathic abilities are more ... adept than mine. He could regrow a limb without any effort if need be. He can sense minute changes in the world around him that will serve to warn of impending danger, and generally will hide all other characteristics. The last is believed to be a genetic form of humility. When his status was confirmed, shortly after his birth, Wyik and I were asked to go into stasis to be available for his return and to help guide him."

The group was silent as they absorbed this. Araime studied Doc for a moment then went to him, after a moment they hugged and for a time stood forehead to forehead. When she went back to stand by Wyik, Araime seemed relaxed, and more at ease, something that no one had noticed was not her norm until now. Everyone else was now cautiously looking at Doc, not the least of those being the Doll.

"Moving on." Doc commented, then looked at Sally, "We need to know what you suspect and have discovered over the years concerning the, for lack of a better choice or words, human trafficking."

Sally considered for a moment then explained her findings and observations.

Most human/alien interaction took place at the Dulce Base in New Mexico. This had been the case before the Roswell incident and was, in part, the reason the fated ships were in that vicinity. Other installations do exist, however, the focal point, according to Sally and Ruvator's observations, was central to and around the Santa Fe National Forest, but more specifically at Dulce. There were and are several smaller habitation locations scattered in the areas and networks between Dulce and Area 51. But Dulce Base was what they had identified as the locus for questionable activity.

The base schematics indicated seven underground levels, but Ruvator and Anexten had been exploring a level nine when Sally lost contact with them permanently. This had been during the mid-seventies, in Earth's frame of reference. By then only four of the original Mithrim crew were alive, and two of those were in stasis. When Ruvator, Anexten, and three others disappeared in that final action, Sally felt it was best to continue her investigation from afar. To avoid further losses she and another Gray had booked passage home. Her companion continued back the Zeti Reticula Star system and Sally diverted to the Geray complex to continue her investigations.

"Now, it seems," she said to Doc, with a decidedly feral smile, "that with the Mithrim's help we may be able to avenge your family and prevent further trafficking in this corner of the universe."

Over the next hour, Sally explained all that she had learned of the hidden activities in the Dulce Base. She identified the varied species that were part of the clandestine operation including the suspected involvement of an insectoid species known to as the Eldrane, their possible base on one of the planets in this system and finally, the level of human support. The latter included how one Ronan Amos Murdock fit into the puzzle.

Chapter 47

During the brief mind-meld, seen by the group as Doc and Araime putting their foreheads together, Doc felt, for lack of a better term, the missing pieces of his existence the past sixty-some years. Once the initial group meeting was over, and Sally had finished her briefing, those present split into groups to tackle the issues. Doc began by approaching, Araime, his sister. Again, he became aware that the Doll remained at his side, and that seemed both natural and expected. Whatever transpired in the next few days, the Doll was an essential part of his family going forward.

"So little brother now is your time to put things right," she smiled tentatively, "no pressure there. Our parents would have been proud of the being you have become on your own. Now I have released all safeguards and blocks, we all look forward to seeing what you can accomplish."

Doc stood for a moment and hugged his sister again. No forehead melding, just a warm hug. Then Doc, the Doll, and the two Dunarians joined one of the groups that included Sally, the rest of the Mithrim crew and a few of the Geray station research group.

They started by considering the information they had obtained regarding the Others' planetary base. Surveillance video was now coming in from the bugs that had hitched a ride on the three escaping gunships. Those single-seat fighters had been part of a larger squadron that had initially been deployed from the unknown cruiser as it faced off with the Mithrim. With their host destroyed, these runners had turned tail. They eventually approached the red planet, diverting at the last minute to its moon Phobos. They had skimmed the barren surface of that moon then began a shallow descent into the 6-mile (9.7 kilometers) Stickney crater. The feeds from the little tracking bugs revealed several habitats and hangers for multiple ships as part of what appeared to be an established base.

Doc had been given a chance to examine one of these little autonomous tracking devices when exploring the Mithrim. He was so impressed that he asked Wyik to prepare one for each of the crew. These small devices were about the size of an old flip phone and on cursory examination looked like a discarded shard of metal or plastic. Instead, they were little AI autonomous surveillance bots. They were capable of using the network of sentinel nodes the Mithrim had distributed in the solar system and when given a task would use all of their considerable skills to hide and report back to the Mithrim. When not in spy mode, they also could be bonded to a person and act as an amusing mobile personal digital assistant.

The conversation then shifted to examine the issue of human trafficking. Statistically, more than eight million humans go missing each year, a large percentage of those are children. While a portion of those reported as missing later turn up or are found to have died from a variety of causes, the sheer number was daunting. 800,000 of those are trafficked annually across national borders alone. The numbers were obviously skewed as a significant percentage of those being abducted we from third world countries. However, according to Sally's research, there had been a recent shift to young adult abductions from the US and other developed nations.

Sally and Ruvator's research had pointed to the

following actions, at least in what they had observed at Dulce: The abductees were captured by mostly human capture crews and delivered to level nine in the Dulce Base. The abductees were processed. Some, it appeared were culled, others released. It had been, during an attempt to gain access to that 9th level of the Dulce Base, that Ruvator, Anexten and their three companions had been lost. Sally had tried to get answers but had been stonewalled and had left shortly after that.

The human teams responsible for the collection of abductee candidates were managed through an organization run by Ronan Amos Murdock. At this point, Tommy began to contribute to the conversation. Tommy had been to the Dulce Base on several occasions to investigate the unusual activity, a comment that was followed by several eye rolls from human and non-human members of the group. It was on one of these visits that he met Ally the first time. He admitted, for no apparent reason, that he was unaware she was not human during that first meeting. They had collaborated on several investigations since then. They had even worked on one case that had included Mike. Mike shrugged when the Doll glared at him, and he accepted the punch to his arm from Amber without comment.

Tommy continued with what he, Ally and Mike had learned together and separately about Ronan Murdock. He apparently had several mansions, one of them near Garrapata State Beach off the Pacific Coast Highway. Every year he would have a massive get together for his Birthday. This year that celebration was to be at the estate in Carmel by the Sea. Generally, these bashes included a wide range of political and celebrity guests.

"Maybe," said Ally with a wicked smile, "We should

attend this party and expose him."

Tommy just shook his head at that and continued explaining what he knew of Ronan's organization. That included information on Ambrose Cobb who served as one of his high-ranking lieutenants. Tommy admitted that it was Ambrose who had appeared with the helicopters when they were looking for the Mithrim. Considering their departure and the circumstances before it, he wasn't sure that Ambrose was even alive. Considering his failure in grabbing Doc and the Doll, if he was alive, he may not in be Ronan's good graces.

During the various explanations, the observations and the give and take, Doc leaned back in a chair and listened. For a while, he concentrated on the chair. It was like a recliner merged with acceleration couch. He liked this chair and relaxed back into it as he continued watching the discussions. The Doll came over, sat at the edge of the chair, studying Doc for a moment before speaking.

"Something is bothering you," she finally commented, more than asked, "You seem detached and introspective. At first, I thought it might have been the realization that you have a sibling. Then I considered it might be that you were spinning plans in your head to deal with the base on Mars. Now I think there is something else."

He patted a section of the chair; it was big enough to accommodate both of them comfortably. The Doll considered for a moment then settled cross-legged at the bottom of the chair so that she could study Doc as they talked.

"Very little of what we are discovering is new information. From what I am hearing, this has been going on before you were born."

That earned Doc an eye roll as he continued, "At first, I thought that the Mithrim was the catalyst, but she has been here, on Earth, the entire time. This group is galvanized and making plans, why now. "

The Doll smiled, "What did you learn when you and Araime did your head bump?"

She studied him as he seemed to be looking for an answer. Finally, she kissed him gently on the forehead as she got back up.

"You are what is different, you are the catalyst, the spark needed to decide how to move forward. Since you rescued me, everybody's plans have been askew. You/we are not visible to the opposition making it difficult for them to focus on a solution, so they are in blind reaction mode. So, let's make some plans, rock this planet and right some wrongs."

Chapter 48

They had two specific issues to resolve and a lesser but equally important issue. Addressing these issues would put a stop to human trafficking, theoretically. In physical order, these could be represented as the Mars base, Dulce Base, and finally, Ronan's criminal empire.

They needed more information about the Mars Base, technically it was the base on Phobos, but it was easier to refer to it as Mars. For planning purposes, it was necessary to understand the number of ships and personnel at that location and if there were other bases in this solar system. The cruiser that they destroyed above Earth's moon was a formidable craft. The Mithrim had been able to dispatch it quickly due to her unconventional tactics and inherent capabilities. Given what they knew, she could stand her own in a showdown with two, and possibly three such craft but they needed to know what to really expect. The ship types, though familiar, were still unknown and none of the current Geray staff could shed any light on the topic.

They had the bodies of the two spies. Well only one, since they were sure the female technician was Teletin. They had sent her body as part of the red herring back to Dulce. Harec's body, however, had not been thoroughly autopsied. Preliminary tests revealed an odd mixture of humanoid and insectoid traits. Sally had alluded that he might be Eldrane, but that still needed to be confirmed. Everyone looked to Amber, who shrugged and indicated she would see what she could find.

During the initial meet and greet at Geray, the Doll had been the figurehead for the group. Doc had remained restrained or at least had stayed in the background in a lesser authoritative position. This was to reduce attention being focused on him. That was no longer the case. While there was some initial speculation concerning the Mithrim's crew, Doc's familial status was blatantly evident after Sally's dissertation. Doc, however, remained reserved and aloof in his observations and contributions. During one of the round table discussions of options for the Mars base, the Doll fixed Araime with a questioning gaze. The young Dunarian looked back instantly, studying the Doll. Finally, the Doll looked toward Doc as she tapped her forehead.

The Doll was not initially prepared for the gentle voice ... thoughts ... that seemed to emanate from Doc's sister, "*I truly cannot penetrate the shield he has suddenly constructed. Our mother had impressive psychic abilities; she was teaching me until I went into stasis. I could sense the power in her, she had pushed me to strive to develop to that level. I mess with Wyik for practice; however, I can't get to my brother's ... center. He is coming into his own, and I only have legends as a reference to what he might be able to do.*"

During this time Sally had begun offering some unusual solutions, much to the surprised reactions from the rest of the Teletin group.

One last thought blossomed in the Doll's mind, she recognized the gentle flowery breeze that she now knew to be Araime, "*He feels ... very ... strongly about you and I sense that feeling is mutual. Trust his decisions, no matter how they may appear on the surface.*"

The Doll turned and spotted Araime, with her back to her, as she followed the discussion with Sally. Sally, once again, was adding a twist to the available options. She was, apparently, more than she had initially been presented when she was accepted as staff at Geray.

Sally was now casually explaining that she could provide a six-vessel strike force with four of those ships being cruiser level ships of the line and the two others would be troop carriers. Oh, and as a side note, the xeno-biologist most had believed Sally to be was really a senior Vlichoir agent. That last casual admission caused an unusual series of reactions from the assembled Teletin.

Ally moved to Doc's left side and was mirrored by the Doll as she slipped to his right. Doc seemed momentarily distracted, then nodded. His two bookends saw a brief return nod from Araime as she had Wyik move toward the Gray in an almost protective or at least supportive move.

Ally began, "For those of you not familiar with the Vlichoir, they are a confederation of peacekeepers, for lack of a better term. Beings with Vlichoir credentials are from many species and bound together under a compulsion to protect and defend." She chuckled," I sound like I am describing a human TV cop show."

Ally went on to describe the Vlichoir consortium. When a Vlichoir agent or group of agents are looking into an issue, they remain undercover. Since they are from a variety of species and skill sets, they generally maintain their cover until they are forced to act on the information they have uncovered. Not all species are fond of being overseen by an agency they may or may not subscribe to. The agents and their actions are not always appreciated. The two Dunarian seemed to have sensed this as they casually bracketed Sally for support.

Sally had probably noticed the edge of tension that appeared when she casually admitted her status. However, it was the only way to validate the resources she could bring to the table. She also noticed the Dunarians' support, but her focus was now directed to Doc.

"Doc, Sosan, I have been direct by the consortium to follow your lead," she said as she studied his features. "I, we, will support and provide whatever resources you need to resolve this trafficking of humans. The resources I can provide will deal with the base on Phobos, you will be free to deal with the Dulce base and other planetside pieces in this puzzle."

The Doll felt the Araime's gentle flowery touch, "*Sosan is the honorific for the legendary members of our species. A Sosan is a result of melding the Dunarian traits discussed earlier. I do not have the words in your language to adequately describe all the traits Doc may have. Doc made a conscious decision as a human to follow a path that allowed him to save lives and aid those around him. That is consistent with a Sosan's nature. I am, however, not sure how the Vlichoir knew his status.*"

Doc was now the focus of all present as he studied Sally then finally commented, "It is getting late, and has been a long day. Sally, can you give me specifics on what the Vlichoir can provide. Lovan, have you heard anything from our little band of escapee's? They should have been debriefed by now. I would like to know what the atmosphere is in the Dulce base. Let's meet tomorrow morning, again, and review our options. Sally, you will stay with us on the Mithrim tonight." Doc added in a tone that indicated this was not up for discussion.

Chapter 49

Back in the Mithrim the crew, now including Sally, headed for the common room. As they headed down the passageway Araime momentarily stutter-stepped, as she felt the bemused presence of Doc, "*I heard your comments to the Doll.*"

Doc assumed that they would get down to business but found that was not the immediate point of order. The Doll, standing by her chair look directly at Doc and with an amused smile said, "What are you?"

The prophetic nature of those three words was not lost an any of those present except for Sally. Wyik told Sally they would fill her in later.

"I appear to be a work in progress," Doc replied, then surrendered by clarifying the 'what' part of the question.

Doc asked Sally what had prompted her to expose him, then his status, and how was she aware of that status. Her answer was simple. She had been to the Mithrim on three occasions, the last one was to meet the newborn Sosan.

Sally had been introduced to Araime and Wyik. She was told their primary responsibility was to shield the infant until he was able to deal with his stature. Had things gone well, Doc and his family would have left Earth. The investigation they started would have been finished by the Vlichoir.

Sally lost track of Doc and the Mithrim when Ruvator and Anexten did not return from their last excursion. She was never privy to the location of the infant Marxten, and the Mithrim had gone into lock-down. Sally had no resources to move forward on the investigation and was being watched. She finally left Earth and joined the Geray complex. When the Mithrim came calling, Sally had not recognized Doc as the infant Sosan she once held. However, when she saw Araime and Wyik again, putting the Mithrim in context, she put the pieces together.

Satisfied with her explanation, Doc moved the conversation along. Araime was a potent telepath. When reunited with her brother, she used that talent to maintain the block to Doc's growth, as their mother had trained her to do. Sally's remarks, earlier in the day, left Araime with no reason to keep that block. The head bump from his sister released the last bonds. These quick answers were, of course, not enough for this group. The Q & A continued in earnest.

Ally immediately resurrected her favorite issue. How was it that Doc had so effortlessly knocked her out on their first meeting? Now, as she framed her question, she glanced at Araime. With a little prodding, Doc admitted that he felt confident he could short circuit most sentient species. This implied that Doc was always in their minds.

Araime laughed out loud at that conclusion. She explained that this gift came with an innate understanding of how to tune out the never-ending din of thoughts. The constant flow from the minds around a telepath would overwhelm them if they couldn't banish the noise to the background. Could he read or even send them thoughts? Yes. Would he do so unbidden?

"No" was the verbal reply from Doc.

During this interchange, the Doll looked pointedly at Araime who continued, "I communicate with Wyik, telepathically, and have recently formed a bond with the Doll, but I would never go into a mind unbidden."

She looked at those around her as she addressed that bond, "The Doll has a strong innate mental presence, so much so that when she looks to me for an answer, I feel obliged to reply."

The group had now focused on the Doll. She smiled, nodded to Araime, then looked directly at Doc for a fraction of a moment before looking back at the rest of the group. His reaction was brief but noticeable, and none of the group outwardly wanted to know what had made their bastion of character blush.

Unabashedly the group then ran through an imagined list of what they believed might be included in the skill set of the Sosan they knew as Doc. Araime, and Wyik contributed when Doc seemed unsure of an answer.

They methodically reviewed the five Metaphysical options. The list included Psychokinetic ability, which included telepathy but also included any external manifestation of power derived entirely from mental manipulation. Next, they explored Psycoportive skills, the ability to manipulate space or time. Onto Clairsentience, the ability to hear or sense anything outside of what was considered an acceptable range. Next in line was Psychometabolic performance; this included strength, stamina, and healing enhancements. Finally, Metacreativity, the ability to create physical objects, including creatures, or some form of matter from lesser sources.

The questions, while focused on Doc, were not necessarily posed to him; he was still growing into the set of gifts. Doc finally explained that as he became aware of a capability, he would update this crew. That did not prevent those present from presenting theories. For example, Sally postulated that Doc could effectively disregard anything that did not kill him outright as a minor annoyance and he would heal rapidly.

Metacreativity seemed the hardest to pin down. Araime explained that in the legends, a Sosan could fashion an impenetrable barrier by drawing raw ectoplasm from some Astral Plane. When asked about the Astral Plane, she shrugged and indicated that she had no clue. When all eyes turned to Doc, he also shrugged.

Through this entire voyage of discovery, they had all taken time to graze on whatever was a favorite snack, under the guise of a real meal. When the interrogation and comments finally wound down, they dispersed to their quarters. Sally had also been assigned a cabin for her visit.

Chapter 50

Doc studied the Doll as they got ready for bed. He was doing his very best to not pry into her thoughts. This would have been consistent with earlier comments concerning privacy. The issue at hand was the Doll. She had, since midway through the previous discussion, been randomly thinking, make that broadcasting a wide range of intriguing concepts.

"You're doing this on purpose," Doc finally said as he slipped into the bed, "to drive me crazy, or just to bug me? Or maybe it's to see if I will take the bait?"

"Nope," she replied as she nestled in beside him, "just making sure that you know I am here. We have a busy few days coming up, and I don't want you to feel alone."

With that, she closed her eyes and drifted off into a relaxed sleep. Doc felt the sense of security she exuded and soon drifted off also.

Doc woke and, to his surprise, was alone. He sensed that he was the last one to be getting up for the day, and that bothered him for two reasons. It seemed that he was hyper-aware of his surroundings and, now, had to consciously ignore his perception of his immediate environment. That environment encompassed the Mithrim. The second thing was that she, the Mithrim, was ready to depart, and he needed to be present. Doc dressed and headed for the bridge, momentarily wondering who else had joined the crew. There was a new distinct presence he could not identify, only that 'she' was with the rest of the crew.

Everyone was at their post on the bridge when he arrived. So, Doc settled into his station where he found a cup of coffee and some form of bread or biscuit waiting for him. Before he could say anything, he felt an overwhelming sense of safety or security. In the past, he might have been startled or reacted in a defensive posture. Instead, he realized he signified that haven in the mind of the diminutive, ebony, cat-like creature as it settled in his lap.

"Doc, glad to see you are finally up," the Doll commented with a smile, "You slept a full ten hours. Araime said you might need the time as your body adjusted. Myth materialized about two hours ago. The Man and the Myth has a certain ring to it."

"Your new companion," Araime clarified, stifling her laughter, "is the final confirmation of your status as Sosan. She, Myth, is the physical manifestation of this vessel."

He needed to understand what this creature they were referring to as Myth was, but he was equally sure it was nothing he could change, so the explanation could wait. With coffee in one hand and the other resting absentmindedly on Myth, the crew filled him in on what had transpired as he slept.

Lovan had begun to get reports from the faux escapees as they settled in, back on Earth. When they had been rescued by one of the searching vessels, these faux escapees had initially been transported back to Dulce Base to be debriefed. Their appearance prompted questions. Why had there been a secure Teletin enclave on the moon and why had it been attacked. Lovan and his team were monitoring feedback from the escapees, with Mithrim's help.

While safely hidden in Dulce, those escapees were being investigated with some speculation about their status. Initially, they had been interviewed/interrogated regarding the station itself, and only to a lesser degree, the attack. Three escapees had been prepped with information concerning the spies discovered. The others were feigning ignorance of those spies. Among the three, with feedback related to the spies was Dezir.

On a different topic, Sally had, also with the assistance of the Mithrim, arranged for Lovan to coordinate directly with the six-ship Vlichoir strike force now inbound. Tommy and Ally also made use of Mithrim's secure communications to contact their respective commands. Their queries were intended to identify any unusual activity since the attack on the Teletin base. They, in turn, explained to their contacts, that they were currently monitoring an unknown group that might be involved with the recent increase of abductions. Tommy and Ally were known to be involved in this deep cover investigation, so their undisclosed current location and status was no cause for alarm.

After bringing Doc up to date, the focus returned to him. The group continued to try to understand his status and capabilities. Araime, Wyik, and to a lesser degree, Sally, had some knowledge of what he might be experiencing. The rest of the crew were concerned. Doc didn't seem his usual self since the final release of his mental blocks the previous afternoon. Then there was the Myth of Myth as Ally put it. This morning, as they each grabbed some breakfast, then headed for the bridge, they discovered the space occupied by a small odd cat-like creature.

This creature had investigated each of the crew then returned to Doc's station on the bridge. Araime and Wyik, though initially surprised, referred to the furry apparition as Myth. They explain that she was a physical, vs. a holographic representation of the ship's personality. Part of the lore of the Sosan included this physical manifestation of any ship they were a member of. The had never seen one before, so they were surprised, then delighted, when the little critter actually appeared.

Myth, her name was more of a label as it alluded to the Mithrim itself, did not seem to communicate directly to any of the crew. Congenial and not aloof when approached, she was just there. When asked why they referred to Myth as female, the immediate reply was all ships are female. A comment that everyone shrugged and accepted without further question.

The crew immediately guessed that Doc was up and about when Myth became more animated and paced around his seat on the bridge. Doc sat with Myth on his lap as he was briefed on the crews' observations.

Now it was his turn to fill in the gaps. He looked around and began with a few questions. His first question; was there any reason for them to remain in the crater on the moon or could they jump back to Earth, to be closer to Dulce. That discussion was short. Nothing held them here. They could deploy devices in the crater to keep Geray hidden and still maintain contact with the escapees, the Vlichoir and the Mithrim. Lovan had already begun to coordinate with the Vlichoir who would be arriving within the day. Geray would remain cloaked, and the inbound six-vessel strike force would also be cloaked. Sally asked if she could stay with the Mithrim for the immediate future.

With those points resolved, the crew directed their concerns to the Doc and Myth. Absently stroking the diminutive creature, Doc explained that he was now finally awake, as he put it. He could feel and understand the power and how it would manifest in him. However, until he tried to use one of these new talents, he only had the theory to go on. Finally, he gently reached out to each of those present so that they understood he could communicate with them in a manner other than vocally while making it clear that he would only do so in emergencies.

Doc glanced to Myth, and all lighting on the bridge dimmed noticeably as a demonstration of his connection with the small furry manifestation. He continued, by confirming the Doll would maintain administrative control of the crew, and all other division of responsibilities would remain as it had recently been defined. Finally, he explained that while he had an overlay of memories, now unlocked, from his parents, as well as knowledge of what it meant to be Sosan, in general, that he was still learning and please be patient with him.

"I'm still in here," Doc tapped his forehead. "I just have a lot to sort out."

The crew's remaining questions were brief. It was time for action. As the discussion wound down, Mithrim rose from the crater to begin the jumps back to Earth.

Chapter 51

They returned to Earth in three short jumps. The first jump brought them to a position relative to the Lunar Orbital Plane. From there they moved to a location on the ecliptic plane, holding station above North America. The last jump was not a jump as much as a transition back to their point of origin a few days earlier. This destination was a point of concern. They needed a place that allowed them access to Dulce but not under the sphere of influence of that covert alien enclave. Sally's input helped move this decision forward.

According to Sally, when she had visited the Mithrim, it was in an underground cavern at the edge of the Guadalupe Mountains. This was near where it had surfaced to retrieve Doc and his companions. Mithrim had rested there for several decades. The Dulce base was at the northern border of New Mexico and Mithrim's cavern near the bottom of the state over 400 miles distant. The gap should provide them cover from prying eyes if a bit remote. To ease some of the concerns over the distance they would have to travel to explore the base, Sally explained that the locations were linked by several passages and cavern tributaries. During the first few years, the original crew of the Mithrim, adapting to their surroundings, had constructed a hi-speed transport system the allowed Anexten and select crew to monitor activity at Dulce. It connected to the caverns that provided shelter for the Dulce base sub levels. It was this transport system that had delivered Sally on her first visit.

When Doc and his group had escaped into the Mithrim, several days earlier, they were under attack from some of

Ronan's minions. Mike at least was curious to see if their aged Ford Excursion had been destroyed or was just sitting deserted. Now, as Mithrim settled into the canyon, they realized just how cramped the area was, and were surprised at the space itself. Out of curiosity, Mike had asked for the Mithrim's specs. Mithrim's airframe was 71 feet tall, her length 334 feet, and her horizontal span (wingspan) was 425 feet. Knowing this, they had been expecting a massive hole in the side of the canyon wall. Instead, all they found was evidence of two burned-out helicopters, and sadly, no Excursion.

The canyon wall looked the same as when they had first seen it. There was no seventy by four hundred plus foot opening in the side of the canyon. Now, of course, they were looking out at the scene from the command deck. This was very different from finding themselves in the shadow a ship blocking out the sun and shielding them from a fifty caliber machine gun.

As they studied at the area, they were acutely aware that the seemingly solid canyon wall was only marginally larger than the span of the Mithrim's manta like wings. Araime rolled her eyes and guided the ship forward toward the canyon wall. The canyon wall shimmered, and the Mithrim continued forward, moving gracefully through an equally shimmering passageway with adequate clearance. Suddenly, they exited into a vast cavern that could have served as a base for two or more of the Seeker class ships. Araime and Wyik were familiar with this base as was Sally, to a lesser degree. Doc could pull glimpses of this temporary operations base from his father's memories. The recent additions to the Mithrim, on the other hand, just gawked in surprise. Regardless of their initial impression, all were anxious to leave the ship and examine this vast underground site.

This base camp had been constructed while her original crew repaired the Mithrim, using the raw material of the cavern itself. All Seeker class ships were equipped with a fabricator designed to produce anything that would be needed on whatever planet they found themselves. During that time, they also analyzed the odd issues and interaction of the multiple species on Earth. They wanted to understand the rationale behind the initial attack on the Mithrim. So, over the subsequent years, the base grew.

The new crew members took their time investigating the base. Three tunnels disappeared into the bedrock serving as a conduit for hi-speed maglev pods. Those pods ranged in size and capacity. Some were designed for passengers, some for equipment and or vehicles. Wyik translated the labels; one was labeled Dulce, one designated Los Alamos, and the third identified as Groom Lake. The one to Dulce could make the 412-mile trip to the Dunarian station below Dulce in under 40 minutes. That station was hidden in much the same manner as the entrance the Mithrim had just used. Even now, it remained undiscovered and could provide access to the caverns below Dulce.

This entire complex had gone dormant when Doc's father had died on the last incursion to Dulce. With Araime and Wyik in stasis, Mithrim had gone into what was similar to hibernation waiting to see if the one living child born on Earth would find his way to the ship. Had he, Doc, not returned to the Mithrim, she would have woken the remaining crew from stasis so that they could, at least, continue to follow the original mission parameters. Now, it seemed, with the Mithrim back to full strength and all living Dunarian accounted for, it was up to Doc to finish what his father and mother had started many years earlier.

After exploring this underground complex, they agreed that referring to it as a temporary camp seemed an understatement. After some deliberation, they decided this underground complex should be named Dunar-Two and that the base in the Stevinus crater should be referred to as Dunar-One.

Exhausted, they returned to the familiar surroundings of the Mithrim's common room. This spacious shared room, lounge, dining area, central meeting area was where they had all gathered to start their new life. When they met here, the first time, there had been some wonder as Wyik seemed to be able to randomly reconfigure the furnishings. Now, this was their safe space with its conference table, random seating, and other generally eclectic furnishings. Wyik, still the acknowledged master at reconfiguring the area, helped Sally to get settled and comfortable so they could start forming plans.

Doc began, "I suppose you are all wondering why I called you here?" and was met with eye rolls and not too subtle retorts.

It seemed that regardless of the species this was a standard comic lead-in to any group gathering of questionable origin. After a few more random quips, they separated the project into three tasks. Shut down the base on Phobos and release any abductees. Shut down the non-human command and control portion of this operation. This was believed to be centralized in the lower levels of the Dulce base. And finally; shut down the human-based component of this operation, believed to be under Ronan's control or management.

Chapter 52
Near Garrapata State Beach

Ronan Amos Murdock stood silently at the fourteen-foot floor to ceiling windows. He was looking out over the cliffside at the Pacific Ocean crashing against the rocks of the cove. Ronan was aware of the reflections of his guests in the glass. Instead, he preferred to focus beyond and recognize the ocean and power of the waves as they crashed against the rocky coastline. That was real power he told himself.

He wasn't alone in the room. Rosy Cobb was sitting in one of the four large 1940s Fritz Hansen Wingback chairs. His new head of security, Kevin Evans, sat in another of the chairs. Seesrtin, Squadron Leader of the two remaining Thurog picket ships occupied a chair. The fourth chair was filled by Rhiyant, a Teletin, sitting with a relaxed air of indifference. Finally, standing to one side of the group were two of the bugs. He didn't recognize these two in their creepy skin suits. He probably would not have known they were bugs, but Rhiyant had insisted that a sensor gateway be installed at the main entrance and exit points of his mansion. He had seen what was under the skin suits.

Ronan had worked with many savory and equally unsavory individuals and groups in his lifetime. He had grown up on the streets of Belfast, survived the gangs and a stint of time with the IRA in late 1969; then decided to abandon nationalism for capitalism and eventually immigrated to the US. Now he was head of a large and mostly unknown International syndicate. He still avoided the drug trade. It was its own devil, and while profitable, was always in the news and under the watchful eye of enforcement agencies.

His products were information technology and human trafficking.

As his organization expanded and strengthened its position by intelligent vs. gang tactics, he learned that aliens, those of an extraterrestrial nature, existed and he adapted. They became a valued customer, for the most part. He had no problem abducting the cast-offs of society and sending them to be used as slaves on different planets. He looked at it as a service to his world, fewer indigents on the streets, and the abductees got to experience new worlds.

He had an arrangement with the Thurog as muscle. They looked mostly like big ugly humans, but they did their job, and that was what counted in his estimation. Then there was his alignment with the Teletin underworld. Teletin was part of a confederation of species and had agreements with the governments of several countries. He chuckled to himself at the assumption that the arrangement would be without intrigue. His affiliation with Rhiyant and his organization was a straightforward business alliance and, until recently, had been without any significant issues.

Then there were the bugs, the Eldrane. They worked through the Teletin, so Ronan rarely dealt with them directly. They were the distribution arm of the products he funneled to the Teletin. They were not even remotely human, or humanoid, whatever. Worse still they wore a skin suit, a living tissue that covered their bug bodies, so they looked human. One of them had been crushed when a shipping container slipped its clamps, and he caught his first glimpse of the bug shell under that skin suit. It made his skin crawl on several levels.

Now, suddenly, the whole operation was threatening

to go left of center. It began with a botched attempt to capture a DARPA scientist. She may have been trying to create super-soldiers, he didn't really care except that her work might produce a product he could sell. That whole operation had gone wrong, and the ripple effect was still being felt. That was the reason for this meeting.

He went through the group, beginning with Cobb's report. A snatch and grab team had been dispatched a few weeks ago to snag Dr. Wing, the DARPA scientist. It failed because of an old IT tech, driving to work, who butted in. They got word that the scientist was meeting her rescuer for dinner at a restaurant by the beach, a team of professionals sprang that trap. That result was worse than the initial attempt. Evidence that they might be in New Mexico resulted in a third failed attempt. At that point, the scientist, her assistant, her bodyguard, the original rescuer, and random other unknowns were, well completely gone, somewhere.

There was a suggestion that they had left Earth on a fantastic spacecraft that appeared out of the side of a mountain, but that could not be substantiated. That third attempt, however, had cost Ronan two expensive helicopters and several highly trained operatives. That, of course, was not nearly as bad as the Thurog having lost an entire ship when they tangled with the mystery spacecraft.

At this point Rhiyant's contacts believed the whole group had ended up on the moon. Ronan might have been amused at that excuse had the situation not continued to spiral downhill. The next chapter in this unusual story was a little unclear because the Teletin underground was not particularly forthcoming. It appeared that spies at a base on the moon had been terminated, the station itself, had disappeared, a bug space cruiser had been destroyed by the mystery spacecraft, and survivors from the missing base suddenly appeared in orbit requesting rescue.

"So," Ronan asked in a calm forceful tone, "Are these incidents all the result of the actions of a female scientist with no apparent clandestine background and an IT consultant who retired as a medic from the Navy 40 some years ago? If that is the case, we need to hire them, or we need to put an end to this before it is completely off the rails!"

Sadly, while none of the attendees had answers. They did all agree that the two unlikely partners and a mysterious spaceship were at the center of the issue.

Ronan's birthday party was coming up the following weekend and was intended to be a big affair held at this very mansion overlooking the bay. It would be attended by the elite in both Ronan's circle as well as government contractors who looked the other way at his reputation. He needed this problem gone by then, or at least not escalating.

Rhiyant assured Ronan that his organization would clamp down on the moon fiasco. The Thurog pickets would maintain a watch from orbit, and the Bugs would ship out any current abductees, then go dark at their base near Mars for now. None present were happy with those decisions, but none of the players could come up with any realistic options.

Once the visitors had left, Ronan asked Cobb to remain behind, the two sat down for a discussion of tactics. He had been disappointed by the failed helicopter mission in New Mexico, but he had known Ambrose for almost thirty years, and his friend was still limping as he recuperated from the debacle.

"Rosy, my old friend," Ronan began, using Ambrose's nickname, to make it clear he was placing his trust in Cobb, "I need you to make sure that my birthday party, with all of the important guests, goes off without a hitch. I want no hint of recent events to surface. If you feel you need them, get some additional backing from Seesrtin, maybe some of his ground troops, maybe even a ship. I trust the Thurog. To them, this is just a business. To the Teletin and the Bugs, this is an ideology, and we all know how that goes when the hard decisions need to be made."

When Cobb left, Ronan turned back to the windows where he could appreciate the power and majesty of the waves as they continued to pound the coast. It was a calm, beautiful day, and it looked like next week would include perfect weather for his party. But you never knew when a storm might suddenly appear.

Chapter 53

Amber had no background in non-human physiology but was supplied a link to a Vlichoir medical team by Sally. With their assistance and a Teletin biochemist drafted to assist her, they tackled the autopsy. As they stripped away Harec's external biomaterial disguise, one of the medical team speculated that the body appeared to be Eldrane. When completed, the findings were consistent with that hypothesis. The body resembled a bipedal version of a Mantis and had been encased in a biomaterial that made him appear to be Teletin. He was wearing a skin suit. When Amber reported the findings, her declaration produced a gasp from both Ally and Sally.

Gathered in the common room, Sally explained to the crew what that meant. The Eldrane were a bipedal anthro-arthropod species or insectoid species vaguely resembling giant praying mantises. They have triangular heads, with bulging faceted eyes, supported on flexible necks and are approximately two meters tall. While basically arthropodic in nature they were an invertebrate species with an exoskeleton, a segmented body, and paired jointed appendages. Unlike the Mantises, they loosely resemble, they had only two legs. And while they did have two pairs of arms, the lower pair of these were vestigial. When in their pure form their Chitin color was a Cadmium Green. Their exoskeletons were proof against most common accidental damage including cuts or scrapes. However, if their chitin is penetrated, they bleed profusely. They could, however, mend broken or cut chitin with a chitin substitute that they exuded like saliva.

All Eldrane are uncomfortable to the point of fear regarding any form of immersion such as falling into a large body of water or being trapped in sand or material that will envelop them. This is because they breathe through openings in their upper thorax and are easily susceptible to drowning if their upper body is submerged. The rigid cuticle nature of their chitin inhibits growth, so an Eldrane replaces it periodically by molting. When dealing with lesser soft body species, they often adopted a pseudo skin that covered their chitin and can be made to resemble the species they were dealing with. That material is porous and does not restrict their breathing.

The universal impression is that, as a species, they are dedicated to expanding their control throughout the galaxy, and they have enslaved several other species already. As part of their continued expansion, they are frequently involved in abductions of the populations of lesser species or races they had not yet subjugated. Their empire is governed by a strict military dictatorship.

"So," Doc interjected, "with their ability to wear a skin suit to hide their appearance, they could mingle in with any group or species?"

The nod from all present was a sufficient answer. This devolved into a discussion of where these insurgents were coming from and how to identify them. Doc was confident, as was Araime and Ally, that they could recognize their mental patterns. This meant that any interaction outside of the current group would require one of them as part of the away team. The next conjecture was that Eldrane were probably the primary end-users for the abductees. They had the requisite science to modify humans to be sold to any species, and this would enable them a modicum of control if they embedded devices in the slaves they sold.

Level nine, in Dulce, would be a perfect hidden section
for them to use to prep their captives before shipment as well
as to conduct experiments. Because they, as a species, were
not part of the confederation, those lower levels would have to
be maintained by traitors within the confederation.

The next task for the Mithrim group was to analyze the
information from the tiny surveillance devices that were still
transmitting from Phobos. Those little autonomous AI guided
devices had successfully set up a series of listening posts
where they could cover the entire base. Once they had
modified their own appearance so that they fit into the
surroundings, they began transmitting tight beam packets of
information back to the Mithrim as well as the Geray 2
complex. These persistent little devices had mapped out the
schedule of operations at the Phobos base. They identified the
communications hub for the installation, and one of them had
made its way to that hub. Once it identified operational
parameters, it created a nest in the main hub.

Any assault on the Phobos installation would require
the Mithrim. The capabilities of the Eldrane ships and
personnel were still an unknown. What was known was that
the Mithrim could hold her own with minimal effort in
support of a Vlichoir task force. Any assault against Phobos
and Dulce would require a coordinated strike. This would
require splitting the efforts and personnel that formed the
Mithrim crew. Ronan's operation could then be dealt with
after the two primary targets were neutralized.

Thanks to the invasive and thorough interaction of the
AI surveillance bugs on Phobos, they had an ongoing status
report of operations at that base. The next decision was who

would go with the Mithrim to Phobos as a supplemental to the Vlichoir task force. Araime, Wyik, Mike, and Amber would crew the Mithrim. That decision made, all present comically looked at Myth to make sure the odd little construct did not have any objection.

Myth looked at each of the four for a moment then settled back into Doc's lap. Decision made and approved.

Chapter 54

Planning for the Dulce complex was not as straightforward as the assist with the Phobos base. This would involve Doc and the Doll. Doc had foolishly attempted to suggest that the Doll stay behind. It was a short discussion. Tommy, Ally, and Sally would round out the team. Ally had the most recent knowledge of the various levels of the Dulce base. Tommy had less access to the known levels but was still aware of the multiple ins and outs of the complex. Sally had less current information but did have prior knowledge of attempts to uncover what was happening on the lower levels. That included the existence of sections below the seventh level.

They began by reviewing what they knew about the base itself. The upper surface of the base was an unassuming government structure. It was situated within a fenced-off open area with the prerequisite Government Property signage. This building offered limited access to the central hub and was intended as a show and tell for government officials convinced they were entitled to full disclosure.

Based on a visitor's access level, they could reach sections of the first three levels and, in some cases, level four. These levels were of little interest to the assault team, as Ally felt their current group should be called. For planning purposes, the team needed to consider how all levels interacted with the entire installation.

Level one was almost entirely garage, storage and maintenance rooms with some offices. It did appear to house air handlers, and other equipment related to the carefully maintained environment of the lower levels. In reality, critical systems for levels four and below were in secure bunkers on level four with redundant systems on other levels.

Level two was an extension of level one. It was also a garage, or possibly could be considered a hanger. It included housing and maintenance for trains, shuttles, tunnel-boring machines and some of the older UFO's that were shown to visiting dignitaries. As with Level one, it also included a smattering of offices.

Level three was the primary office level for the complex and included most of the command and control offices. Most was a generalization, as with all government installations, some offices had restricted access or were spotted on lower levels.

Level four was the first of the ultra-level locations, and while still shown to some dignitaries, access was severely limited. This level included Human Aura Research as well as research related to Dream Manipulation, Hypnosis, and Telepathy. Theory and application went hand in hand on this level with studies and training for tasks as simple as lowering a subject's heartbeat with Delta Waves to introducing data and programmed reactions into a subject's mind for those with implanted biodevice chips. The Doll lightly moved her thumbs over the implants in her palms and smiled. Her implants, linked to the Mithrim, were mission-specific and could be re-tasked instantly.

Level five was rumored to have large vats containing liquid nourishing solutions for several species. Access to the level was severely restricted. This section was said to also have several rows of cells holding men, women, and children, presumably human. While these claims were not substantiated, this was one of the areas they needed to consider.

Level six was privately called "Nightmare Hall." It contains the genetic labs. It was here that several crossbreeding experiments of human/animal/interspecies were conducted. This included the use of fish, seals, porpoises, birds, and mice that were vastly altered from their original forms. Rumors abounded that there were multi-armed and multi-legged humans and several cages and vats of humanoid bat-like creatures up to seven feet tall. Ally rolled her eyes as they discussed this section but did suggest that they investigate the work done there carefully. Based on what they were hearing of human trafficking and the viability of human DNA, benign studies might be carried out in this section, whereas in level nine, those same studies were more pronounced and or horrific.

Level seven was an unknown to Ally, Sally, and Tommy, each of whom had limited access below level four. As with any top-secret installation, especially one that included an interstellar cast of characters, rumors abounded. Not the least being that this level contained row after row of humans in cold storage, including children.

The confederation had chosen the Dulce base for its central location to several smaller sites scattered throughout the underground networks between Dulce, Los Alamos, and Area 51. The Dulce Base currently was home to the largest repository of extraterrestrials and equipment in North America. The five of them simply needed to penetrate its defenses, and gain access to the secure sections to expose unrestricted trafficking of human beings as genetic fodder for interested extraterrestrials buyers. As this understanding percolated in the minds of those in the planning session, they lapsed into silence.

Araime finally broke the silent retrospection, "It looks like your assault team has its work cut out for it, I'm glad all the four of us have to do is attack a fortified moon."

"We have an edge," Sally said after a moment. "We have much more information than we had before the earlier attempt to expose this travesty. We also have a Sosan, and I still have contacts in the area."

Over the next few hours, this group of nine formulated options.

The Mithrim team had the advantage of numbers. They would be operating as a unit with a highly organized Vlichoir strike force. This, coupled with the detailed information regarding Phobos base operations activity from the little AI spies should make their part of the operation painless and straightforward.

On the other side of the equation was the Dulce Assault team. They had only limited access to Dulce through two known agents, Ally and Tommy, a Vlichoir agent, with a range of resources, and Doc and the Doll.

The first part of their plan involved gaining access to the Dulce complex. Tommy and Mike had gone dark, as had Ally, from their respective branches of the clandestine community. This gave them an excuse to resurface and report to Dulce for a debriefing. Sally, on the other hand, had departed Earth some time ago and her reappearance will raise questions.

Sally had that covered. She had maintained an ongoing relationship with two quirky Jicarilla Indians that had migrated to live off the reservation on the outskirts of Dulce, New Mexico. The pair had allowed their home to serve as a base of operation for Anexten, Ruvator, Sally, and others trying to resolve the issues at hand decades ago. As such, one of the maglev tunnels from the Mithrim's base went to a small cavern below their home. Doc, the Doll, and Sally decided a visit was in order.

Ally and Tommy took a different approach. Among the resources available in Dunar-Two were several vehicles. Some were obviously of Dunarian design, but a few were domestic models for the various periods during which this complex had been active. Among those was a pristine 1979 Jeep Wagoneer. Doc, Tommy, and Mike had it up and running in short order.

Ally and Tommy loaded the Jeep in one of the maglev pods and took the tunnel to Los Alamos. Once there, they climbed in the Wagoneer and drove to the secure section of the Los Alamos National Laboratory and presented themselves. They explained that they had some intel on Ronan and bummed a ride on one of the underground trams to the Dulce complex. That tram was also used to transport cargo, so they were able to take the Wagoneer with them to Dulce. They all had a plan.

Chapter 55

The ride on the maglev to the stop outside of Dulce was uneventful. They covered the 400 plus miles in 38 minutes. Inside the transport pod, there was no impression of speed or any indication they were racing from one end of New Mexico to the other. Since this little excursion was to gain initial insight concerning the Dulce complex, they traveled light.

Ally and Tommy had left for Los Alamos the previous evening, with the intent of catching a government ride to Dulce in the morning. They realized that Dulce was going to be one of the puzzles they would have to resolve based on the feedback from Geray 2. This joint CIA-Human-Alien Confederation headquarters was located under the Archuleta Mesa in Dulce, New Mexico, close to the Colorado border. Part of the base was situated under the Jicarilla Apache Indian Reservation itself. The main entrance to the base was approximately 2.5 miles northwest of the town of Dulce. With the travel time, they expected to be at the station around lunchtime. This would give them an excuse to head into town before any meetings and surreptitiously run into old friends. The plan was to meet Doc and the Doll at the Players Sports Bar & Grill then head back to the base for a visit.

In the part of the base hosting the CIA and Joint investigative section where Tommy and Ally worked, Spyder had been a legend. Whenever Tommy was there, he would frequently refer to his summers with Spyder and his pseudo uncle, Martin. The initial plan had been to introduce that pseudo uncle. They quickly realized the flaw in this plan was that Doc no longer looked his physical age. They agreed that

Doc could be introduced as Martin's son and the Doll as his wife. Next, Ally, with the assistance of the pseudo escapees from Geray, now back at the base, managed to get some cover credentials for Doc and the Doll. These credentials provided the clearance to access the compound, as visitors, provided they were with Tommy and/or Ally. Ally also learned that Dezir, for his actions during the assault on the Geray complex, had been given command of a new experimental small tactical assault craft with a crew of ten.

The plan was to position Doc where he could integrate the memories he had from his father. The secondary objective was to see if they could spot any Eldrane.

The two couples met for lunch. Ally handed over the credentials she had been passed before she and Tommy left to go into town. Then they all piled into the Wagoneer and headed back to the base.

Once at the complex, they were ushered through security and chatted with Tommy and Ally's friends and co-workers. These were beings that had heard of Doc and were delighted to meet his son and his hot wife. The Doll, going for a tourist vibe, was wearing stylish loose-fit Patagonia Stand Up Shorts that showed off her long-tanned runner's legs. She was also wearing a strapless tube top. All male and some female attention was focused on the Doll. This whole visit was based on misdirection.

The group was visiting offices in level three when Doc got a hit, as he put it. He picked up the mental pattern of an Eldrane, possibly two of them with a group preparing to enter a lift to the lower levels. What happened next was a surprise to three of the four Mithrim spies.

They had been swapping tall tales with some Teletin friends of Ally when they felt additional thoughts in the corner of their minds. They suddenly understood that one of a group behind them, at the lift, was Eldrane and that individual was about to experience a fainting spell. This insight was due to Doc mentally reaching out, and was followed by a commotion as a tall individual collapsed. Everyone turned in the direction of the disturbance and moved to get a closer look.

The Doll's cover was that of an ER Nurse with a military background, so it was logical for her to approach the fallen individual. She calmly took control of the situation. While she was turning him over, he shook out of the stupor and looked around with an embarrassed expression. His facial expression was not missed by the team. What was overlooked by the rest of the onlookers was that the Doll gifted the fallen Eldrane with one of the little AI bugs, as she helped him back up. The diminutive little electronic spy immediately blended in with its target's clothing. Not wanting to miss a chance, the Doll gifted another of the little bugs to the fainter's companion who Doc also identified as Eldrane.

The fainter looked confused but explained he had missed lunch. That seemed a reasonable answer, and everyone went their own way and back to what they had been doing before the distraction. Each of the four Mithrim team had two of the small AI devices with them. They released these into the wild as they left. Tommy and Ally submitted reports concerning their observation of Ronan's operation while Doc and the Doll were given a lift back to the Wildhorse Casino & Hotel where they had booked a room to cover their activities.

Later that afternoon, the four members of the covert

operations force (they were trying out team names) and Sally met to review what data they might be getting from their little bugs. They had decided, early on, that they needed a new name for the devices since it was confusing to talk about bugging the bugs with ... However, they still hadn't come up with a better naming convention yet.

They temporarily focused on Doc, acknowledging his sudden entrance into their thought patterns. After some discussion, they agreed that it was appropriate for the situation and left it there. Then they considered Doc's validation of the two human appearing beings that he had identified as Eldrane.

"They were definitely the same species as the spy Harec," Doc replied to their questions. "I could feel the difference in the thought resonance. I can, also, blank those thought patterns in much the same way as I originally did to put Ally to sleep. How many I can subdue at one time I don't know, but they have no mental barrier as do some of the Teletin and other species I tested when we were in the complex. I noticed that the being that I identified had a very human reaction and facial response, but I assure you that it is a highly evolved pseudo-human mask. More like an entire outer shell that has been developed while studying human physiology and reactions."

Once they began to review the transmitted data and images from the spy bugs, they knew the decision to use them had been the right one. They now had clear photos, a floor plan, and actionable intel on levels six through level nine. The images of level nine exposed a series of holding cells and research labs for genetic manipulation the Confederation would frown on if it was made known.

A strike force was already committed to the Phobos base of operations, but the Dulce installation on Earth would require more finesse. Sally spent an hour working through channels and was finally rewarded with access to an additional specialized covert strike team of twenty elite commandos. They would be delivered to the canyon near the Mithrim cavern the following morning. Sally suggested that they return to Dunar-Two to meet the strike team and brief them.

During their research on the Dulce base they found records, in the archives, of a 1979 battle that nearly exposed the whole complex. That had since been covered up. They needed this operation to be as clean as possible and with as little exposure to the general population as possible.

Chapter 56

After dinner and some further review, all four headed back to Doc and the Doll's room in the Wildhorse Casino. This was just for show, and shortly afterward they all slipped out to the Wagoneer. They picked up Sally, then took the maglev back to the Mithrim. They had already reviewed the info from the various data feeds but wanted to be able to study the data using the tools available on the Mithrim.

During the short trip back, Doc realized the Doll was studying him. He knew that despite the enhancements she had recently received through his ship, she could not read his mind, but he felt like she was looking into his psyche.

"You're worried about me in the coming action," she finally said, barely above a whisper. "I don't think you're concerned about my ability to handle myself, just that I might be hurt. It could happen, but you are not going without me at your side."

There was no reason for him to answer, he could see that she had made up her mind, and ... there weren't any options.

It was just before 8 pm when all nine of the current crew were back in the common room of the Mithrim. They started with the intelligence they were getting from the i-Spys on Phobos. Amber had come up with the name i-Spys, and it was unanimously accepted. Several of the Phobos i-Spys was now integrated into the primary data storage system on that moon and could, therefore, provide them redundant access to everything from routine communications to command and control information.

A regular shipment of abductees was scheduled the second week of any given month. Transfers of modified abductees were planned for the third week. Until abductees were shipped, they were maintained at the base in stasis pods. The shipment intended for the previous week had been postponed. According to the manifests, they now had an excess. There were over eight-hundred abductees in stasis scheduled to be shipped when the embargo was lifted. A decision had also been made to stand down until the rash of unexplained incidents subsided. That decision had come from Eldrane management in the Dulce complex. According to the information they now had, that senior management position was held by an Eldrane named Lisarra. She was responsible for the overall direction and administration of the Phobos base as well as Earth installations.

They continued to break down the information, still focusing on the Phobos base and the Earth side non-human based installations. They found it interesting that the only facility on the Earth's moon was Geray. The Eldrane documentation indicated that the moon was considered too close to Earth. The Eldrane had been aware of the Teletin base and made sure that there were always several spies in residence. The small installation that Dezir and Ally had destroyed was only an emergency staging area. Lisarra had issued orders for the attack on Geray, in response to the emergency beacons launched by the spies at the base.

Had the beacons contained more information, she might have considered an alternate response. The fact that only one had gotten far enough to broadcast a partial message before being destroyed convinced her she needed a more pronounced reaction. Lisarra had already tasked an Eldrane heavy cruiser to investigate the earlier loss of one of the Thurog cruisers. The Thurog had been hired as backup muscle for Ronan's human trafficking operation. That operation had become increasingly profitable.

The Eldrane cruiser had been transitioning to Earth's orbit to assist the remaining two Thurog medium cruisers holding station above the North Pole. When it was redirected to investigate the emergency beacon, it was destroyed. Lisarra wanted answers.

Before the Mithrim had left the cavern, making her presence known, the Eldrane local force had consisted of three heavy and two light cruisers, four smaller corvette class pickets and was augmented by the three Thurog medium cruisers. There were other smaller support craft such as this tactical assault craft Dezir and Ally had destroyed, and two medium cargo haulers. Now with the appearance of the Mithrim, Lisarra's forces had been reduced by one Eldrane and one Thurog cruiser, and a network of spies in Geray, yet she still had no answers. Her solution was to have her forces stand down until she could get some answers, then determine a plan of action.

Lisarra's authority only extended to the non-human forces. The human element in this slave trade was through an arrangement with Ronan's extended organization. Homeless, runaways, disenfranchised individuals, and specific phenotypes were targeted by Ronan's international organization. Once acquired they were taken to a local staging area for transport off-planet to Phobos and eventually to the stars. In the United States, collection points were across the North American continent with ultimate transport to Dulce,

New Mexico. There were additional backup facilities and support in Los Alamos and Groom Lake.

The Eldrane were meticulous in their record-keeping, and the i-Spys now had access to all that information. Doc noticed Sally had lapsed into an uneasy silence. After a moment, he paused the discussions to engage the normally gregarious Vlichoir super-agent.

"Sally," Doc began, "what's bothering you. I would have expected more enthusiasm?"

Sally gave a little shudder, then seem to calm herself. She suddenly seemed closer to her real age. "Marxten ... Doc ... Sosan, I met your mother before you were born. After she passed, I remained friends with what was left of the Dunarian crew until this ship went into hibernation. During the final sortie into Dulce, I lost some very dear friends, including your father, and Alura's grandfather."

She continued, "At that time we were desperately trying to get actionable intel we could use to expose and put a stop to what was the beginning of this now extensive operation. Now, several tiny AI devices are supplying us with information that would have made all the difference and saved so many lives. This technology existed then, but the circumstances that allow us to use it didn't."

"I am okay, I just wish I could turn back time. When this is finished, I think I might return home and retire," she said with a heavy sigh.

After a moment Doc smiled, a comforting smile, "Then we need to get it right this time, no mistakes, no loopholes, let's finish our review and get a good night's sleep. The next few days are going to be interesting."

After further consultation with Sally, she was reassigned to the Mithrim coordinating with the Vlichoir task force in the assault of the Phobos base. As they continued their discussions, the crew learned that Sally, at one point in her life, had commanded an Alution frigate. There was no doubt that the Phobos part of their plans would be in good hands.

That left the Dulce base and Ronan's organization.

Chapter 57

They decided that the Dulce base and Ronan's organization should be tackled separately. Whereas the actions against the Phobos base and Dulce needed to be coordinated and simultaneous action. Communication between Dulce and its satellites was in real time. The base on Phobos, despite the distance from Earth to Phobos, operated in near real time. Phobos was 48,000,000 miles from Earth depending on their elliptical orbits. The communications protocols used by the Eldrane allowed from 1.5 to 10 minutes for a one-way signal and was nearly twice as fast as regular radio communications. At this time of year, and taking the elliptical orbits into consideration, signal time for one-way communications was under 5 minutes. That meant that Dulce would be aware of any move made against Phobos in short order.

Both locations would need to be hit simultaneously. The teams would need to coordinate their attacks. If they were successful, Ronan's organization, on the periphery, would not be alerted and could be tackled after the two primary targets were subdued.

It was getting late, so they all retired to their individual quarters. The next few days would probably not allow for a relaxing, carefree night. While most returned to their own quarters, Sally followed Doc and the Doll to their quarters, asking if she could have a few moments of their time. Once there, she sat down and expressed her concerns. Sally had seen the previous attempt to shut down the abductions end badly. She recognized that they now had superior intel and resources, but she was just voicing her concern.

Sally's final comment to Doc was, "You, above all, are a crucial part of this operation. As a Sosan, you need to draw on all the resources you have available. If you have abilities you have not explored, now would be the time to confirm them."

With that ominous proclamation, she sighed, bid the pair a good night, and left for her room.

"No pressure," the Doll said, after Sally left, and turned to study Doc's reaction.

When the Doll woke the following morning, she remembered her 'No pressure' comment to Doc and nothing more. Looking up, she saw him sitting in one for the floating chairs watching her. Before she could ask, he told her that he had slept well, and he was sure that things would work out. She had questions, but all she got in return was a wry smile. She had only known Doc for the past few weeks, but she knew that smile meant she would not get an answer until he was ready.

She took another moment to take stock of her surroundings. Her clothing was neatly folded or hung in the refresher, coffee was on the table at her side of the bed, and she felt well-rested. She thought that she had been fully dressed and in a different room of the cabin, in her last conscious memory. She studied Doc as she considered that she seemed to have misplaced a snippet of her memory and wasn't sure what that meant. She decided that trust was the answer she sought, and she trusted Doc.

Once again, the crew gathered in the common room and checked the current reports from the i-Spys. There had been no significant changes in day to day operations at the Phobos base, no extra security, no request for additional ships. Those at the station were satisfied to sit and wait out whatever storm was coming. On the other hand, the Dulce base seemed to be experiencing controlled pandemonium. Of the eight i-Spys they had released yesterday, six of them made their way down to levels seven, eight and nine. The other two had tackled the communications center on level three.

Mithrim now had access to all communications networks for the Dulce base. They had also identified and could separate the base communications chatter from the separate communications on the Eldrane channels. Tommy and Ally tested this by followed their typical communication protocols. They surreptitiously inquired if there was any new news on Ronan's upcoming birthday bash. The results were both amusing and informational.

Their inquiries about Ronan moved up the chain and returned down with reasonable answers. CIA and Teletin covert teams reported on the upcoming extravaganza, including projected guest lists, and security protocols.

On the other side of the house, results of their request they would never have seen were far more informative. The Eldrane reports covered resources currently in play at the mansion, including Ronan's request for additional support from the Eldrane, the Thurog, and from other assets that include two Teletin, two CIA and one other player neither were familiar with.

During these early stages of the morning review, the Doll continued to study Doc while attempting to recall the chain of events after Sally's departure. Finally, without anyone noticing, she pinched his thigh and stared at him, willing him to answer her. Doc continued to appear as though he was following the information being presented and never looked her way. However, a new world opened in her thoughts.

"I will always answer you when you direct your thoughts to me, the pinch is not required." She wasn't experiencing a faux verbalization; instead, she just knew ... that was it, she knew what he meant.

"It is vital that I can control and use the gifts I have now come into. I felt it was safe, because you trust me, to experiment ... ", that concept was vague and nebulous. *"We started the experiments together. I explained my need to refine my telekinetic abilities. We began getting ready for bed, so I practiced control by gently undressing you, it seemed an amusing and provocative approach to our burgeoning relationship. When I had placed and folded everything, I floated you over to and placed you in our bed. Finally, after we discussed my next proposed action; I took control of your autonomic systems, rendered you unconscious, and carefully removed all memory of the event. When you were sleeping peacefully, I suddenly felt guilty and spent the rest of the time in the chair, exploring who I am."*

"And what did you learn," she said in a whisper, she needed to at least hear her own voice."

Again, she felt, not heard, *"I am ready for our part in this coming confrontation."*

The Doll flushed with momentary excitement and something that she could not explain. To the outside world of the common room, she and Doc appeared to be following the discussions and review of the success of i-Spys.

A little before lunch, the group was alerted that a

stealth combat shuttle had arrived in the canyon. Mithrim dispatched a small drone to meet the vessel, then to escort it back into the main cavern area.

Sally made the introductions, and they all relaxed over lunch. Doc, the Doll, Tommy, and Ally, who would be dealing with the Dulce compound, used the time to get to know their newly arrived support. Araime, Wyik, Mike, Amber, and Sally, who would be with the task force targeting Phobos drifted off together to review and prepare.

Chapter 58

Cdr. Branko Golub was in command of the strike team that had been drafted to support the assault on the Eldrane contingent in the Dulce complex. Branko, in turn, handpicked his team with the understanding that they would be coming up against Eldrane. He was confident the task force cruisers, were a sufficient match against the Eldrane ships at Phobos. He did, however, express his regret at not being able to see the Mithrim in action. As his team settled in and grabbed some lunch, Branko spent some time walking around the outside of the ship, admiring her as she sat quietly in the cavern.

Cdr. Golub was a Lyssa Royal. The Lyssa Royal was a Lyran subspecies that might be considered humanoid, but whose physical appearance resembles that of a six-foot-tall feline. They were not a feline species of cat people, but a humanoid species with feline qualities. Among those characteristics were increased agility and strength. His handpicked team included seven more of his species then an impressive collection of elite operatives from other species. All members of this team had been in more than one encounter with Eldrane, and the next few hours were filled with stories about their various exploits. While the anecdotes were informative in themselves, they were invaluable for the intel they provided on Eldrane tactics. This helped Doc and his group outline how to approach the lower levels of the Dulce base as they began to review and propose options.

The information from the i-Spys, in Dulce, included access to the records that Lisarra maintained on her staff and security teams. As a result, they knew the number of individuals they would be dealing with, their areas of responsibility, weapons, and the security codes to the areas where required. They also had access to the schedules and other pertinent information, including the origin and allegiance of the personnel at the Dulce base. That information identified those who were Eldrane spies in skin suits, as well as who were assisting them. Lisarra, it appeared, kept detailed notes and dossiers on her employees and associates.

While it almost appeared that this was going to be easy, both Doc and Cdr. Golub reminded the group that they were assaulting a secure installation. The combatants they would meet would have the home ground advantage and were known to have a pronounced disdain for the 'soft-bodies' they would be fighting. Planning would be essential for them to pull this off.

The strike force was also aware that they would be outnumbered three to one. The records they had obtained from the i-Spys broke down the personnel in the compound as followed. There were thirty-six security personnel, thirty-two scientists, and administrative personal that were identified as Eldrane. Despite the skin suits they wore, this was a species that had their own built-in armor and had, regardless of status, been brought up as warriors. Mixed into this lethal contingent were fourteen other human and non-human individuals. There were others on the edge of this criminal organization, but the fourteen they had identified were invested in this deception and would not merely give in. That meant that their strike force of twenty and the four from Mithrim's crew were up against a force more than three times their numbers.

Doc remained mostly silent as the rest of the team reviewed the disposition of forces and the layout of the several levels they would have to navigate. Finally, he asked if he could give those present a short demonstration of what he had recently come to embrace as his capabilities. While Ally and Tommy were taken aback at Doc's apparent recently discovered abilities, Branko's veterans smiled broadly and went back to revise their plans to accommodate the Dunarian Sosan as a resource.

Tommy and Ally had been reviewing their specific and joint contacts for the past few days. After the recent updates from the i-Spys, they did a final review. For the plan to work the team couldn't just walk into Dulce and begin shooting. The number and variety of beings in the base was extensive. In the big picture, the eighty-plus individuals they had to deal with were a small percentage of the total population. Dulce was a joint command including representatives of the eight council species, those included administrative, scientific and other staff. Then there was a human contingent that included CIA, NSA and representatives from the clandestine services of several countries with their complimentary military components.

They had considered notifying the appropriate agencies but based on the information they now had, it seemed that Lisarra had already developed a contingency plan should someone or some group attempt to expose her operation. That contingency plan would if allowed to run its course, destroy most of the base. Her plan, however, was based on full disclosure of the operation at the command level of Dulce. It did not, as far as they could determine, consider a precisely focused strike.

That was their plan, but they would still require some form of coordination, or they would be confronting the Eldrane while trying to explain their actions on the fly. That part of the plan fell back on Tommy and Ally to identify critical personnel that would listen to them, agree to their plan, and be able to run cover interference for the operation until they had Lisarra. With her captured, they should be able to convince the rest of her group to surrender without precipitating catastrophic destruction of the whole complex. And, of course, they had less than 24 hours to come up with and put this plan into action. The last restriction was the knowledge there was a pre-planned move of the current abductees from Phobos in twenty-six hours.

Sally sat in for some of the initial planning, while she would not be present, she knew a great deal concerning the factions in command of the Dulce complex. They reviewed daily schedules for the target personnel. The thirty-six security personnel covered three shifts equally. Those shifts were a day shift beginning at 07:00 - 15:00, swing shift from 15:00 - 23:00 and a night shift from 23:00 - 07:00 the following morning. When not on task covering levels eight and nine, the off-duty personnel were quartered on the eighth level. The science and admin personnel only worked two shifts, day and swing. Lisarra, however, apparently roamed the area till after midnight on an irregular basis.

Scheduling the strike during the latter part of the night shift sounded ideal, but supervisors on the night shift of the complex's departments were not their best choice for several reasons. Again, thanks to Lisarra's obsessive nature, they had tracking data on all the base's personnel. After reviewing departments and staff, they decided the swing shift offered them the best options and opportunities.

Chapter 59
Kustar Base, Phobos

Juksar finished sending the confirmation to Lisarra, the Exalted One, that the scheduled fleet freighter had entered orbit. They would begin transferring the current chattel within the hour. He knew that the local time, at the part of the human planet where the Exalted One was, would be 2200 hrs. and that she would surely get the message in a little over 5 minutes.

He turned to his adjutant, planning to have that worker follow-up, when the battle alarms sounded throughout the Phobos installation. An unknown ship had appeared in a low orbit directly in front of the freighter. All Eldrane ships of the line including freighters were heavily shielded and armed, so the freighter fired on the unknown.

Suddenly the freighter was gone, turned to atomized debris. That was the last thing that Juksar remembered. His communications array went down, even as a distress alarm was being broadcast to Earth and the Eldrane homeworld.

—————————— **Mithrim** ——————————

Araime brought the Mithrim out of jump space 10 Km above the Eldrane freighter, they had arrived earlier and joined up with the Vlichoir strike force with its four cruisers and two troop carriers. The Troop carriers had already begun to transfer assault troops groundside. When the freighter popped into the system, the timing was right. It would be 2200 hrs. in Dulce, New Mexico, or zero-hour.

They made the short jump to the lower orbit, and as the freighter slammed on its shields, powered up its weapons and fired, they hit her with a full charge from their forward batteries. The results were satisfying. As the freighter broke apart, Wyik transmitted the destruct command to the i-Spys on the planet. The two in the communications network started a chain reaction that took out communications, and most of the base power conduits. That should soften up the base for the shock troops that had already begun to deploy.

It was midday for those on Phobos, so all local personnel were going about their regular routines, the loss of power and communications caught them off guard. However, the Eldrane were a warrior species, and they recovered quickly. Away from the prying eyes of other species, none wore any of the body coverings. All wore light armor covering their external chitin. Since this was an airless moon, they also wore breathing pads covering their spiracles should there be an emergency. Those in the warrior caste grabbed their weapons, and the maintenance and journeyman classes headed for the damaged power station.

Three of the Eldrane ships burst into orbit, two of the heavy cruisers and one a light cruiser. The four corvettes rushed to join this battle group, they had been stationed as pickets along the outer orbit and had been bypassed by the incoming Vlichoir force using Mars as cover.

Two of the Vlichoir cruisers immediately moved to engage as did the Mithrim. The other two Vlichoir cruisers were providing cover for the shock troops now on the ground and meeting stiff resistance. The smaller cruisers made short work of any ground-based weapons installations typical for

Eldrane facilities as well as any mobile weapons platforms and combat shuttles.

The rules of engagement for interstellar battles are typically measured in hours as the combatants' launch weapons at interstellar distances and attempt to hit targets. Targets that may be several hundred kilometers away. Targeted vessels do not stay in place for a particle beam to bridge the distance. These targets also tend to avoid missiles or rail gun munitions hurled at them. As these weapons close the gap and if they can chase their goal, they are usually met with a point defense system. Rarely were the actual combatants at the ridiculously close range these ships found themselves.

For the Eldrane, not used to up close and personal combat, this became an immediate issue. Their point defense systems were intended to deal with projectiles or missiles that were traveling at finite speeds. Instead, they found themselves facing particle beam weapons that bridged the short gap between the vessels at light speed and were not subject to point defense systems. The Vlichoir ships, with the Mithrim's aid, had been able to appear at the ecliptic of the Martian moon with weapons online and prepared to engage.

One of the Vlichoir cruisers immediately took substantial damage but remained on the line. Conversely, not all of the Eldrane vessels were destroyed or disabled in this initial engagement. A remaining Eldrane light cruiser with two of corvettes attempted to fight free and escape to safety. Their mistake was to try to go through the unusual mystery ship that had moved to intercept them. The Mithrim proved that to be a costly mistake.

The ground action took a bit longer. As the conflict

escalated, it became apparent, to the remaining Phalanx Commander of the Eldrane units. He was faced with two issues. One was that he could not successfully destroy the stasis units with the chattel that had been scheduled to ship that very day. His standing orders were to not to allow any of these beings, especially the genetically modified ones, be examined. What he didn't know was that this directive had been discovered earlier by the i-Spys. The first Vlichoir units on the ground were already on station when the freighter sent to retrieve the abductees was being destroyed. Their mandate was to protect those abductees and establish a solid defensive line.

The second thing the Phalanx Commander realized was that only their personal weapons systems were operational. The station had fixed weapons batteries and some mobile systems. Those weapons were designed to receive guidance from the hardened tactical combat systems. Those hardened systems in a secure bunker were not operational, and, for some unfathomable reason, could not be brought back online. The maintenance teams sent to investigate never reported back.

The entire Phobos base was secured and under Vlichoir control in less two hours. Relative to New Mexico time, the station was secured two minutes before midnight. The only communication from the base had been the confirmation that the scheduled fleet freighter had arrived.

Sally transferred to the flagship of the Vlichoir strike fleet. She initiated medical support for the abductees that were not in stasis and strict supervision for those in stasis units. She then relinquished authority for the Eldrane prisoners to the Fleet Admiral in command of this Vlichoir strike force.

The Mithrim and her crew of four returned to Earth in two jumps where she eased back into her berth in the cavern.

Chapter 60
Dulce, New Mexico, Earth

Captain Marion Anderson, USAF looked at the unit team leads on the evening shift. She knew that this was an unusual situation, but she trusted her CIA contact. Marion's units were responsible for the roving patrols on the lower levels, four through seven, of the Dulce complex. She had a counterpart for the upper levels, one through three, and Tommy had said that they were already alerted.

Her teams were accustomed to dealing with their alien counterparts, and, the three Teletin evening shift units were also here at her request. She took a deep breath and passed on the intel that she had been given. During the briefing, Tommy and his counterpart Alura, part of Teletin counterintelligence, stepped in to answer questions. Captain Anderson was proud of the responses from the mixed group. They all nodded, asked some intelligent questions, and accepted the answers.

She knew that there would be no problems as she overheard one of her TSgt's and a Teletin Ranger. "So, we can shoot anyone not in Vlichoir tac gear, right?" The Ranger smiled and gave the human a high-five.

Tommy and Ally moved through the level one entrance. They both wore Vlichoir tactical gear, a dark blue-black suit of body armor, and a full helmet with the dark face shield up. Not all the articles attached to the tactical harness were readily identifiable, but some were. One was a small but lethal appearing tactical rifle, the other a small hand weapon more substantial than the snappers. No one doubted the lethality of this team. The two known members were accompanied by two, possibly humans, also in identical tac gear but with their face shields dark. These unknowns moved confidently with the CIA and Teletin agent, and it was apparent they were in charge. The guards at the entrance had been briefed and ignored the four. The four disappeared into a lift to the third level admin offices.

They stepped into the atrium on level three at 22:01 and headed for the admin offices. A tall, broad-shouldered Aghartian stepped out of one of the offices holding a communications device. He suddenly dropped to his knees and fell forward, like a marionette whose strings had been cut. A sentry on site, looked at the two pairs, then moved forward and bound the Aghartian with a force-tie around its wrists and ankles.

―――――――――――――――

Cdr. Branko and his team left the maglev pods and deployed near a section of rubble in the cavern. They applied the breaching charges and punched through the south wall of level nine at 22:00 and immediately headed for their targets.

Branko's group had been disbursed into three six-man teams. Each team included five members with Z89A pulse rifles. These small light-weight assault rifles were equipped with magazines that contained 160 armor-piercing flechettes. The sixth member of each team carried an XC300 heavy-duty Plasma rifle. Branko accompanied by an XC300 operator rounded out the twenty-man strike force. Branco and his gunner made for the lift at the center of this level. They were followed by one of the six-man teams. The other two teams laid down cover fire as they engaged the second shift Eldrane security team that had suddenly realized they had company. It was a one on one match, and the Eldrane were not expecting an attack on this level near the end of their shift. At 22:02, all lighting for levels 8 and 9 was extinguished by a fastidious pair of i-Spys.

At 22:05, Doc and the Doll entered level eight using a little know lift that went down from level three to level nine. Tommy, Ally and a four-man team that included Captain Anderson lagged systematically sweeping levels four through seven. They were looking for the previously identified traitors still on site at this late hour. Doc and the Doll had forged ahead when they received confirmation that Lisarra was currently on level eight, in the dark. The HUD displays in Doc, and the Doll's sealed helmets had been set to identify all known species in the complex as well as the Eldrane that would not have usually been ID'd.

Branko and his XC300 gunner joined up, as pre-arranged, with Doc and the Doll. The other six-man strike team moved towards the barracks area to deal with the off duty security teams. Unlike their counterparts on Phobos, these Eldrane did not have emergency patches covering their spiracles so sleeping gas canisters were being lobbed into the barracks area to reduce the bloodshed.

Doc and the Doll were after Lisarra. She was, they had been informed an Exalted One. Among her species, she was an important dignitary, and while not necessarily in the acknowledged good graces of her homeworld, she was a powerful entity that needed to be neutralized according to Sally. The i-Spy tracking her communications confirmed that she was still in contact with someone, and that turned out to be one of the two remaining Thurog cruisers. The i-Spy indicated that she had just ordered that ship to jump to Dulce and open fire on the base. The Mithrim was still in play at

Phobos and even with its abilities would not be able to intercept.

Doc contacted Tommy and within seconds was informed it was covered, so he returned his focus on locating the Exalted One. Amid the confusion, and the staccato buzz of the Z89A assault rifles, Doc was able to neutralize several of the scientists as they charged out of various labs at his group of four. That information apparently spread quickly as the scientific teams began wearing headgear Branco had previously identified as designed to block Teletin psychic abilities. Some of these worked and soon more elaborate versions appeared that seemed to partially block Doc's ability to neutralize specific Eldrane.

During this entire time, the battle continued for the eighth level. They had suffered one of their first losses as one of the Vlichoir troops had been hit and succumbed to his wounds. However, the double-team approach had resulted in a successful takedown and control of the ninth level. Only two of the on-duty Eldrane had survived and were being held. The strike team that had lost one man remained on the 9th while the second unit of six came up into the eighth level.

During that shift of forces, Doc received a message from Ally. Dezir, now in command of a new experimental small tactical assault craft had challenged the Thurog cruiser, and it had backed down. Dezir then intercepted a message that the Thurog cruiser had been ordered to jump to Phobos and found that amusing.

Suddenly three warrior class, two scientists and a being they all assumed must be Lisarra stormed forth from one of the labs. They carried a makeshift plasma cannon and opened fire on the group without any warning. The effect was not what any of the combatants on either side expected.

The Eldrane had emerged from a side lab, already presumed cleared. Their initial shot with the plasma cannon was directed at two of the Lyssa from one of the Vlichoir teams. It only vaguely affected its target, knocking the troops off their feet. The second shot never came to pass.

Doc spun to see the six attackers with elaborate protective headgear. As he continued to turn, he thrust his right hand in their general direction, his palm forward. A shimmering veil appeared and seemed to absorb the first blast. Doc continued to complete his turn toward the six figures. There were sparks and an explosion as the makeshift plasma cannon imploded and ceased to exist. Despite the pyrotechnics, there was an eerie silence. All six Eldrane were flung back into the lab like limp dolls, the headgear exploding away from their heads.

One of the scientific staff and Lisarra remained alive, both pinned to the back wall as though glued in place. Doc walked up to Lisarra and stared into her faceted eyes. All present were silent, unsure of what he might do. Lisarra's head moved for side to side as she focused on Doc. It was apparent he was communicating with her, but nothing broke the silence.

Finally, Doc turned and walked over to the Doll. Behind him, the limp form of Lisarra slid down to the floor.

"We are done here," Doc said to no one in particular, then to Branko, "I am sorry for your losses." Finally, to the Doll, "Tell Tommy and Ally, we are on our way up. We need to return to the Mithrim."

The Doll looked at the time display in her HUD. The time was 22:48.

Chapter 61
Near Garrapata State Beach

Ronan was in his study; he could see the grounds outside the raised patio. The guests were beginning to arrive, it was his birthday, but he had an uneasy feeling. Ronan had expected to hear his recent shipment had left from the base on the Martian moon. He also anticipated some of the Eldrane and others from the Dulce base to arrive this morning. Neither of these expectations was forthcoming. In fact, he had heard nothing at all from the Dulce base today, and that was unusual.

Ambrose came in, as he was staring out at the ocean. Rosy also confirmed he hadn't been able to reach any of their contacts in New Mexico. They should still be fine. The extra Thurog security he requested, as well as additional ground support vehicles, was staged in one of the warehouses. On the other hand, Rosy was accompanied by one of the lieutenants from the Thurog ship in low orbit over this coastal region. That individual was requesting an audience. That could not be good.

——————————————————

"You are sure this is going to work?" The Doll asked quietly as they turned keys over to the valet. She didn't sound concerned, just curious.

Less than an hour earlier they had taken possession of the Bentley from a CIA garage outside of Carmel. From there the four had driven up the Pacific Coast Highway (PCH) to Ronan's estate, a little past Garrapata State Beach. Tommy and Ally already had cover IDs and invitations to Ronan's lavish birthday bash, new ID's and invitations were produced for Doc and the Doll.

To the casual observer, they were just two more affluent couples arriving in a long line of luxury vehicles waiting to pass through the private security. After clearing security, they joined the growing audience headed along a walkway to the open lawn with its covered tables and refreshments. The four easily blended in with the cream of government and private A-list individuals. Doc and Tommy were both in summer casual tuxedos, Ally and the Doll both wore full-length designer gowns that caught the eye of most male guests. Whether this was due to the striking overall presence of the two tall attractive assured women or to a slit that opened their gowns on one side to the top of long, lean thighs was anyone's guess. The Doll's gown was a sapphire blue that complimented her exposed, tanned legs as she casually strolled arm in arm with Doc. Ally was wrapped in an emerald green that served as a counterpoint to her long crimson hair. They had brought gifts, as was expected, for their host's birthday. Those gifts had been scanned by security and were being carried for them to one of the many tables. Doc ensured that the package contents were appropriate in the mind of the security personnel when they scanned the neatly wrapped boxes.

This was Tommy and Ally's show. They had imagined, planned, and re-planned this operation for the past three years. In the past, they had been pulled back due to a lack of resources, evidence, or several other aspects needed to convince their combined agencies to give them the green light. This was the second time this event had been in Carmel. Since this was Ronan's fiftieth birthday, an extravagant celebration with an auspicious guest list had been planned. They would have preferred a less elaborate venue, considering the previous evening's joint action. They had little choice but to go forward today, or they might again lose the element of surprise.

This was going to be a delicate operation, they couldn't just roll in with sirens and arrest Ronan with an audience that included government officials, captains of industry, and select celebrities. They also had to consider Ronan's security force was top drawer and included an off-world component. That component included an interstellar medium battle cruiser. Yes, this had to be handled carefully despite Tommy and Ally's desire to grab a microphone and shout, "Gotcha!". The Vlichoir and the eight species that formed the Confederation at Dulce considered Ronan Earth's problem. After last night, they now had what was needed to put these several decades of embarrassment behind them, and wanted to do so quietly.

The four strolled forward with a cautious reserve. During a brief review with the Mithrim crew, in the earlier morning hours, there were still some questions, but Sally had departed with Cdr. Branko and his team. All present at the debrief agreed that Sally was more than just a minor player in interstellar politics. Next, despite urging, Doc remained silent concerning the few moments he had spent in Lisarra's mind. Reports that they received, as they were getting ready for this party, were that the ordinarily confident and controlled Exalted One was maintaining her silence; however, any mention of Doc caused her visible discomfort. Doc remained reserved and waved off any direct questions saying there would be time to go over the particulars. So, as the four walked across the tailored lawn to join the other guests, the Doll remained as close to Doc as was possible.

Ronan sat silently behind his large teak desk. He

listened carefully to Lieutenant Fresst from the Thurog ship in a low orbit above the estate. After their initial report, he had Ambrose call in Evans, his security chief. When Evans arrived, he was accompanied by the unit commander for the Thurog security forces. This was a ground unit assigned to rotate to this estate or whatever residence Ronan might be for any period. With the heightened security measures, he was getting mixed and disturbing signals.

Lieutenant Fresst began by confirming that they had lost contact with the remainder of the privateer fleet late last night. Their sister ship had been summoned to Dulce where it was challenged by a previously unknown Teletin tactical assault craft. To avoid an incident, they had made a jump to Phobos for back-up support. Now, with no further contact, they were being considered lost. His Captain, Seesrtin, would hold station, per their contract, but was expressing his concern by sending Fresst to meet with Ronan.

Ambrose confirmed that there had been no contact from Dulce today. On the other hand, nothing seemed amiss locally. No sudden police or government presence was charging done the PCH to gain access to this compound. All of the guests had been screened, and no names from the watch list Evans maintained had triggered an alarm. Ronan had grown up on the streets of Belfast and made it this far by trusting his intuition, his gut feeling, and that gut was uneasy.

Maybe he would consider retiring. He stood and motioned to Ambrose and Evans to walk with him; it was time to head out and greet his guests.

Chapter 62

Ronan stepped out of the back of the main building and took a moment to take in the view. There were tables and chairs set in small groups, attended tables with all manner of spirits, and fancy little useless party snacks. To one side were two long tables with gifts intended to impress him. He paused for a moment and considered that there might be some genuine people here, so he stepped out to be sociable. As he walked around shaking hands and accepting well-wishes his entourage consisting of Ambrose, Evans, and oddly, Lieutenant Fresst, stayed close by.

He had known Rosy from Belfast when he was beginning me to grow this organization. Evans had been handpicked by Rosy, so he felt secure with them at his side. After a few moments, he noticed two attractive couples standing near the gift tables. The two pairs seemed to be watching him. He thought they presented an odd juxtaposition of casual indifference as they watched him, but never missed any move he made through the crowd. Rosy was the first to put part of the puzzle together.

"Thomas Conner!" He spat out, "and I will bet that is his alien counterpart."

Ronan placed a hand on Ambrose' shoulder, "Calm down, if they managed to finagle an invitation, we should see what they are up to. We hold the high ground here."

Ronan recognized Tommy as they closed the gap and continued to study his companion. He was sure her name was

Alura. He smiled and wondered if that was the Teletin's real name was or just a pun on her very alluring features. He knew her species were like human chameleons or something like that, but as he got closer, he was confident it was her. As they closed the gap, Evans and Lt. Fresst moved their hands towards their weapons.

Had he blinked Ronan, would have missed Alura's reaction, even then he had to make some assumptions. She wore a full-length green gown that appeared to leave nothing to the imagination. There was a slit up one side, possibly to her hip or at least high on her shapely thigh. When she moved or shifted her stance, every inch of a long leg was visible. When Evans and Fresst had moved towards their weapons, Alura's hand had somehow parted the split and returned with a snapper. It was now visible against the bare thigh where her hand rested, the active charge indicator showing the red kill vs. the amber stun setting. She smiled.

"There is no need for aggression on either side. Let's discuss why you are here," Ronan commented in a casual matter of fact manner, then noticed what he had missed.

He had been so focused on the striking redhead and her CIA counterpart; he had completely overlooked the second couple. The other woman was undoubtedly as stunning as Alura and somewhat exotic with a slight Asian cast. Like the Teletin, she wore a full-length gown with a slit up the side. He decided that it was the plunging neckline that drew the eye and distracted him. He assumed the snapper in her hand pointed at the Lieutenant's head came from the same impossible location as had Alura's. She smiled as she motioned a no, with her head, at the Thurog officer.

Evans and Ambrose made a stand down motion to the

young ship's officer. During this exchange of glances, one of the roving servers approached the gift table, and Ronan watched in fascination as one of the presents unwrapped itself. The server reached into the open box and pulled out a very lethal-looking compact assault rifle of some unknown origin.

Tommy broke the silence, "Allow me to introduce my colleagues. I assume you have already recognized Ally Veseranna. The gentle-hearted woman with her snapper pointed at the Thurog Officer's head is Dr. Karen Wing, she prefers to be called Doll. Her companion is Martin Brensen, a retired Navy Corpsman. He is an old family friend, and his friends call him Doc."

Ambrose commented through clenched teeth, "This is the pair that escaped some weeks earlier."

Tommy smiled and continued, "Perhaps, if you had left the Doll alone a few weeks ago, we would not be here now."

Ronan watched in fascination as a second server approached the table, and another present unwrapped itself with the same end result.

Ronan assessed the situation, and re-joined the conversation, "Doc, Doll, please accept my apologies for what appears to have been a poor decision. Doll, Dr. Wing, our intent was never to harm you, just to offer you a chance to join our team and continue your excellent work in genetics. Can I assume you're missing assistant and the Marine Corps officer assigned to protect you will be making an appearance here also?"

As he spoke, Ronan pressed the panic button grafted

under the skin of his right hand. He assumed that Rosy would have already done so or would do so soon. The signal would put the estate on lock-down and alert the ground-side units as well as the ship in orbit. He assumed that the snapper pointed at the Lieutenant's head was because this Doll thought the Lieutenant was getting ready to alert his ship. Ronan could appreciate the title, she was indeed a Doll, and apparently a lethal one.

Ronan continued, "While it appears that you have somehow gained access to this private party, and successfully smuggled some weapons and two back-up personnel, I see no other movement, and my guests have not yet been disturbed. If you stand down now and leave, we will call this a draw. If not, the forces I have just alerted will begin to move in, and this will not end well."

He waited for a moment to let his words sink in, then another moment for some of the security units to appear then another moment. Ally, that was what Tommy had called her, leaned back against one of the tables. The Doll leaned casually against Doc's shoulder, never dropping her aim on Lieutenant Fresst.

There was a murmur from the assembled guests. There seemed to be something going on near the shoreline in the distance.

Doc smiled and commented as though it was an afterthought, "You should turn to see what your guests are trying to figure out."

Ronan turned and looked out toward the Pacific Ocean. They were on a small plateau overlooking the ocean. Maybe a quarter-mile out, the sea was boiling as a something rose from the surface, water flowed back down as an immense glowing manta ray-like ship rose into the sky, maybe a hundred feet above the still churning sea, and moved toward the shore. The Thurog officer made some startled, maybe shocked sound.

Behind him, Ronan heard Doc comment, "Yes, that is the ship that disintegrated your Captain Massrten's ship a few weeks ago. She is the Mithrim and is my ship. She returned from Phobos last night after assisting Vlichoir ships in destroying the Eldrane base there. You don't want to upset her crew."

Epilogue

San Francisco Chronicle
Prominent International Financier Arrested

Washington (AP) - Ronan Amos Murdock, a prominent international businessman, was arrested yesterday at his estate in Carmel by the Sea. Those close to the mogul, and in attendance at his fiftieth birthday celebration were shocked ...

ENQUIRER
Alien Intervention

(Carmel by the Sea) - Even as the authorities rushed in to capture Ronan Murdock during his fiftieth birthday bash, guests were capturing cell phone pictures and videos of Alien Flying Saucers coming in to protect the mogul from ...

FACT-CHECK.ORG
National Enquirer Wrong Again

We have reviewed the recent supposed cell phone videos of a single "Flying Saucer" coming out of the sea at the Murdock estate. The mysterious ship is a photoshopped and doctored image from the 1953 version of the "War of the Worlds" ...

Made in the USA
Las Vegas, NV
03 July 2022

51057984R00182